A Flickering
Mindlight

A Flickering Mindlight

Dean Vyas

authorHOUSE®

AuthorHouse™
1663 Liberty Drive
Bloomington, IN 47403
www.authorhouse.com
Phone: 1-800-839-8640

This is a work of fiction. All the characters, places and events are used entirely fictitiously or else they are from the author's imagination.

Published by AuthorHouse   11/21/2012

ISBN: 978-1-4772-4649-8 (sc)
ISBN: 978-1-4772-4650-4 (e)

Dean Vyas graduated with an honours degree in
Industrial Design, 1994, from Cardiff Institute of
Higher Education. He is a religious fellow and had a
Catholic upbringing. He regularly attends Church.
His hobbies and interests vary from time to time
but include hanging out with friends and going to
the cinema. He lives in Cardiff, Wales, UK and can
be found on the web at www.deanvyas.com

For my Mum, Dad and Sister

'Now that I in my contemplation of these matters have witnessed the extent to which the spirit of intimate human contact assumes the form of sensual pleasure [or, the degree to which the demands of this world are associated with sense gratification], I have entered this silence. Happiness is the natural state of the living entity and therefore I have definitively put an end to all of this.'
Srimad Bhagavatam; Canto 7,
Chapter 13:27—Bhagavata.org

'For out of the heart come evil thoughts—murder, adultery, sexual immorality, theft, false testimony, slander. These are what defile a person;'
Bible; Matthew 15:19-20—NIV, 2011

'As Jesus and his disciples were on their way, he came to a village where a woman named Martha opened her home to him. She had a sister called Mary, who sat at the Lord's feet listening to what he said. But Martha was distracted by all the preparations that had to be made. She came to him and asked, "Lord, don't you care that my sister has left me to do the work by myself? Tell her to help me!"

"Martha, Martha," the Lord answered, "you are worried and upset about many things, but few things are needed—or indeed only one. Mary has chosen what is better, and it will not be taken away from her."'
Bible; Luke 10:38-42—NIV, 2011

'But seek first his kingdom and his righteousness, and all these things will be given to you as well.'
Bible; Matthew 6:33—NIV, 2011

'Nay, but as when one layeth
His worn-out robes away,
And, taking new ones, sayeth,
"These will I wear to-day!"
So putteth by the spirit
Lightly its garb of flesh,
And passeth to inherit
A residence afresh.'

'Impenetrable,
Unentered, unassailed, unharmed, untouched,
Immortal, all-arriving, stable, sure,
Invisible, ineffable, by word
And thought uncompassed, ever all itself,
Thus is the Soul declared!'

**Excerpts from the Bhagavad Gita,
Chapter 2, poetically rendered by
Sir Edwin Arnold (1832-1904).**

Prologue

"I can see it like a shadow at his feet, and it makes me go all gooey. So small and imperfectly formed. We must have it!" The last sentence snapped like a steel trap.

"If you would allow my humble opinion, I think he's unsuitable, Ms. Lock, I believe he's a wriggler—"

"There's no need to be concerned about that, Ms. Seymour, I know he isn't, I can smell it on him from a mile away. He's a consignment ready to ship." Her mind wandered briefly, "So delectably misshapen . . ."

"The rivers have been overcrowded of late, Ms. Lock—"

"I was speaking metaphorically. Put your thinking head on, dearie, there are more modern ways—the revamped lift shaft? I'll arrange that he travel with me personally. I would enjoy having him alone in my company. Anyway, don't worry about all the nitty gritty." Ms. Lock walked over to the black door and closed it, cutting the umbilicus of light into the room. "It's a matter of the utmost secrecy until they've been briefed. I don't want any leaks, anything that might dissuade him from the natural course."

Lifting a slat in the maroon blinds, she peered into the office beyond, as light shot through like a spear into the murky room. It seemed to sting her eyes. Quickly she let the slat fall again.

"When will you brief them?" (The question really meant, "You will brief them now!") She sat back down at her desk and waited for the affirmative response.

"I haven't contacted him yet. I'm new to the administration—had to memo the others in the chain. It took a bit of time explaining my authorization—"

"You are testing my patience, young lady. That's not what I told you to do. I want you to pool your energy into the task at hand, not fanny around with trivia. I will advise the others in due course." She clasped her little silver, fork-like pen and scored the paper in front of her. "He's in receipt of the calling card. I sent it to him myself three days ago. Check your e-mail for his response. He will have certainly bitten."

"Yes, Ms. Lock."

"After your meeting, at the day's end, be sure to make him sign this." She passed the document over the desk. The young woman reluctantly took hold of it.

"It's the binding agreement between us, which you will issue on my behalf. It has my signature. Then, when I have him alone with me, he won't be able to turn back on his commitment, made in writing."

"Ms. Lock, he's still undecided, we should give him time to come around to us—"

"No, my dear, he's hardcore material, I know, I've been scouting him for some time. The decision, the finishing touch, will be made when he signs the contract." She leaned forward slightly over the desk. "And remember, my pretty; you are my emissary to the outside world. I appointed you for that purpose. I require that you use *every* means at your disposal to ensure that he ends up on our payroll." She eyed her subordinate's figure eagerly.

"I have my doubts, Ms. Lock, as to his veracity—"

"You are not employed for your opinions. Your opinion is *my* opinion. Your loyalty is to me and is total." She swiveled to the right. "I can't wait to get my mitts on him. Have him in my hand, and then let him spin the wheel," she mused, then cracked back to her previous thought process, "And one thing, don't let this one slip through your fingers like the others did. He must be ours by Tuesday."

"The others were unsuitable, Ms. Lock—"

"So you say, but be sure not to tell me the story of *the one that got away* after your tête-à-tête," she picked her fingernails with the pen's prongs. "Lead him into my lap and I will reward you accordingly, as I reward all my acolytes. I'll review your salary or you can have an extended holiday—perhaps you will be permitted free time to spend in my personal company." Her eyes slithered down the young woman's well-proportioned breasts to her shapely calves. "If you're 'good' that is. But if you disappoint me," her eyes bit like cold, red steel, "I'll have your pretty head on a platter!"

The young woman took a single step back, unable to speak.

"He'll make a loyal servant, slave to the wage. Tell me, how much did we decide we would pay him as an incentive?"

"I don't remember, Ms. Lock, we didn't finalize."

"Tut tut! I remember it was enough—for now. I want you to raise it—at the meeting, by perhaps five or six thousand. No higher or else he'll become suspicious. Do you understand?"

"Yes, Ms. Lock."

"Once he's through the gate I'll personally show him the inner workings of the corporation . . .

"One other thing, is there anyone—an acquaintance—who could be aware of his pending . . . employment? Anyone who at this stage could deter him from making this career move? I know of no one since that woman left. Give me your report."

"I believe not, Ms. Lock, my sources reveal the same."

"That's very good, isn't it?" It was a rhetorical question. "Ohh, I so look forward to having him under me, under my authority—"

"But there may be someone—"

The sealed room filled with a low-pitched growling, from an undeterminable source.

"What do you mean, there may be one?"

The young woman's defiance seemed short lived, "There may be one other of his acquaintances that has fallen by the wayside . . ."

"Then we need not worry about that, eh?" She skewered the eraser at her right hand with her pointy pen and leaned back on her chair. "I want this one sooo much, you wouldn't believe how much. And he's as good as ours if we do it right. That's certain."

"Yes, Ms. Lock."

"I want him presented to me at twelve o' clock Tuesday for our informal interview, during which I will make the final judgment. Thence, I will take him with me in my own transport down into the inner sanctum, to start him in his new role within the organization. Do I make myself clear?"

"Yes, Ms. Lock."

Chapter 1

Bouncing along on a space hopper, gripping its horns tightly, teetering on the verge of falling off, but never quite. Alongside scampering, a small group of children, huddled and singing together and chattering with excitement. Difficult work this, jumping energetically uphill, he thought to himself. The lactic acid invading his legs, made them feel as though they were twice their weight. Wobbling on his inflated seat as he struggled, it felt as he laboured to raise and lower each leg in turn, that he was leapfrogging through soup. The denims he was wearing were clinging, partly due to their being sodden with sweat and partly due to the fact that his muscles had swelled with the leg pressing exertion.

He continued up the centre of the road, smack bang on the intermittent white line that separated the two lanes for traffic, the eye-catching brilliance of which suggested the prescience of a graphic designer Colossus. They wound their way counterclockwise up the hill at a slow and perfectly steady pace, but for him a painfully slow one. The kids were happy enough though—it appeared as though they were totally unaffected by the wearying climb. They scrambled along on each side of him.

When nearing the top, on what was so gradual an incline now to be virtually a plateau, the children still chatting noisily, he stared at the view looking into the far distance. He gazed in wonderment through the cubic miles of pure, crisp air. It was breathtaking. He could see the crevasse plummet down, the rocky drop with a dusting of gravel. It tinkled down it every now and again, halted only by the odd outcrop of tufty shrubs that were sparsely scattered over the pitted stone. He could see the tarmac boa constrictor, which clenched the hillside, spiral down below and at the bottom, the thin stretch of beige and off-white shale was unspoilt by the presence of a single distracting soul. The ocean—a deep azure, with subtle, translucent green colour changes in the gentle waves as they heaved and waned. And the lead gray sky juxtaposed dramatically with nebulous clouds, building and layering heavily before his eyes, heading toward the west, an unsubtle hint of an approaching storm. He took in the air with heaving breaths, absorbing that view.

On regaining perspective of his own situation in all of this scenic glory, he suddenly realized that the children had disappeared. The emptying of the air of all human sound filled him with a strange melancholia. But he distinctly heard the space hopper snigger. Only for brief moments he thought about this, then the space hopper, in a jolting blur of red rubber, like a huge, demon possessed egg, continued forward of its own accord, with him still astride. He could see where it was leading as the gradient unflattened—a dark, thickly wooded area up ahead, rolling over the remainder of the climb.

Kieran abruptly awoke and tried to retain the dream in memory, in order to analyze it. He had a feeling that it had some significance but then after a few moments

6

remembered what important things there were to do in the wide-awake world, and let it go. But not very reluctantly—like the impulse to show affection to someone taken for granted.

Perhaps he would never recall it again. With just the ephemeral residue of the experience remaining, he fumbled for the alarm clock by his bedside. National Sport Fm was better than those rotten music stations, but not much better than the alarm's buzzer. He turned it off.

It was funny how quality sleep always evaded him during the night but in the morning, he was turned into a chunk of driftwood gliding down a dreamy river. There was to be no lie-in. It was Monday, 24th November, 2003, and the interview was for 9:00 a.m. Nothing could blank out that sinking, Monday morning feeling, the feeling of having one's hand caught in a relentless iron mangle, to be wrenched up to the shoulder by the day's end and expecting to be wrung through entirely by Friday. Nevertheless this would be a "historic" Monday, he reminded himself and so he propelled himself forward.

Frowning, he rubbed his mushy eyes, the eyelids ingrown into pulverized orbits. He stretched out his long, spindly, gilt wish-spoon body over the presentation box double bed and breathed in that distinctive (but of late, usual) smell of stale, sweat-embalmed sock a few times, with breaths that could have been deeper, and finally with that "yoga" mustered energy, shoved off the blankets in one go.

Chapter 2

Staring at himself in the mirror, eyes still bleary through the oily film smeared over them, he scrutinized his reflection through the flecks of toothpaste. He preferred not to look at it, the dark bags under the eyes and the graying hair were something of a deterrent, but today this would be particularly necessary, the means to an end. He examined in detail. He had formed an opinion about the importance of physical appearance (which was really superficiality), and the first impressions it gave. But without the attention of the *Babylon 5* makeup crew, he couldn't see himself scoring very highly in respect of this belief. He was tempted to reach for Alice's Body Shop foundation in the cabinet, but abstained.

He looked tired—staring into the dull blue dots on raspberry ripple that were his eyes. *Very* tired. A fact identifiable from every facial feature; the sallow, greasy complexion, the pores on his nose, the mottled, clammy cheeks and the cluster bomb detonation acne over his face's lower hemisphere.

The sink filled with hot, though not hot enough, water. "Any day now I'm going to knock wet shaving on the head—grow a fucking beard." How many times before had he told himself that? He never took his own advice though.

Apparently, the opinion was that bearded individuals gave prospective employers the jitters. A fellow wearing a beard had something to hide other than his chin. It implied insincerity. It was a refusal to display facial expression, which in turn defined the person as a secretive type. Perhaps antisocial, with ulterior motives, maybe even hording plans to bring about the collapse of a harmonious, efficient office. Who could say exactly what that facial fuzz meant? But it *was* an ideal place to hide a small spanner.

Kieran very well knew why he didn't take his own "advice". He knew the game like the back of a pay cheque, and knew that all related complaints were procrastination. He continued complaining anyway, and let the pimples impress on his jawline like meteorite showers over a Jovian moon, where he ritually scuffed and scratched off his facial fuzz.

Kieran's special shaving flannel swirled in the water, and he draped it over his face. It felt quite invigorating and revived his mind. The heat seeped into his jaw and he savored this short sweet moment before he would engage in the "hacking of the bristles". After blobbing foam over his chin in precautionarilly large dollops, he took a sharp intake of breath, and then delicately began to tease the brown bristles away.

"Don't need it, don't want it," he grunted while dragging the razor over his stretched skin. It rasped in defiance of the care he took to avoid cutting the flesh. After a few tender minutes, he beheld the finished result. Just the customary little piece of toilet tissue on that perpetual and persistent red blob on his chin. *Rather like a cherry on a bakewell tart,* he mused.

A minor tweak to the ruler straight fringe and he was done with that confounded mirror and face, satisfied that he had made the best of a bad deal. In all honesty, Kieran thought, to get the result he really wanted, he'd have to sleep through the winter. Not a possibility, the interview was for 9:00—two hours from now. Hurriedly, he splashed the razor into the not-so-hot water, as the million pores on his chin began to sing, and millions of tiny bristles clung to the sink at the waterline.

Aah, the trials and tribulations of city living. Living to work and working to live. *Nothing new there,* he thought. But surely in these high-tech days of machines and computers, shouldn't the necessity to work be something of an anachronism, receding into the depths of time? The activity of distant ancestry? Surely leisure time should be the selling point of the early twenty-first century.

But no, not a bit of it. The gas and electricity bills scattered over the coffee table he viewed beyond the bathroom door in the living room were testimony to the fact. Work—effort followed by reward, was the order of the day, as it had been for every day of mankind's existence (or at least since recorded history), only differing now in *character* rather than quantity.

He looked through the bathroom window over his garden, as the thought reverberated in his mind. The fog was building at ground level and the terraced houses beyond were barely visible. It was a gray, not blue, Monday, and every physical feature of the world he could see outside the bathroom window suggested the same. The grass was a green-gray, the walls a red-gray and the surrounding buildings—they were just gray. Grayness imbued everything, but this wasn't because of the fog. It was because it was Monday and Monday was a day when everyone engaged in the gray activity of work. But then he thought, "a necessary evil," reminding himself of this particular Monday's significance.

"Don't much care for them, but those bills aren't going to *evaporate,"* he muttered to himself. He scowled in their direction and then scanned the rest of the living room while walking in. "What a sorry mess."

The plant stems (in better condition they would be described as "the flowers"), breathing their last from the demoisturised air, buckled in the radiator heat, like long dull-green liquorices, almost invoked pity within him. As if in defiance of his lack of assiduousness, the petals dripped off them as they stood dying, and mockingly settled like crispy confetti on the floor. He considered whether he would look for the watering jug later that evening, but then wondered whether it was worth keeping them at all.

Flat tidying had always been a regular activity when he was cohabiting with Alice, and she did most of it. Now the flat had almost become a reflection of his disheveled mind, the result of the brutal upset caused by her departure. At the same time, he hadn't been able to muster the energy to clean it up. It just wasn't a priority for him anymore.

The living room especially had become something of a place of mourning. The litter served as the reminder of his ex-lover. He considered briefly the symbolic meaning of this metaphor but didn't pursue it too far, having one eye on the time. No time to be analyzing that which isn't relevant to the task in hand, he cajoled himself. No, instead he wistfully embraced the mess and accepted it as the poignant memory of a failed love affair. Another event in an aspect of his life that was perpetually failing. Another stain on the tapestry, which embellished the story with its own, miserable significance.

Chapter 3

Having finalized a few niggling details, Satan stood patiently at the entrance of the modified lift. It arrived and its doors swung open, revealing an interior large enough for three people, covered in sheets of mirrors. Satan strode in, multiplying a few times by their reflections, and waved a little device containing unknown technology below the lift control panel. An aperture opened up, revealing a second control panel.

Satan pressed the button with the lighted downward triangle, the polished steel doors swished closed, and the lift, with a stomach turning lurch (though in Satan's interior there was no human digestive apparatus), descended. The Devil watched the digital floor counter display change without expression, down from twenty. For a long time there was no change in the readout, it being stuck on "basement".

The digital display went black, as the moving cubicle crossed dimensions. Then the red digital readouts returned to the display, from floor minus one, onwards.

At floor minus two hundred and fifty, Satan's body began to snap, crackle and pop, as it morphed in form from the one chosen for the earthly rendezvous, into the one he preferred—male, reddish-black colouration, dagger teeth, horny head and so on.

Now Satan looked at his reflection on the mirror walls of the cubicle to fiddle out any anomalies in his hellish appearance. He was turned out well enough. The shape-shifting creature that was Satan rocked on his long, spiky feet a few times, keen now to be out of the confined space.

The stifling metal box, barely containing the Devil's expanded material form, slowed from its fantastic speed.

The gratuitously maleficent black eyes observed the floor level display:—955,—956,—957,—958 . . .

Just before floor minus one thousand, Satan prodded the keypad with an oversized, gnarled nail. The lift cubicle came to a standstill at that floor. The doors slid open.

Satan disembarked. To his left, into the smoky, gray-brown yonder, an endless row of lift doorways identical to the one he had just exited, and to the right, the same. They were the openings to lift shafts of all the parallel Earths and all the other planets that utilized lifts.

There were other, more antiquated ways of reaching Hell, for example the rivers Styx and Acheron, but these were falling out of popularity with Satan.

He set foot on one of the countless landscapes of Hell, having decided that this one would be the most appropriate for his new acolyte, the *man in question*.

Satan, through his slick, black-balled eyes, looked onto the vast vista that was a fraction of his heinous dominion. It was a floor of Hell on which the woeful incidents and activities would be comprehensible to earthbound life forms, but only just.

Before him, sprawling in a spectrum of agonies, was a portion of the mortal creatures of the universe.

Everything that was condemned to Hell was a mortal creature. A soul with some sort of material body encumbered upon it, which would eventually disintegrate for whatever reason, always horrible.

The only time a soul, within or above Hell, parted entirely and finally from a material form, was when it had reached a state of purity (of good rather than evil), at which time Satan would lose all interest in it, as it could never again be annexed for Hell. This was a very remote possibility for those in the Underworld, as low down in the league of goodliness as they were.

Satan languished in Hell by choice, but (the exception to the rule) his body wasn't mortal. And it could be regenerated into any gloriously wicked form, whenever he chose to do so. The association with Hell was a chicken and egg thing with him. It was a continuation of his existence, just as much as he was a manifestation of Hell.

His consort for this particular sector of Hell, comprising ten individuals of various shapes and sizes (one as small as a cat, another as large as an elephant), in various stages of decomposition, dashed limping and hobbling to his side.

"Hail, Satan!" they cried, more or less in unison.

Those of basically human corporeal form, with a sleight, lifted their arms from off their rib cages in the vain hope that Satan would be charmed by their vulgar odours, and concurrently less inclined to kill them.

Alas, he noticed nothing above the acrid smoke from burning bodies.

One of the odious bunch, Arzoley Kyam, asked with a sickly, wavering voice, "Lord Satan, what brings you to the one thousandth plane?" (Satan, during his time in Hell, dwelled more often than not in the even deeper layers.)

Satan said, "I am expecting an earthly mortal to join our world." He referred to the dimension of Hell fondly as his *world*, because worlds, more than any other habitat for mortal creatures, provided the best hunting grounds to prey on fallen souls. "I look to find him a suitable location on this plane."

A vile, slave master stooge, Sarmosa, asked "But my lord, why have you come in person? You usually call up a floor level attendant, on whose floor the mortal will be placed, to collect it and find for it a suitable location."

"True," said the Devil, "for most, I allow my capable floor keepers to arrange the whereabouts of the newly fallen, in Hell."

Trollix Crabtree, a senior floor level attendant, asked, "Then why, sire, the attention to detail with the positioning of this one?" He readjusted his semi-exposed brain, which tended to swill around when he moved his head, before Satan's response.

"This particular mortal has so much potential. His mindset is so very promising," he said in a growly kind of way. "If it is nurtured, he is destined for great things." Satan looked proudly ahead at his panorama of horrors. "I cannot leave anything to chance. I cannot permit any mistakes and so, myself will arrange the setting."

One of the helper fiends, Magnanimana, said "But level one thousand seems quite a drastic drop for someone fresh off the Overworld, sire."

During her asking of the question, the entourage released farts (a risky business) slightly louder than was their intention, hoping that the perfume would more endear them to the Prince of Darkness, standing as closely by as he was.

Alas, still Satan noticed nothing of the intermingling fragrances above the stench of the burning bodies, but he had heard the superfluous and impertinent noise from one of his servants. He raised his trident and pointed the end of its handle at the guilty party. Energy frazzled around the pole and spurted over the flatulent stooge. He fried on the spot, the skin charring as the molten layers of fat oozed through the fractures in it, splashing onto the rusty iron plating they were standing on. Satan turned off the heat when the raw viscera was exposed through the black rags of skin. Keretin was no more. Perhaps the rapidity made it a merciful death. Perhaps not.

Casually, Satan continued, "I agree—for most, the shift in abomination from usual life suddenly to an earnest one on a deeper plane of Hell, would be too great." He placed his scrawny, viciously nailed hands on his jagged hips and looked to the brackish sky, carefully weighing his explanation. "Of course, if a mortal is misplaced in too grim a level of Hell, the experience can jump start their *moral* centers. It may well jolt the mortal back onto *the path of light* (to coin a cliché), so that eventually they end up describing their time in Hell merely as a lesson learned, as they continue to gravitate towards the light source."

"Why does this mortal differ in respect of that, sire?" asked Magnanimana, with a humble bow.

With a smile of admiration not for her, but for the man he spoke of, he answered, "He has in place the atheistic philosophy to be able to plummet to unprecedented depths.

"There are floors I have created, which as yet have not a soul on them. He can be the first living entity to forge ahead onto these, can be my number-one, *pioneering* living entity."

For Satan, a mouthwatering prospect, because he existed solely to corrupt souls, which he did by cunning temptation, or torturing a soul's material body in multifarious ways. Corruption had more to do with the soul's response to torture, rather than its actual endurance of it. For example, Satan could set up an environment to cause starvation of a material body, encouraging the soul to mobilize the body to cheat, steal, murder, to acquire food. End result—a further reduced soul.

An impure soul always carried a material body—which could then be tortured to death—a very nice feature as far as Satan was concerned. When death of the material form was reached, it didn't mean that the torture sessions were over. Not at all. It just meant (more often than not, the way Satan played it) that the soul reacquired *another* material body, which could be tortured to death, and so on and so forth.

Satan elaborated the virtues of his protégé to his servants in waiting. "He has the underlying belief system (though he hasn't fully acted upon it yet) that has permitted him always to discard the subtle illumination in his earthly environment, that would keep him on the *opposition's* path, he being *God*." He rotated his head like a tank turret, a shadowy beam swinging over the intent faces of the macabre, hodge-podge collective.

"I want to get him up to speed quickly, want him to fulfill his potential sooner rather than later. I can only achieve that aim by strategically torturing him. He can handle level minus one thousand, I know he can. The convictions he has emplaced in his mind mean that he will be able to accommodate the depravity he will experience here, and not change his underlying philosophy. He won't turn to the light. He will slide inexorably further down!"

With that, the Devil turned his head again to his despicable assemblage and grinned a grin larger than the width of his red, jutting face—teeth like tusks poking irregularly through his tensioned lips, his eyes with a copious thatch of black brow resting above, narrowing to black slits.

Chapter 4

After dressing and breakfasting on coffee, Kieran paused for a moment to contemplate the meaning of all this preparation; shaving, aftershave, the suit, the tie—all that rigmarole and the meaning of his role in society as a paid worker. Who, ultimately, was he serving, *other than himself*? What was the real value of the service he gave? Tracing along in his mind where these questions led, he tried to imagine who, in the long term, would truly benefit from his "service". What impact would he have in his role in the greater scheme of things?

An insect struggled and flipped along the carpet like a Mini Cooper over a rock strewn quarry floor. It erroneously sought respite at the pronounced heel of Kieran's glossy black shoe and squeezed through underneath. Contempt flickered lightly in his mind.

He struggled to answer this self-generated question but couldn't for the life of him figure out the answer. Perhaps his question was unanswerable by himself, or the great guru on the mountaintop. He was not indispensable. He wasn't saving any lives. He wasn't visibly making any profound contribution to society that was immediately apparent and for this reason never really felt any deep sense of achievement.

A nomination for the Nobel Prize was not in the offing. Did that make him insignificant to society as a whole? A microscopic component, within a larger entity, in which the relatively minute contribution he made meandered around the labyrinth, dwindling into obscurity?

Whether he could ever have any real value in this massive tangle he felt was debatable, or, being as reluctant to engage in discussion as he was, at least something to reflect on privately.

What he did know, though, was that his gut was of importance to him after skipped meals, including skipped breakfasts. That was beyond any question and not requiring any analysis. As a mild feeling of discomfort rippled through his spleen, he instinctively reached to feel over his thigh, to seek the reassuring edges of the little bottle of pills that would, after it arrived fully, erase the pain. Then he pulled away his hand from the bottle as though it were electrically wired, in fear of his subtle addiction.

Conjecturing some more, Kieran at least knew the *obvious* reason to work, which was to earn, in order to satisfy his own material requirements. If he was not of any real value to society—and this opinion was beginning to crystallize in his mind, then at least his own existence as a worker was for *himself*.

Alice, his ex-lover, would insist every living thing had a purpose and should be respected—plants, animals and people. Everyone had a vital part to play in the great scheme of things, which would be of benefit to all the other tenants of "Gaia"—this role decided by a celestial landlord as it were. No one was redundant. Every life was interdependent with others, presently and in the future.

Kieran agreed to differ. He'd only ever scratch Liz Hurley's back (though he never revealed his fascination), a prospective employer's, or *her* back (because to him, she had lovelier legs than Liz Hurley's). But not sweaty plebs, flying squirrels or arctic lichens. To scratch anyone else's was unnecessary and sordid. It was self-belittling. She was a Communist gone mad. She'd have the zookeepers sharing the cages with the pythons and rattlesnakes. She'd have a welfare state that extended to the insect race (he inescapably envisioned a human size earwig signing for Jobseeker's Allowance).

With that, he lifted his shoe and leered down on the bug like a wrathful deity. He brought his foot down over the condemned insect and rotated, hoping he would hear crunching as its exoskeleton burst. Instead he pushed it into the pile of the carpet, trapping it between the fibres. Still satisfied, he left it to die slowly from its multiple fractures. *"What on earth kind of purpose did that piece of shite have?"* he thought to himself.

It wasn't really Kieran's intention, or primary concern, to make a contribution to society in any way. But it was a sick irony that half the time, a person's attempts to satisfy his own requirements contradicted his desire to make such a contribution. But apparently that was just how it was. It seemed to Kieran, that to get and keep a job, one had to resort to such foul methods. Had to be so insensitive towards other candidates—sometimes had to lie and cheat and deceive the very same society that person was supposedly serving.

But he was *compelled* to satisfy his primeval survival instinct. *So what* if, in all of this confusion, he was insignificant. How much more significant could anyone else be? Seen that way, robbing, cheating and stealing wasn't so bad. Kieran's theory was that, in the final analysis, everyone was actually driven by the same urge—of self-satisfaction—of selfishly making secure *oneself.*

He snapped back onto the most pressing requirement. Shifting his body weight he darted for the coffee table, rummaged amongst all the paperwork and fished out the all-important interview letter. Without it, *how would they know who he was when he arrived?*

A little crumpled, the A4 page was, in a manner of speaking, his passport into Candlelight Ltd., and from there, surely his passport to success. It would usher in a new age of prosperity for him—undoubtedly. He had to pay back those loans.

The business had failed some time ago but the legacy of debt lingered—the studio, the computer workstation, the drawing board, etcetera. That, though, he could sort. What was more than ever getting the better of him now was his *frame of mind.* The last few months had been the most stressful he could ever remember in all his thirty-three years.

"Not to worry (from today onward)—just the medicine I need," he thought, grinning at the sheet. He slotted the paper into the briefcase compartment. Pacing to the door, he grabbed his coat and looked back at the living room one more time.

Outside the fog was awful, worse now. A couple of times Kieran caught the pavement for lack of being able to see it, but both times, in less than cat-like fashion, had managed to maintain his balance. The fog and the shoes—"these fucking shoes," he cursed at regular intervals—new and very stiff, with a chunky heel that dragged and scraped the concrete on every step, nudging tough leather into the skin over his Achilles tendon. They were becoming raw. He began to position his steps more carefully in an effort to prevent more blistering.

Kieran jostled through the first of many stations he would enter on his way, that foggy morning. Over the tannoy, a message that one of the trains had stopped for some urgent (but as yet unknown to the announcer) reason. An unexpected delay—the train would not arrive for another eight minutes—but even so, one he was prepared for. Luckily, the extra effort of dragging himself out of bed with the sheer willpower of one obsessed by a pay packet meant that he was early.

But he *was* impeded by the gnawing pangs in his stomach, which arose whenever he exerted himself. He'd skipped his medicinal fix earlier, which wasn't a good idea. The brisk walk to the station ensured he would need a double dose to calm his ulcer satisfactorily, and it was nagging for it now.

Even so, Kieran bore it instead. He bit his lower lip for a few moments, trying not to let others see, until the aching subsided. The truth was that he *didn't want the bastards to get him down*—he didn't want to become dependent on spectacles to see. If he conceded to those, next he would concede to the use of a walking stick, then a wheelchair. He needed to remain strong, to stand upright, otherwise he would slide down a slippery slope into the pit of the unfit, and would be quarry to be taken advantage of by the survivors.

Chapter 5

Satan continued to ponder his new arrival. It was a brainteaser all right, though Satan's thought process wasn't confined to a small lump of organic matter called a brain. He was a supernatural being. His thoughts were interwoven with the entire fabric of the dark half of the cosmos.

He was never casual with *other* mortals—but a few lost to "the light" (a term he even used himself, to simplify the concept of moral lifestyle resulting in avoidance of Hell) was inevitable. The way Hell was bundling in the squalls of fallen souls, that negligible loss didn't *really* matter.

But the soul Satan was currently fixated on was worth ten other fallen souls—rather like a super-sized and unflawed diamond amongst tiddly, common gemstones.

He imagined that jewel on his finger.

At the same time, he considered revising the allusion of *morality* with *light*, based on his understanding that oftentimes, wickedness proliferated in environments that had been *revealed* in light.

Whoever heard of an immoral fetus, which was ignorant of the outside world but was perfectly contented in its lightless, simple environment? Surely no crime could be considered, let alone committed in such a circumstance—There is nothing visible that someone might desire in a dark shop window, but turn on the lights . . .

Perhaps darkness and consequential ignorance *was* bliss.

Then again, thought Satan, it was probably a *double-edged sword*. Light shed on worlds revealed temptations, but it also revealed the means by which to avoid them.

But those earthbound humans traditionally thought of Hell as a dark and dingy place. So many painters over the ages had portrayed it that way. There was no truth in their representations. Not necessarily, because Hell was split equally between submergence in light as it was in darkness. It depended on whichever was more conducive at a particular time, in a particular region, to debasing the interned souls there yet further. Satan saw no reason to pay homage to what was a human fallacy, by turning out Hell's lights. He thought to himself he might even turn them up higher.

Oh, and as well, he'd have to check up on the fetuses—whether they really *were* quite as innocent as he had only seconds earlier assumed . . .

The Devil particularly liked to watch humans suffer in Hell because, of all the mortals there, human ones were the most vain. They had believed that the benevolent force of nature, which they referred to as "God", was human in shape. True, from a human perspective, God was indeed human in shape but from a pig's perspective, God was pig shaped and from a giraffe's, giraffe shaped (because he understands their needs and desires from their own point of view).

Humans on Earth (the place from where they originated) considered other life forms as substandard, for having a lesser affinity with God. Now fallen in Hell, the Devil liked to batter them for that underestimation of other living creatures, as a result of the humans' vanity.

All the way up to the horizon could be seen the array of mortal creatures, that had morally deviated to the extent that they were now resident on this landscape of the Underworld.

There were people but there were also bacteria, plants, insects, fishes, birds and other animals, including dinosaurs—earthly varieties of all these and alien ones (by human standards). There were mortal creatures that were outright alien species (including synthetic constructs, such as self-aware robots), in countless number, which bore no resemblance to any living thing that existed, or ever existed, on Earth.

But for his select theatre, most often Satan chose human players—adult men and women.

The Devil growled to the level one thousand maintenance stooge, "Bring the throne carriage!"

"Yes, Devil sir!" said Trollix Crabtree.

Satan never used telepathy to converse with those in Hell unnecessarily, let alone the rest of the universe. He considered that doing so would dilute the epitomal evil of his mind. He used his telepathy only to conduct constant warfare against the mind of what humans called "God".

His pug-faced, Prince of Darkness, wannabe cronies did the telepathy instead.

Satan's mobile throne arrived, carried by three score grubby, naked humans, male and female, five heavily tarnished robots, a large glistening black beetle, with a Frisbee sized fluorescent green dot on each of its retracted wings, and a black, bear-like creature with what appeared to be jellyfish tendrils flopping from its face. The division of wretched creatures, on whose shoulders Satan's throne carriage was burdened, were squeezed together like matches in a box. A couple were on fire too. They budged and jostled through the swirling waves of condemned life.

A blanched, emaciated crony of the Devil that circulated with a few others around the carriers of the throne platform, momentarily separated from the group, into the smorgasbord of wretched life, and returned with a human. It jabbed her forward with a dagger and forced her down on all fours in front of the throne platform. Satan had presently chosen to be the height of two end to end male humans, and so when he stood off from the lift foyer, using the crouching woman as a step onto the throne platform, she was crushed into the burning coals, and his taloned toes gouged deep lacerations over her back.

With the second step, he was on the throne carriage, a raft-like structure of lashed Tyrannosaur thighbones. His cortege clambered aboard by whatever means was at their disposal, having first to tread the scorching coals to reach the carriage. A larger stooge used a rough and ready ramp, while the smallest made clever use of abseiling equipment to alight. They positioned themselves five on either side of the Dark Prince as he settled himself down onto the bony throne.

The stately seat was made entirely of organic materials; the glued husks of small insects, and here and there those of larger ones. Human bones were structurally placed in its framework for added support. There were visible elements of alien body parts—dried, flayed, checkered skin over the seat and armrests, and coiled, parched, dark purple entrails at the backrest. The fabrication glistened in slimy greens, russets and nearly blacks.

Satan sat forward, emblematic trident in one callous fist, resting its pole on the bony floor, the other hand under his chin, his elbow dug into the armrest.

"Summon the buggers!!!" boomed Satan at the janitors of the one thousandth floor of Hell, even before their feet could simmer down from their scorching.

Though in anguish, they swiftly obliged the Prince of Evil, by telepathy.

After some thirty seconds, a procession of mostly humans and a few aliens came before Satan's throne carriage, carrying their moving stage, and steadied. It was a platform dedicated solely for the purpose of sodomy. On it, men, the odd, smaller-size dinosaur, a dozen gorillas, a sprinkling of hitherto natives of the planets Skenrab, Darthaar and Quastar 7, three sheep and an aardvark, engaged in the act. The one hundred or so had been specially selected beforehand for this activity. They had, since their arrival, on the ends of sharp poles, been forced to do *it*—non-stop. Amongst the cluttered, writhing, slapping bodies, some lay dead on the blackish gray lattice platform, exhausted by their endless task (but of course their soul was simply migrating to another physical body in the thick of Hell—*no escape*!).

A few more, fresher bodied souls were poked up toward the platform. They clambered up crude, short ladders to the stage and without dilly-dallying, found a victim with which to engage in sodomy.

A couple of the ghastly helpers of Satan dragged out the corpses with large iron tongs. They tumbled over the edge of the stage-set like rag dolls, into the smoldering coals, their flesh nearest the heat blackening and crisping.

Satan watched zealously, quite impressed by the way they were performing, for he was a keen bugger himself. "You there! Faster!" he bellowed at one of the pairs.

They did as they were told.

The Devil's decaying overseers threw some crusts of bread onto the stage. The sodomites, without stopping, clambered and collected the pieces like hungry, conjoined pigeons. They ate without a pause in their physical exertions.

Satan wondered. Could the man whose soul he would soon possess, be placed amongst these? Perhaps for a month or two? Satan was amused by the idea but could not decide for sure whether the man would be suited to partake in the *buggery traveling show*.

After observing proceedings for about a half hour, more or less silently, he ordered his assistants to get rid of the spectacle. His servants, with a telepathic command, caused the mortal creatures—men, women, aliens and beasts, on whose shoulders the stage was rested—to shuffle off miserably. They would display their wares to whichever one of the Devil's senior executives next demanded their attendance.

As the float jostled away, Satan cruelly shouted in a grating tone to the performers, "Don't slow up, or I will see to it personally that your winky and baps are lopped off!"

They redoubled their efforts, even as the Devil detached his attention.

Satan snarled to his uncivil servants, "Let's get it moving!"

His slimy, rotting-fleshed cohorts carried out the command. The throne carriage lurched forward.

It progressed half a mile, when the Devil ordered the carriage to stop at a pen of dinosaurs, into which some impish tormentors were spraying various acids and corrosive liquids, as the wayward prehistoric creatures screeched in abysmal agony.

An unsuitable environment for his charge, thought Satan. He'd be torn apart instantly. The torment would be too intense and too brief. Satan reckoned it wouldn't lower the standard of the man's soul, wouldn't be a "constructive" experience for his student.

He sneered again at the executives standing at either side of his throne, simultaneously swiping at Banjogong Crisps, scooping off a few sizeable chunks of putrid flesh from his shoulder. The executors got the throne carriage moving again. Missing the fragments and the mobility of his arm, Banjogong picked them from off the seesawing, bone, carriage-floor, and gingerly replaced them in the liquid troughs on his shoulder.

They passed by a dull, steamy field, covered with suspended iron grating. There were pathways beneath, along which various mortal creatures, including many humans, stoked the fires. They wheeled barrows brimming with petrol, collected from some interminable source, along the network. Wherever the fires were low, they tipped their load into the faltering flames, which then exploded with new life. Often when this happened, parts of the barrow pusher's anatomies were badly scorched. Some less fortunate fire tenders were engulfed in flame and never came back out of the fiery pathways to replenish their wheelbarrows with fresh fuel.

On the iron grating, above the field of fire, were a myriad of earthly aquatic animals, large and small. Immoral shrimp, jellyfish, starfish, ordinary fish, octopi, sharks and whales, all tossing and turning on the immense grill, the steam pouring from them billowing high into the air above.

Satan liked seafood.

Perhaps the man of promise could be stationed here, as a fire attendant. It would be soul-destroyingly rigorous but possibly a bit too hazardous. The idea was to reduce his spirit further, not shock it into changing course.

Chapter 6

Kieran determined the rest waiting for the train and on the train journey, would give his poor gut an opportunity to settle and if necessary, he would take the tablets, that poisonous remedy, when aboard.

The train guard allowed him through with a token glance at his ticket, and Kieran made his way to the platform, leaning forward slightly, trying to relieve his intestine. He was irritated and tired—extremely—he was mentally exhausted, and physically devitalized.

In the last twelve months, he had lost that many pounds. Well, he at least still had full mobility when he took his medicine, even if his batteries were drained. His doctor, after an investigation into his condition, had told him that he needed to avoid stress and prescribed him a strict diet and the pills. *The comedian*—avoid stress? It would be easier to avoid a train while roped like a damsel-in-distress to the track. The peristalsis reflex maliciously sent waves of hot lead through his intestine and he cursed under his breath in a fairly undamsel-like manner.

By his feet a pigeon pecked for crumbs. It was a scrawny old one, quite ugly, he thought. He watched it haphazardly pick the tarmac, sometimes at nothing at all. He considered pigeons to be vermin. He eyed the white splatters around the bench he was seated at, and scowled at it. Was there any sanity rattling in that twitching head that he could understand? Its existence to him seemed so pointless. While looking for a single redeeming feature, he noticed the missing toes and feathers, and then chased its head jerking around to catch a glimpse of its eyes, those tiny, beady, dead eyes. He could find no redeeming features. A grimace settled on his face as a smidgeon more contempt rustled in his mind for the little starver. He grunted (but inaudibly) and then jabbed his foot at it, wincing as the crisp blot of blood sticking the sock to his heel came away.

The pigeon fluttered its wings and hopped off.

Kieran hated animals and that scavenger just reminded him why he never kept pets, despite Alice's continuous harassment. But she never liked seeing birds in cages, which is what Kieran wished upon those flying parasites. To be captured and jammed in cages, for man's wants, to serve some useful purpose. He wondered what pigeon meat tasted like and whether their eggs were appetizing. They could be farmed like battery hens, contained and productive, harnessed like wind or wave power, consumed like fossil fuels or any other natural resource.

Apparently some people fancied the flying blighters as pets. All pets were lousy but surely they would be the lousiest. Nope, no animals stinking out the flat. Absolutely not.

Alice was always watching the Discovery Channel, almost as though it were a consolation.

The platform was thronging with working folk, who had all set out with the common purpose to secure a comfortable future for themselves, having accepted the *king's shilling*. Somehow, instead they stood in the front line of foot-soldier/clerks on a battleground; prim in their uniform, marching forward unremittingly in their unbroken lines, transfixed on their distant objective (as set by their superior officer/employers far behind them). The one bristling with the hooks and barbs and spears, of work-related, emotional breakdown.

Onwards they go, their minds sprayed with gunshot and spackled with canister shrapnel, disintegrating before their own eyes, but unable to break away to safety, not because of loyalty to their comrades-in-arms, but because they're caught between the *deep blue sea* and the *devil to pay*, for desertion, or *resignation*:

Marching forward to die, wistfully resigned in a manmade Hell.

Kieran stared along the congested platform at all the expectant commuters standing behind, by mere millimeters, the long white line that stretched the length of the platform, delineating the danger area before its edge—*the point of no return* . . .

He considered the distance the train would be from that white line on arrival and was struck by the incongruity of behaviour of the crowd. How was it, that bunched up as they were, there was no fear in standing so close to what was potentially an impending disaster? Almost as though they were not even aware that at any second, a steel juggernaut would rumble over the track? That thin white line separated those nearest the edge from a very sticky end.

Did they know who stood behind them? What were the chances of one of the crowd pushing forward, for whatever reason, either by accident or maybe even *intentionally*, causing a domino effect with a fatal ending? Kieran felt there was so much irony in this behaviour.

Where there was public concern, even outrage, displayed at the potential long-term effects of BSE, or the risks involved in flying, how was it that these people could teeter on such a precipice voluntarily, and with such confidence? Life was so full of these inconsistencies and contradictions, he thought.

Taking it further, what if someone *did* push? What if someone *did* fall? He went on to consider the type of injuries someone would sustain if they were that unlucky toppler . . .

Of late, Kieran was always having these morbid thoughts, and didn't really make any effort to check them. "No harm in morbidity. Expect the worst, prepare for the worst." It was all about damage limitation in the long run, and the best way to avoid damage was to stand away from the edge.

For Kieran, the wedge between himself and the white line would provide the necessary protection, and this morning would ensure that he acquired it, at Candlelight Ltd.

Kieran looked again at his poxy-waged brothers and sisters, standing en masse, seeming more like shiny pins pricking the white billowing fog cushion, not knowing which among them, at stress breaking point, would be plucked away from sanity, into the air by the fingers of an invisible, Olympian seamstress. He viewed them insentiently, degrading them while promoting himself, and mused—*or like the shiny steel bristles of a brush, to scour the grime and flaky oxide from the eroded worthless artifact, the place of their employment. Some of them to kink and snap away from their wiry kin, with no one's realization or concern.*

Through the white mist, the train materialized and stopped without event. The commuters poured out like grains of rice from a burst bag. An equal number of grains struggled onboard, along with Kieran.

"Hate early morning starts . . . this is ridiculous . . . busting my back for money . . . damn bills!" The rumbling grumbling came as a steady stream through his mind even though subliminally, he knew the importance of today. Navigating the underground was no problem for Kieran. It really was second nature to him now. The minimal attention required to orienteer through the network of train routes allowed his default train of thought:

"Collar's too tight . . . blasted train's crammed . . . next to his armpit . . . stifling in here!" He gritted his teeth behind peaceful lips, as he was sure so many others of the po-faced commuters on these sunrise trains were doing.

On this train, he *had* managed to secure a seat. Thankfully, as of all those he was to journey on, this one would be the one he would travel the furthest with. Before parking himself, he'd swiftly lifted from the space behind the seat, next to the window, the *Astronomy Today* magazine, that some stargazer had discarded on his way to office.

Yeah right! Point your telescope to the stars through the bars of your prison. It won't give you their freedom.

Another one of those incongruities.

He flicked through the pages, only in order not to have to stare at those taciturn faces, which he seemed to meet whatever direction he looked in.

There was a contrived behaviour on these journeys that was, without exception, imitated by all, which Kieran was a master of. It was the art of being discreetly uncivilized in a civilized environment and making it work to one's own advantage.

Firstly, the seat's identification before acquirement:

Kieran had swiftly recognized the opportunity, as soon as its possessor had shifted in anticipation of the next train stop. This was even before the train had begun to slow down! Kieran was waiting and yes, gradually its rotund possessor lifted himself up, both arms pushing on the rests.

The profundity of the moment didn't pass Kieran unnoticed—he half imagined a blue whale heaving off the ocean's surface, the watery wake resembling the slightly moist, uncreasing imitation leather seat. Evidently, the Discovery Channel had left its mark on his mind.

Kieran's mouth made a faint crackle as he opened it ever so slightly. That much he could allow himself to reveal. But he made no movement, nor did anyone else standing and waiting.

Secondly, the skill was in the timing. Here was an empty seat, uncoveted as yet, but for which there were many desirous. What to do? He looked slightly to his left and then his right, intuitively knowing that the other suitors were doing the same. The gesture implied a concern for politeness—*are you requiring the seat?*

But before one could reasonably expect a response, Kieran had made his move towards it, and parked himself successfully, much to the annoyance of the competition (which, even so, didn't display any annoyance).

Also rans, he thought and dismissed them from his mind, even as a subtle grin lingered on his face.

Chapter 7

There are countless worlds in countless galaxies but of all the habitats of mortal creatures, the world called Earth provided the Devil with the richest pickings. And humans were his passion fruit. "They're such sophisticated buggers!" thought Satan. He *loved* to hate them.

Still appreciative of the dinosaur's brute viciousness, he just found them a little too mentally ineffectual—thick basically. No more were forthcoming from the blue planet anyway. Humans, on the other hand were so canny, and in large supply. They were Satan's flavour of the era, and would remain that, unless the promising self-aware machines underwent a surge in evolution.

The good and evil actions of humanity were the greatest consequentially, for those within their own species and other species. Their advanced intellect surpassed that of any other living creature's in the universe. The expression of *their* wicked desires could be multiplied greatly by their appliance of science.

Humans induced greater dynamic fluctuations of morality versus immorality between and within species on their home planet, than did any other single life form that shared it: They could ruin a species' natural habitat. They could cause, and *did* cause, the extinction of innumerable species that cohabited their planet.

They had the technology to annihilate themselves and everything else on Earth and had, on at least one occasion, come close to doing so.

And whenever levels of stress were high, many mortal creatures made mistakes (while it had to be said, others transcended above the hardship). People were so ingeniously adept at raising their stress, and those of other creatures, that Satan *loved* being around them. He felt like a seagull behind a fishing trawler. The harvest of fallen souls was considerable following in their wake. Humans seemed to catalyse life on Earth into choosing a camp—Satan's or the *other* one's. They were instrumental in Satan's great haul of souls from Earth of late.

And that wasn't all. Humans were mad-keen on going beyond their planet and into other territories out in space! Satan wondered what they would dredge up if they were to begin the colonization of other worlds in other galaxies. It was an exciting prospect, and all because they were able to acquire *material power*.

Satan pondered over the form of mankind's mental makeup. He stretched his imagination and said, "Definitely more in *my* image."

The slave undercarriage trudged on through the bleak landscape filled with horrors, bumper to bumper.

The Devil refocused his mind on issues more current. He appeared irked to his cronies on the throne deck. They feared for their lives, in his erratic company. His eyebrows formed a wide black V as he strained to the tedious task of finding a replacement for the late "great" Keretin, an additional problem to the more major one of finding a place for his esteemed newcomer.

"Bring a replacement for that one, whatsisname? The one I fried?" asked Satan ratily, and looking puzzled.

Banjogong Crisps offered, "Keretin, sire?" He nursed his gushing shoulder with a hand.

"That's the one. Bring a replacement for that piece of crap!" demanded the Devil, annoyed at ineffectively expressing his wish.

The remaining nine looked to each other with sideways glances of uncertainty and fright.

"Who would you have in his place?" asked the cyborg Noctonomicus, whose metal parts had part oxidized to a mat black and part corroded into bubbles which wept a turquoise residue.

Satan gesticulated with a punch of his pitchfork-toting arm. "I don't know, dammit! How about Kermid?" he asked agitatedly.

"Kermid, sire?" asked the deadpan cyborg.

"Yes, you know, Kermid Splain!" He flicked a forefinger at the machine-man as he said it. "The one I dragged down kicking and screaming three days ago."

Kermid was a prospect. Satan delivered him to the thousandth floor personally. But not so hot that Satan was bothered *himself* to find him a place. The soul in man's clothing, soon to arrive, was a far more important individual.

There was momentary silence. The squad of nasty gimps, most of whom were humanoid, *knew* it was racial prejudice. Humans, humans, it was always humans who the Devil more often than not chose to be surrounded by. Not that they held a gram of loyalty for their species. They were just bitter that they themselves were human, and so the brunt of Satan's sadistic attention.

Satan substantiated his decision. "Yes, Kermid's the one. He's doing well apparently. Displaying an admirable degree of callousness to others tortured alongside in his dungeon. His savagery quotient has shot up!" Satan relaxed a little, now that he'd settled for someone.

He looked deep into the choked atmosphere as he said, "And I think his tendency to physical violence will translate nicely into calculated mental violence—when he's trained in telepathy." A little smirk appeared, in approval of himself.

"He'll make a useful assistant, though I have doubts as to whether he's management material—probably not devious enough," the Devil's slicing raspy voice subdued as his mind wandered in further consideration of the replacement.

Normally when Satan chose humans, it was only so that he could indulge his torture fetishes through them. Being chosen as a servant of the Devil would seem to be deliverance from such a fate. Rather, it was a worse one. True, those who were selected to wait upon him hand and foot wouldn't normally meet their physical demise so abruptly under direct torture. But they would witness the accelerated, moldering decay of their material bodies instead, in the Underworld's flesh and steel dissolving atmosphere. They thought of themselves as being comparatively lucky, but they were mistaken.

There were no privileges in Hell.

"Plingo Braintree!" Satan shot a scowling look at the pintsize master of telepathy on this plane of the Underworld.

The crimson crustacean gave a little hop on the moving deck and crackled something to the Devil.

Satan never gave the cursed souls in his possession *affectionate* nicknames—only ones to differentiate between the multitude of turds in his vast fire-and-brimstone toilet basin. The irony was that he *abused* fallen souls in Hell out of hatred for the traces of morality remaining in them. But he *respected* their presence in Hell. And he absolutely *adored* them for their evil potential.

He said to the crablike creature, "Speak English, you silly thing!"

Satan insisted that all his menservants should be able to communicate in English. American English was fine, but it had to be English. This because the administrations network of the netherworld would otherwise break down. If the creature did not have the intelligence even for rudimentary comprehension of the language, it had no place at his side as a personal aide. Anyway, if it didn't have that lingual understanding, it wouldn't have the degree of wickedly directed intelligence either, required for the onerous task. Any mortal considered would have to satisfy *both* criteria.

If a prospective executive did not have the vocal equipment to enable speech in the language but otherwise understood it, design whizzes like Noctonomicus the Cyborg could knock up a voicebox-gadget for the individual. For that matter, he sometimes produced *brain enhancers*, so in theory at least, it was possible for *any* life form to have a position at the Devil's side—just so long as the soul had satisfactorily progressed up the ranks of wickedness. Even so, it was a rare slug that attained the position of *grand inquisitor* or *slave master general.*

Plingo Braintree was naturally brainy, but had such an electromechanical device to assist his speech. The scarlet crab, originally from planet *Deneb 3*, in a solar system within the Andromeda galaxy, hooked one of its pincers over its shelled back, and tapped a brass button. The gizmo, about the size of a box of *Milktray,* came to life, lights the size of penny coins, flicking on and off in a retro, early *Star Trek* sort of way. Simultaneously, from the central grill of the device came the translation of Plingo's dialogue. In a debonair voice, it said, "Plingo Braintree at your service, Lord Satan."

The Devil looked at the carapaced creature, about as big as a large tin of *Quality Street*, with interest. He said, "Now, Braintree, you're a bit good with the old *telepathy*, I want you to train up this *Kermid Splain* when he arrives, so that he can perform his duties as my servant in the way I expect." He uncoiled the spring of one half of his black moustache as he said it.

Plingo acknowledged with a humble crouch. "Yes, Master," he said suavely.

The Devil's moustache sproinged back as he let it go. He looked to the gathering of horrid shites. "People, I'll have Kermid brought here and I want you to focus on getting him trained up for the job. You can be as snide towards him as you like, just so long as it doesn't affect his ability to do his duty as an executive of mine, in this here part of Hell."

The late "great" Keretin, whom earlier Satan had melted, had been a master of torture design of the archaic, traditional type, using basic building materials. The Devil was disgruntled now that he had laid him low, without realizing how soon he would miss his service; Satan knew he'd need suitable "quarters" and tortures for the *man in question*, due into his custody, if none of the ready-mades would do. He wasn't expecting the replacement for Keretin, Kermid Splain, to be of any use in that respect.

The Devil could chase up Keretin's spirit, which may by now have found a suitable physical body in some region of Hell, but only through extensive telepathic investigation undertaken by his *soul database* compilers. If Keretin's soul had already been logged, the "soulsearch" engine of Hell's computer network would show the Devil its location.

But the transmigration of Keretin's sinful soul would only have occurred an hour or so earlier, so wouldn't yet be logged on the database. Besides, Hell's computer network had been part "corrupted" (irony of ironies) by the mysterious CHERUB virus, and the database had been affected.

Anyway, Keretin's new body probably wouldn't have the same design genius brain of its predecessor, so he wouldn't be worth looking for.

The Devil strained a half-smile of resignation, a couple of teeth ejecting from his parted black lips. *Oh well,* thought Satan, looking at the bumbling degenerates around his throne, *we'll just have to see if we can squeeze blood from this bunch of stones.*

Chapter 8

Kieran's enthusiasm had vaguely waned since setting off, due to weariness and concerns about Candlelight Ltd.'s female director, a Ms. Lock (of the Iceni tribe, he mused). Alice, his ex, was demure in character, he assumed due to the upper hand he took in their relationship. That was how he liked it. But what if he had given *her* the upper hand? "Give a broad power and see the contrast in attitude," he wondered.

The proposition seemed so much more exciting a couple of days ago, even earlier that morning: The opportunity to work within a company which really did pay very well *but* which required someone to start up with them immediately, and "hit the ground running", the favourite cliché of many an employer at interviews. Someone who *really knew his stuff.*

What Kieran knew very well was graphic design—straightforwardly a graphic designer. They required a straightforward graphic designer, with extensive professional experience in graphic design. The job, he thought to himself, would be a doddle. With the amount of experience he had, all the hard work he had poured into his career in the attempt to *get to the top* (though he had never really reached the top financially), it was inevitable that he would have the skills sought after. *Just give it your famous Kieran*

Handshake and Smile, and you'll be away, boy! he thought, then checked himself before headmistress Lock. Nevertheless, horny handed from toil invested in jobs that never really satisfied him in their remunerative reward, he was itching to milk this one, believing the job would soon be his.

What Kieran didn't understand was why there had been such a delay before Candlelight Ltd.'s invitation to him. It was a complete mystery.

About five years before, his own graphic design studio venture folded, and he was compelled to join the herds, looking for employment.

In his earlier jobs, he was earning a pittance, as a result of not having the right qualifications and experience in use of the latest industry-standard, desktop publishing software. He even made an attempt at going freelance for a brief period, the wages from employers being so measly, but his business failed. In desperation he sent out, over the course of the following years, salvos of speculative letters asking employers about work opportunities, while at the same time giving details of his own professional experience as a graphic designer. He rarely considered in depth *who* he was writing to, which was probably why he applied to Candlelight Ltd. They weren't strictly a graphic design studio. He only hoped that his ploy would result in better-paid employment.

It did, marginally at least, but only after making slight alterations to his CV, where he gained a graphic design degree and another six years of office experience, working for the biggest graphic design agencies, involved with the most prestigious clients.

He went from being a layman to being a computer graphic design *maestro*, all with just the deftest touch of his fingers over a word processor keyboard.

In other words, he *lied* his way to a better job. Now, owing to his burning desire to excel and five years later on, he *was* closer to being the design genius he had claimed to be, if not inspired, at least very competent, which was why the job was as good as his.

It seemed to Kieran that Candlelight Ltd., a subsidiary of a much larger corporation (according to the brief information accompanying the interview letter), was one of those companies he had approached many years before, without his recollection of having done so. It was peculiar but that was his only explanation for the out-of-the-blue interview letter he had received, which he promptly replied to, confirming he would attend. He did this by e-mail—they gave no phone number.

The letter that confirmed Kieran an interview was to the point, but something about it played on his mind, apart from the fact that the director of the company was female. The *woman* thing was a sticking point for him, however—while there was no doubt in his mind that a woman *could* get a driving instructor to pass her, either by squeezing his willy until he climaxed, or until it turned agony blue, whether she could actually *drive* was a different matter. He was nervous about which way inclined the woman director of Candlelight Ltd. would be. Did she hang to *his* left or right?

He grabbed out the letter from the simple black briefcase by his feet. It was not so easy as the train shunted on its tracks. While he was there he took out an apple too. The empty stomach wasn't helping his ulcer. Kieran had a bite before rereading the letter in his hand:

Mr. Kieran Nichol
21 Erraway Street,
Tewsbury,
London.
TW1 9BW

Ms M. Lock
Director,
Candlelight Ltd.,
Office 7
Floor 20
Shepshire High Street,
Glebeton,
London.
GL26 8FK
candlelight@shadow.com

19th November 2003

Dear Mr. Nichol,

Following your application for the position of senior graphic designer within Candlelight Ltd., we would be pleased to invite you for an interview.

Please attend us at our address (as above) on 24th November, 9am for an informal discussion.

I look forward to meeting you.

Yours sincerely,

Ms M. Lock
Director
Ltd. Candlelight.

The letter was one of the briefest he'd yet seen for such a proposition. *They* would receive him collectively, as suggested by the term "we" but then the letter ended "I"— *"I" look forward to meeting you*, seeming to emphasize Ms Lock's final authority. Did that make her a bit of a dominator?

This thought was slightly disconcerting but it was the misarranged company name at the page's end that was the cause of his mild *puzzlement*. "Hmff. You're excused," he thought but not really having much sympathy for the typist.

He took another nibble at the apple, as drops of its cargo sprinkled onto the paper. It was another distinguishing feature amongst the many others that had collected on the grubby page, but didn't disguise it from being the *golden ticket*. Three bites later he put the page back in the briefcase, with a few more fingerprints and crinkles.

Chapter 9

Kermid Splain arrived, escorted by two of his ex-dungeon masters. They rose onto the throne carriage and unlocked his fetters. He was dressed in a sackcloth tunic.

The bruiser dungeon masters asked, "Will you have him clothed or unclothed, Lord Satan?"

The Devil twitched around his head, briefly considering. "I think there should be some uniformity in the dress (or lack of it) of those I choose to have at hand. I will have him serve me in the nude, just like all the others," he said surely, with a nod.

They proceeded to rip off his tunic.

"My, my! What have we here?" Satan's eyes lit with malignant glee.

Splain appeared in fine fettle. Satan would see him decline to the gutter from a dizzying height.

"Begone!" said the Devil to the guards, and they left.

Satan liked his entourage to appear naked before him, to see the effects of the strangulating acrid atmosphere on their defenseless bodies. They were executives, but that didn't exempt them from Hellish torment. He liked to see the most closely held possession of those materialistic souls—their bodies—perform as a *pain machine*; constantly breaking down, plastic and metal disintegrating, flesh dangling, puffing and sloughing off. Their miserable predicament he found endlessly amusing—how they wished for a body that didn't malfunction, while desperately tending their own ravaged one.

Satan loved to see them spinning the wheel, and wonder why they never got anywhere. They couldn't see that they had to get off first to be able to go places—be free of physical suffering. Put differently, they couldn't see the woods for the trees. To Satan's sadistic delight, they behaved like moths that had missed the moon, frying slowly on a forty-watt bulb instead.

One relatively trifling problem was resolved. Kermid for Keretin. But Satan was still at odds as to where he should park the precious mortal man, unlike any other, that would come into his possession, within a matter of hours. The Devil's brain, networked to the entire dark side of the Universe, was hurting now with the mental strain. He looked hither and yon as his throne carriage continued meandering about the thousandth level of Hell.

As one might expect, there was a lot of roasting, boiling, frying and baking of wicked creatures going on, what with there being such an abundance of the element of fire in the place. Persecution by fire was indeed an old favourite of Satan's, but he also liked to experiment with other forms of torture, and liked a change every once in a while.

His ingenuity was in his often-subtle application of temptation and tortures elsewhere in the universe, to corrupt the victim's soul without their awareness, but in Hell, he didn't have to arse around with such guile. The sophistication in the *nether regions of immorality* was required in the inventing of unique torture methods, of a far more savage variety than those he devised for use say, on Earth.

Even so, on floor one thousand of Hell, there was an upper limit imposed (by Satan himself) on the pain factor possible by any torture method that could be used. Those on lower levels were infinitely more horrendous.

He asked his executives standing about him on the throne carriage for suggestions, based on a theme. "Boys and girls, now, tell me what would be your proposal for an appropriate manner by which to torment the newcomer's body and soul?" His hands resting on the armrests, he pushed out his elbows, leaned forwards and snappily looked at each.

One of the putrefying bunch, the cyborg Noctonomicus, put up a hand. "Flaying, sire?"

"Too passé," Satan said dismissively.

Magnanimana with her hand up, "Slow poisoning, Lord Satan?"

"Far too boring for my taste," the Devil said, his hand from under his chin waving her off. "No, this is not what we want—*or not what I want*. I want the focus on an idea within the theme. Try again," his hand back under his beardy chin, frizzling the fibres.

Hand up, Zipodemozzz Naan—"How about electrocution?"

"Be more specific," Satan said, turning to him and placing a finger over his gloss black lips, pointed to his hooknose.

The tremulous gurgle issued from Zipodemozzz's disintegrated throat, "Well, Lord Satan, we could strap him to a chair and send a million volts surging through his fastened body?"

"To what end?" asked the Devil, resting on a single elbow, finger to his lip, somewhat despondent.

Zipodemozzz's gurgle, "Well, it's torture, innit?"

The Devil took in a deep breath and inclined his head a little.

"Oh, how very jolly splendid," he seethed, looking hard at Zipodemozzz now and forcing a grin that was equally a teeth-bearing snarl.

Zipodemozzz cowered, bracing himself with his arms stretched over his face and head.

Satan breathed out—the gassy blue exhalation visible to all, and mellowed.

"*Zippo baby*, the torture 'system' you just described, would render the man's body a crispbread in two point five nanoseconds." He looked to skybound puffs of smoke from the various bonfires in the vicinity as he elaborated. "The pain would be so intense, that as rapidly as he would evacuate the contents of his bowels, so he would in similar time give up his intellectual reasons for choosing the dark side of existence."

The air was thick with the lament of the doomed, but not even one on the throne carriage dared a silent fart.

"Desperate men do desperate things, my friends. The man would pull out from the closet of his mind the god that only two point five nanoseconds earlier he thought of as a *fool's hope—a make believe saviour!*" Satan looked back at the stooges.

"Ooohh, aaahh. Yes, Lord Satan," they nodded respectfully from the waist towards him and each other, in reverence of this illuminating tidbit.

Zipodemozzz Naan reentered, genuinely perturbed, "But Devil, sir, as soon as the voltage was turned down, he would return to his cynical, pessimistic self—"

Instantly, Satan whipped up the trident in his right hand, twirled it like a cowboy twirls his Colt 45 and pointed the butt at Naan's nose, a couple of inches away from it.

The sickly collective cringed in morbid expectancy, some looking away from what would shortly be well-baked Naan bread.

The devil squeezed the metal pole in his hand and slowly a trickle of plasma pulsed down it from his fisted grasp. At the butt of the pole it fizzled, and a little spark of blue lightning darted from it, onto the fleshy chunk that was Zipodemozzz's nose.

"Oh *God*, please don't hurt me anymore, please! *God* help me!" his desperate gurgle made the Devil worshippers wish Satan *had* made more of the moment. Then just as quickly as the traitorous plea left Zipodemozzz's rotting lips, he fell to his knees before Satan. "Oh, Great Devil, you are my lord and master, only you I adore . . ." he beseeched.

The Devil lounged back on his throne, fingers splayed under his chin, elbow digging into the rest, and sighed. "Rise, Zipodemozzz. I'm not going to destroy you, well, not today anyway, because you made a good point. It appears you *have* returned to your true master, after your little crisis. Very good."

Naan rose, an arm folded over his puffed chest, the other behind his back, looking at his colleagues smugly, apparently having won the favour of the Prince of Darkness after all.

Satan keeled back on his seat and hoisted the trident above Zipodemozzz's head height. He hurled his fork holding fist at him. The butt of the trident cracked into Zipodemozzz's forehead, so that his upper body vibrated until the embedded pole shuddered to a standstill.

"Your crude electrocution torture is still a gamble, Zipodemozzz," said Satan smoothly. "The man may equally decide that the reason for being relieved of the pain was due to the acceptance of God in his life"—which would be truly the case, Satan knew—"which would then only reinforce his newly acquired faith."

Zipodemozzz, too much taken by surprise to whimper in the usual way, said simply, "Devil, sir, you've caught the butt of your trident in my head." He looked up cockeyed at the intricately textured bar.

Satan crouched forward, facing him, small startlement on his face. "Oh dear. It seems I have indeed misplaced my trademark!"

Zipodemozzz Naan gyrated crazily as Satan leaned back on the handle and yanked, recovering his property. It dislodged with a muffled pop. The thin, weary skin on Mr. Naan's head hadn't ruptured, but there was a great dent on his forehead where the ornamental butt of the Devil's vicious trident had impressed itself.

Satan addressed the collective once more. "Okay, chaps, joking aside, I like Zippo's electricity idea—we could maybe make it our theme. But with one proviso: We've got to do it in a way that won't overwhelm the precocious sonofabitch we'll soon have in our fold. The pain must be about bearable. And, it's got to be more elaborate than just a set up where he might be wired to a generator and electrocuted to death. No, it's got to be more artful, more sophisticated than that. Got it?"

"Yes sire/Master/Lord Satan!"

"Now," said Satan, commandingly, "hop lively. I want you to knock up a rig, on which we'll torture the newcomer, based on Zipodemozzz's electrocution theme, and my expansion upon that. Get to it!"

"Yes sire/Master/Lord Satan!" they cried, their telepathic instructions already splattering out from the throne carriage to those within the teeming labyrinth who would assist in the diabolical project.

Chapter 10

Kieran went by vital statistics and this was a pedigree race hound. He recalled the accompanying document that had come with the interview note. The way it was worded practically stated the job was his! Working his way from the tail to the head—the salary they would pay, was more than one-half times greater than any he'd yet had for starting similar work—and was an indication of the beast's long-term potential.

The early bird really did get the worm. His few career successes over the last eleven years were as a result of heeding this adage. And the few missed opportunities over this time only instilled in him a wilder, primal desire, to be first at the table, first at the carrion—to work himself harder to be competitive in this, as he believed it to be, cut-throat market, almost to the point of being cut-throat himself. And there he had been earlier that morning, wondering in what way he made a *contribution to society*—what a joke, considering his attitude towards other careerists, supposedly seeking to do the same.

He'd sent Candlelight Ltd. an e-mail, without reading their invitation twice.

Yes, he really had been quick off the mark and this fervent attitude did not conclude with the employment market. He ventured that it would be wise to extend it to life in general, because, after all, his career was his life, unfortunately, and he might as well be consistent.

In this respect, Kieran considered he was only behaving in the way that made humans the dominant species on the planet. The question and answer of argument had been resonating in his head for years, and now he had fleshed out his hypothesis of how and why humanity had reached the pinnacle of all life on Earth . . .

As far as Kieran was concerned, successful modern day humans displayed similar behaviour (if disguised) to that, say, of the caveman, their ancestor. In nature they were identical, and that went for the ancestors of the caveman also, all the way back to the single celled amoebas (which apparently was what all life originated from) of his secondary education biology class.

Yes, those primitive people were a good means by which man's nature could be illustrated. What was their motivation in life? What was their reason for hunting mammoth, finding caves and making fires? It wasn't for fun. Obviously it was purely for survival, no fuss and no frills: And not necessarily as a team either. The caveman had such limited foresight that often they couldn't see how teamwork could be of personal benefit. Thus it was limited and short lived.

An individual only cooperated if the benefit to himself was obvious. Anything not promoting their *personal* survival, *as individuals*, would be irrelevant activity and for that reason was never engaged in. It was all ruthlessly business-like and they were professionals in the business.

There was no etiquette or drawn out protocol, no please and thank you—a grunt would do, *if* that. No long good-byes—a grunt would do, *if* that.

There was no self-sacrifice for another, no free medical treatment if one was mauled by a saber-tooth, and no social security to supplement them when their hunter-gatherer takings were low for a week.

Kieran wagered that there were no tears shed when one of them died, that was if they were *capable* of crying. They may even have been disposed of violently by their own clan, for not pulling their weight in the hunt, one of those odd occasions when the Stone Age man worked alongside his kin.

And kissing and cuddling? Sex was simply rolling on and off. Basic and functionally effective. It had more to do with caveman primitive urges than any premeditated family planning—simply an evolutionary trick by which to continue the species.

This seed of mankind, thought Kieran, was a very good way indeed of seeing the simplicity of life, because in his opinion, the Stone Age man was so *very obviously selfish*.

They were at odds with a hostile natural environment. Nature in the raw, wild and chaotic, was their enemy. Poorly protected as they were, they could perish in the freezing nights. They were not on top of the food chain. Hundreds of predators could make a meal out of them at any time. Their struggle against the environment was so intense, that any embryonic possibility of their having a civilized community was precluded. They were *forced* to take advantage of each other under such hardships, were *driven* to rob, rape and steal from each other, to be able to live another day, as individuals, even as their victim expired. They were *forced to remain selfish*.

Antisocial behaviour spurred from the individual's natural instinct to survive.

And survive the cavemen did, establishing the foundation of all the generations of men that would follow. They, primitive man, were ultimately successful.

Kieran's train of thought continued to rumble: Now why on earth should he, or any other human being on the planet, pretend to be something other than what they really were?

True, the natural world was a tamer place than it had been in the day of the caveman. There was food, shelter and warmth due to urban planning, agricultural, technological and all the other developments, which were meant to benefit the individual through intelligent exploitation of the natural environment.

The animals (in the developed world at least), were subjugated: in controlled countryside, on farms, in zoos, in laboratories, or kept as domestic pets. Their numbers and behaviour were strictly observed. They were culled if necessary, which was just the way Kieran liked it.

But when push came to shove, when the modern day privileges didn't suffice, men reverted to their true nature, which was that of their primitive ancestors. *Call a spade a spade*, Kieran thought. *I know you want it, and I know you'll get it, if I don't get it first*.

For sure, man had become more sophisticated, but politics was simply another tool used to secure one's own selfish interests, and that went all the way from the kids in the schoolyard to the prime minister. If any successful man propounded anything other than that, if they had convinced themselves of anything other than this fact, then they were either deluded—in which case at some point they would be forced to realize this—or else they were lying through serrated teeth. Kieran wasn't thinking about the farcical successes supposedly enjoyed by those indoctrinated into religious institutions, where these gullible followers gave all their worldly possessions *away* to gain happiness. They weren't players. They weren't even on the board.

In the profile of every successful politician or businessman, one thing was common, and that was the ruthless way in which they tracked their objectives, their prey, at all costs, that assured their success. Kieran was certain there was no way he was going to change his modus operandi for the sake of indulging in experiments in futility.

And why should he, Kieran Nichol, adulterate this winning formula for life, tried and trusted by many a millionaire, when life was so short? *You only get one crack at this*. The sun was still shining for him *now*—in a manner of speaking (his mind felt like a urinal, his body, the plumbing). He had to make the most of the remaining dregs of virility that pulsed through him to work, work, work, earn, earn, earn.

Only three months earlier, Kieran's partner had left him. He felt very angry about the incidents that led to their separation and the issues surrounding it.

Alice was twenty-nine, four years younger than him. They'd been growing apart for some time but Kieran could never really pin down the reason. Towards the end it became very messy, but he couldn't let her go.

She had torn herself away and left *him* with this bloody wound. It would take years for it to heal, if it would ever at all. She was entirely blameworthy. Unreasonable. He had planned it all out so meticulously and she had spoilt everything.

"Taking seventeen thousand a year *clean*. Ungrateful. Inconsiderate. Working myself into the *ground* for her! No gratitude. What more could she ask of me! Ten-hour days, six days a week, *struggling* up that ladder! A *senior* graphic designer and for what?" The trickle continued through his mind, the anger redirected through blame but not reduced. If ever he found himself in another relationship, there was no way he was going to be quite so attentive to the other half's sensibilities and requirements. "You'll only be led astray," he concluded, as the ache in the pit of his stomach suddenly turned into a sharp twinge.

Suppose he *did* spend more time with her, what value was there in restaurant meals, cinema going and ice-skating? Why should he put up with her dreadful hippy music when he hated it and most other music?

But then that wasn't really what she wanted, was it?

Anyway, her friends were so tedious. No way he was going to spend time with her in *their* company—Charlene and Thomas, *that pair*—as they talked about "Ulysses" their dog, the human behaviour expert of the canine world, or the reconstruction of their conservatory, the regularity of which in their conversation suggested it were the renovation of no less than the Sistine Chapel.

Not too fussed about her other pals either, he thought.

What was more important—building for the future or living it up now? You *have* to think about the future. I don't care for *nightclubs* and *parties*—I'll leave that to the late teens.

But she didn't want that either. He briefly considered that perhaps he was missing the point.

"What do you mean?"
"You know what I mean."
"I don't know what you mean!"
"You *should* know what I mean."

This was the gist of many a hollow argument, meant to amend their flagging partnership. They became corrosive to their relationship, as reiterant as rust over unchromed steel. They only brought the brittle end closer. She was always reluctant to spell it out, believing this sort of thing was either known innately, or not at all. Comprehension wouldn't be brought about by any deliberate effort on her part.

Often she described him as evasive, redirecting his focus, hoping to resuscitate what might be a withered understanding, but he insisted there was no basis for her accusation, and reminded her that all the toil and trouble he abided was for them both—for their continued relationship.

On the odd occasion when Kieran *had* eked out a direct reply to his plaint, it was to no avail. What she said, those placid words, weren't the water to a flagging rose she hoped they would be. What she told him filtered through the grill on a gutter, the pure droplets of her philosophy, her outlook on life would enliven his senses, heighten his reality, but their effect was superficial and short lived. It trickled through into the vessel of stagnant detritus that, *self-admittedly*, his mind was, not washing it away, but only temporarily diluting its foulness.

She would become distant again, and he would ask once more, "What do you want from me?"

"If you don't know, you'll never know."

Not that Kieran really wanted to understand *anyway*, at least, not at the time. He just wanted to appear to be concerned, devoted to *them*. Her ideas never detracted from the efficacy of his own philosophy, because hers wasn't one. It was self-delusion (which could lead to self-destruction if he wasn't there to balance her), a *Deadhead* attitude harking back to flower children, who were now either destitute and drunk, or accountants. But she could be that way. He didn't mind, and he could support her in her state of misguided innocence. She could remain blissfully ignorant for as long as he could provide the essentials.

Unfortunately, that wasn't the arrangement she wanted. She wanted him to *believe* in her outlook on life, to *adopt* it, to *advance* it, not just nod and smile at her as if she were Daddy's favourite. He supposed she wanted him to become a kindred spirit.

If she wanted *that*, she would have to become so on *his* terms. His way of life left him feeling rough, but that was unavoidable—to eat meat was to invite heart failure, but not to eat meat was to starve. As far as he was concerned, she wanted to have greater leverage to direct their shared existence *her way*, which just couldn't happen. It would be like a Tory government conceding to the Green Party—or the

Monster Raving Loony Party, he thought dismissively, same difference.

He and Alice were the basis of a nuclear family (in the middle of a nuclear war that was modern living, in his opinion), and there was no way he could jeopardize that by allowing her to take the helm.

But she was gone now, and so was the family.

He was not going to concede he was in error, by calling her and besides, she seemed sure of what she wanted, when she said farewell.

He wondered how she would survive without him.

Kieran opened his briefcase and finally pulled out the little bottle of tablets. The childproof cap was simple, swallowing those hamster pellets wouldn't be. As such, his resolve to bare the pain was gone. He clenched his jaw and resentfully gulped down the tablets.

Chapter 11

The Devil was standing taller on the deck than all the ghoulish assistants bar one—it was a human he had turned into a woodlouse that resembled a wooly mammoth (in size). It was another project on a theme, similar to the one underway, that spawned "Woodlouse Man", that theme being *superheroes*. Of course, Satan had envisaged in Woodlouse Man the ultimate *supervillain*, with suitably ultimate superpowers—as everyone knows, a woodlouse has twelve penises.

The Devil thought he'd be a positively super addition to the Buggery Float. Unfortunately, the substantial insect failed to live up to expectations. On stage he just preferred to curl up into one big, black, armour-plated ball. It was a complete non-event. He was difficult to torture too, for the same reason.

So despite not having proven himself in the field of vindictiveness, Satan kept Woodlouse Man close by. He'd see his brainchild rot slowly, fumigated in the noxious gases of Hell, like his earthly cousins one hundredth his size. Satan would get his money's worth, one way or another.

"Hup to, hup to! Keep it moving you 'orrible lot!" spat the Devil at his cohort.

It was a paperless design project. All concepts and engineering problems were discussed telepathically between the black magicians simpering at Satan's heels. The summoners on the throne deck organized the lesser slave masters, crawling over the hot cinders of Hell below, to get their butts into gear. A procession of about thirty suffering souls were assembled at the right of the Devil's throne carriage. Satan's prosecutors bustled them forward into an area of forest over a rolling region of the sulphur-shrouded landscape.

The Devil watched the hustle bustle of his slave lumberjacks semi-interestedly. He saw the bobbing torchlights disappear within the blackened, skeletal trees.

Just twenty meters in front of the throne cart, a gang of slave workers dug trenches, shoveling the soil to the sides in heaps. They formed conical shapes like shady Christmas trees, the glowing coals bedded in the earth a parody of red fairy lights. The sweating, dirty creatures toiled in the eerie glow, whipped across their backs for the shortest pause in their exertion.

Satan looked at the diabolic ecosystem he had painstakingly assembled, in which human beings were so prominent. No artist or cartographer during his time on Earth had ever seen it, let alone painted or mapped it out. Satan recalled Hieronymus Bosch and his belly shuddered as he guffawed—so much wallpaper for a child's bedroom.

He returned to his throne, lounging back, observing the fruits of extreme fascism ripen before his very eyes. He closed the lids over the jet eyeballs. Flaring the nostrils on his wicked, aquiline nose, he sucked in the noxious, soot ridden air, fragrant of burning flesh. It invigorated his mind.

Opening them again, he peered to the distant west. An interesting showdown was taking place on a field cratered by explosions. From the right of the pockmarked mud strait rushed a few hundred football hooligans from all earthly nations, completely naked, apart from the foot attire they wore. Rushing from the left, a tribe of Neanderthal men and women, with their personal effects—clubs and spears and stones, clad in mammoth fur.

The two clashed together at the centerline of the pitch. But it wasn't an irresistible force meeting an immovable object. First the hooligan bigots repelled the Neanderthal surge. Then in retreat, the Neanderthal men and women were violently butted, punched and kicked to the ground, flailing their weapons uselessly within the torrent. Half concussed, mired in the mud, they were set upon by the packs of soccer-rioter fascists, kicked in the head until dead. For all their instinctive brutality, ancient man couldn't match that of the demented Homo sapiens.

It was a harrowing, sickening vision, even to those well accustomed to the sights and sounds of Hell, as the ones in the throne cavalcade were. Their attention had momentarily been stolen by the spectacle. They wondered, *Could this irrepressibly wild mob become the future rulers of Hell?*

Satan, steepling his forefingers under his chin, his elbows against his side, appeared fascinated. "Well, well. A *very* impressive display from *them*. Not just a colony of *pissants*, as I previously thought. More . . . *ants*!" He popped his head around with this realization. "Army ants even!" he said, feeling enthusiasm.

"So what next? They're not really suited to administrative work. Not even one of Noctonomicus's brain enhancers could boost them sufficiently—the retardation is too great. But I would like to pay them a fitting tribute just the same—for their sheer savagery for savagery's sake." He lowered his heavy brow, pouted and pinched his lower lip.

The surrounding crowd of lowlifes waited on tenterhooks, some literally, for Satan to declare his award to the football thugs.

He tangled his Fu Manchu beard around a long forefingernail. "Perhaps the dinosaur pen?" He unwound the hairs. "Naah!"

The sickly workforce held their bad breath.

His eyes beamed blackly as his monobrow lifted. "I propose we treat them to a meal! And make them the chief ingredient!" He looked around swiftly for the accolade.

None was forthcoming. Instead bemusement.

"I propose we serve up . . . a curry. They'll make a *fine, hot curry*! Applause now please!" he swiveled around his head, scowling down.

Hoots and handclaps.

"Yes—a hot, football-hooligan Vindaloo—medium rare. Howd'ya like that?"

The fiendish slave masters were forcing a Mexican wave. It convulsed like a swallowed egg down the gut of a snake.

"Verilly! It's the favourite cuisine in this part of Hell!"

The approving whistles and clamour belied their terror. The previous occasion they were forced to eat one of Satan's Vindaloos, they weren't able to crap for a week and their asses burned when they finally did.

Satan's shiny red face leered. "We can be liberal with the pain—they'll never turn to 'the light'," he

71

waggled his index fingers in the air to form inverted commas. "Perhaps the next body their promising souls find will have a brain to boot!"

Above the slave labourers being pushed to the brink of death, black vultures circled, expecting easy meals. They would have their fill, but the meat would be saturated with virulent bacteria and toxins that would overwhelm even their hardy immune system.

Satan watched a few swoop upon a corpse and do what they do. Then he sighed and turned again to the activity. "Get on with it! Didn't you know there's no rest for the wicked?" Satan laughed nastily at his own droll repartee.

The slave workforce scurried like leafcutter ants over the building site. Unfolding before the crimson governor and his officers was the machination that would be the introductory torture for *the man in question*, shortly to set foot on the unhallowed soil of Hell. It was nothing too elaborate and very low-tech. The scaffold was assembled from the recently forested timber. When completed, the telepathic designers intended it to be a rough and ready, simple and effective solution to Satan's most pressing concern.

The Devil, attempting to languish regally on the throne, was defeating his efforts with constant restless readjustments on his seat. He was finding these preparations so very tedious to watch. He made his presidency over the process more tolerable by diluting it with pleasant thoughts of the *fine curry* he would serve up, to reward his worker's stalwart efforts. As they hoisted, winched and levered the wooden trusses, he knew the curry was well on the way to fruition.

The ingredients had been earlier rounded up, thence processed. Round about now they would be dolloped into the pot, foot apparel and all, along with the chilies—so many, many chilies. He imagined the richly textured stodge curdling in the old black cauldron and inhaled the creamy, dreamy steams belching from it. He absentmindedly smiled as a thin snake tongue slid over his black lips.

Magnanimana, once a Trilurian queen, bleated to Satan, "My lord, the apparatus is near to completion," bringing back his attention to the thingamajig coming together on the smouldering turf before the throne carriage.

Satan narrowed his eyes judgmentally. Between two supporting frameworks was a long beam to which some workers were fixing ropes. The ropes dangled from it at intervals. Satan was skeptical of his design team's utility, seeing the rustic edifice that looked like nothing more than a simple gallows. It seemed they had flopped. He assessed the possibility of quickly flinging them into the curry, but then refrained from such a rash action. It had been enough of a piddling task to find a replacement for the late "great" Keretin, who, if he hadn't been meltified by Satan, could've come up with something that was half decent for the torturing of the *lost* but *now found* soul.

He sighed and said resignedly, "Very good, Magnanana—Magnesia, no, Magnina. Oh, why did I ever give you such a difficult name!" His face was redness times two. He looked at her with a frown. "Thank you!" and issued a firm kick to her buttock, causing her to tumble and fall, sprawling over the edge of the carriage.

No one bothered to help her back to her feet.

Arzoley Kyam, previously a high-ranking state official of the planet Plishul, ventured to the foot of Satan, bending on one knee as much for stability as suppliancy. "Good sir, the device is indeed almost complete but requires a few mortals for the set piece and demonstration."

"Jolly good, Arzoley. Who shall we choose? Let's make things simple for ourselves, shall we? See that bunch taking a breather," he flickered his fingers at the exhausted chain gang gasping the corrosive air, those that hadn't collapsed under the lash of the overseers. "You may utilize them." He brought his hand under his head, resting his elbow on a knee.

"Oh, thank you Lord Satan, how very convenient." He bowed profusely as he edged backwards.

The unthanked workers were encircled and apprehended by the companions they had laboured alongside moments earlier, without the energy to put up any sort of fight. They were trussed up in groups of threes and brought up to the dangling ropes on the central spar across the scaffold, with a manpowered crane and pulley. The trios were fastened in position to the ropes, so that their feet were about two feet from the mottled glow of the ground.

The *servants cum designers* of Satan took their attention away from the contraption, satisfied that it was finished. They looked to their master apprehensively trying to perceive his temperament.

He said, "This had better be good, guys," and rested his bearded jaw gently on the top of a hand, briefly seeming placid, waiting to be entertained, with a *let's see the performance and then we'll decide what to do with you* attitude.

The faces on the throne carriage were trembling.

Sarmosa, a lilac humanoid with festering sores of pale blue, quite bravely tried to coerce a positive attitude from the Prince of Evil. "Oh Lord Satan, we are most certain you will not be disappointed . . ."

A pair of the vultures had keeled over and their bodies spasmed with departing life. Another couple teetered among the shreds of flesh and bits of bone as though they were filled with *special brew* rather than meat. The lucky ones that had managed to get aloft, rather than soar gracefully, scuttled haphazardly through the air like monstrous moths, while others of the fitter ones swooped upon the newly dead.

Sarmosa crooned before a pensively postured Satan, seated on his throne of many skeletons. "Sir, would you permit the show to commence?" he enquired.

"Don't let me hold you up," rasped Satan. He flubbered his lower lip and lolled his head slightly on his supporting hand, waiting uneasily on his chair for the start.

Sarmosa turned and curtly double clapped his three fingered hands, the fingers on one, filled with a raging infection, bulged like sausage balloons. Eight strangely attired humans approached from out of a ground level smoke contrail. A thin, highly reflective, diagonal strap from their shoulder to their hip ended with a similarly shiny holster, which housed a strikingly high-tech gadget, formed of crisp, geometric components, highlighted in the reddish, glimmering light. As they turned into the sad congregation around the wooden structure, on their backs could be seen a contrivance that resembled an oversized, silver-foiled, packet of butter. There were fine, long, zigzagging wires slotted into its bottom facet. They converged into the handle of the geometrical gizmo in its sheath.

It was merely coincidence that in this district, in this plane of Hell, life existed in a very primitive context. Satan and his entourage could travel a couple of miles west and come within a quadrant of the landscape choc-full of the most cutting edge technology—dedicated exclusively to the purpose of demoralizing (with the end objective of corrupting further) the souls of the condemned mortals.

A few of Satan's whip swinging overseers suddenly jarred, as though their brain were being rollicked by some phantom claw (it was actually the less than gentle telepathic instruction of their managers on the throne carriage). Then they forcibly shooed the dejected crowd, that had been standing at the scaffold looking toward the Devil's carriage, like starving peasants before a feudal lord. They scuttled to the side supports of the construct.

The odd, shinily equipped eight moved onward toward the scaffolding. Each one stood before one of the naked trios, suspended from the crossbeam. They turned and looked toward the throne carriage.

The protracted ceremony made Satan grit his teeth and roll his eyes skyward in irritation. Those standing timidly on the throne carriage heard his long rolling growl, thinly disguised as an exhalation of breath. Banjogong Crisps, whose arm was still covered in lines of syrupy, beetroot-coloured blood from his ripped shoulder to his fingertips, was the first (but only by microseconds) to telepathically blurt the order to start to the mysterious eight, at the wooden scaffold below.

They synchronously turned to the bound bundles, and lifted the gizmos from their holsters. There came a low-pitched thrum from the power units on their backs, barely within the range of hearing. At the underside of the backpack, the generating power crackled energetically, and sprang along the coiled wire to the instrument in their hands, which they held by an insulated handle. The strange electricity engulfed the gadget above the handle, casting cool blue light upon the trios dangling from the scaffold, and the subdued gathering.

The wielders of the energy rods raised them. Then one slashed a woman huddled in one of the roped trios, midway across the scaffold. She shrieked in pain as the blue-white, ragged light clung, drawing scribbles around her body. As soon as her cry ceased, another scream speared through the air, as one of the other human "notes" was seared from energy applied by a "musician's" stick. Other screamed "notes" and a tune began to emerge as another and another applied his weird, electric prodder.

The Devil's scaffold and its surroundings were bathed in the sickly, powder blue light, as the dangling bodies incandesced, nerve burning energy forking from them to the timber members of the "musical instrument". Some smoked and cracked.

The series of whimpers, squawks, screams and groans of different pitch puffed through the tangible air and engulfed the throne carriage. Together, end-to-end, the exclamations of agony formed an air-splintering tune. It was the earthly king of swing, Hank Zinatra's "Los Angeles".

Said Satan, "Yeah, I like it! Yeah baby!" He hummed along to the blood curdling tune and karaoked the chorus, ". . . It's up to you, LA, LA!" clicking his fingers while swinging his fist, like a maraca in time to the music.

But for others a distance away, it was about as *easy listening* as fingernails scraping over a chalkboard, multiplied a thousand times. For those nearer it was even worse. Unbearable to hear or *watch*—it was an atrocity of a visual spectacle too. Such was the nerve-racking power that cauterized the notes out of the sufferers dangling from the abominable musical instrument, they squirmed and juddered. Projectile vomit squished from their gaping mouths. For that matter, something poured from every orifice—blood spilled from their ears, noses and eyes and even their skin pores. From below, an abundance of poo and wee was forthcoming, as they contorted and twisted above.

One of the barbaric musicians delayed a note too long. The aura around the victim whitened brilliantly.

"EeeeIIIIAAAAAAAH!!!" she screamed, just before her midsection exploded, like a water filled party balloon (only it was internal body fluids that splurged in airborne ripples about her). The reamed sections of her body tumbled down, as the rope that bound her and her former partners, immediately slackened. They too flopped, through the hoop that had previously secured them, onto the glowering earth. None of them rose from the semi-molten ground.

Satan was riled by this occurrence. Until that moment, he was finding the rendition of Ol' Gray-Eyes' hit very rousing, was really having a *good time*.

Now as the musicians below (telepathically conducted by Satan's stooges on the throne carriage) tried to hold the tune together, it was very obvious that the instrument was three notes short of a virtuoso performance. Ruffled, one of the power rod wavers played a duff note. Instantly Banjogong, disoriented by his blood loss (in buckets from his reconstituted shoulder), pushed out some telepathic pain of his own, toward the discordant musician—the sharp twinge of imaginary forceps to the core of his brain! The musician buckled and staggered. The arrangement fell to pieces as the other players panicked.

Satan could be heard to hiss through his clenched teeth. Simultaneously his brow bunched about the top of his nose, in anger. Fretting big time, the terrified servants of Satan on the throne carriage whirled around to face their wrathful master, so they could better decide what evasive action they should take.

Satan rammed the base of his trident onto the lashed Tyrannosaur bones of the throne deck, one, two, three times, with loud, ringing BANGS. The cacophony petered out, the last dregs of nerve-racking energy, like white-hot veins and arteries, wriggled around the bodies of the *kings of swing*, swinging pitifully to the last on their frayed ropes, as a few sad squirts of poo and wee shot from them, like the remaining washing liquid from squeezy bottles. One final wheezing groan and the dismal performance was at an end.

The Devil just looked dead ahead at his broken toy, frowning a very heavy frown, puffing out angrily with bellowing cheeks. He watched with great intensity for ages, as the living crap on the throne deck cringed and cowered in terror. Then the black frowning mouth gradually bent, to form a massively unsettling smile, teeth jutting out everywhere.

Chapter 12

Kieran stood before the entrance of the tower block and for a moment looked skyward, trying to catch sight of the apartment floor that would almost certainly be his new workplace. Straining to look through the fog, he couldn't see beyond the third floor. He narrowed his eyes to sharpen his focus but then instead proceeded to the automatic, glass sliding doors that engagingly opened before him.

Despite feeling physically frayed and experiencing the advances of nervous tension, he walked through with a certain optimism. He was in the process of securing his future.

The attendant at the reception desk gave him a cursory glance and allowed him to go through.

Kieran took the lift to the twentieth floor, where Candlelight Ltd. was located and arrived on its landing.

I'm all right! Would you believe, I'm going to be early by at least five minutes!

"Yippidiiii," he mumbled dryly. Simultaneously the word echoed in his head, rather more loudly, "YIPPIDIIII!" While ostensibly calm and well spoken, inwardly he bubbled with sardonic jubilation. More often, it was furious obscenity, like pernicious gas within an apparently "good egg".

It was 8:50 and he was due at Candlelight Ltd. at 9:00. He was chuffed about that, but fairly depleted, and his gut was burning from having run in a somewhat stumbling manner, the remaining distance from the station, despite having taken the painkillers.

As he walked along the corridor, a pungent smell of rose or heliotrope or something (he was happy that it was a flower), filled his sinuses, as a blue aproned cleaner walked by him, in the opposite direction, but his eyes locked onto the door through which was his new workplace.

The corridor was so long! His footsteps ticked the countdown to *a new experience*, he thought to himself in cynicism. Certainly, having an extra five thousand pounds in his pocket would be a pleasant experience. Really, he had long ago come to the conclusion that one job was much the same as another. This one would be different only remuneratively.

Swirling through the *event horizon* into the mysterious *singularity* of adventure! He recalled the astronomy magazine he had browsed on the train. The mental metaphor didn't really kindle within him the enthusiasm he thought it might. He walked on anyway—outstanding bills were enough of an incentive to go on.

On the verge of startlement at the remaining gulf between himself and the room, he suddenly became absorbed by the beckoning space. At the same time as the relief at reaching his destination filled him, so did a pervasive feeling of interacting with another entity's energy, as though the office was alive, and within this feeling, another impression of brain matter seeping away from his head, sucked into the nearing room.

The office somehow seemed detached from everything, except *him*. It was no longer part of the tower. In fact, nearing it, he felt separated from Glebeton, and London, in fact everything else he could fumble for as a reference in his mind. A feeling of separation in both time and distance. Even so he did not necessarily feel afraid—more apprehensive and yes, intrigued. At the same time he knew that he was meant to be *there* and refrained from analyzing further to remember the whereabouts of this place. He felt this question was unimportant.

As he neared, the door ahead opened invitingly. He hastened his stride onward.

An oversize wedge heel clipped the carpet fixing at the door and he found himself tumbling to the floor. Flustered, he considered the reaction this dramatic entrance would provoke from his colleagues-to-be. But before he raised his view from the level of the floor, a young hand reached and grasped his own and he looked to the owner.

"Are you okay? That was quite an entrance!"

With the tiredness, stomach, heels and finally this seam splitting fall, he was tempted to flatly say, "NO!" and "FUCK OFF!" He restrained himself, aware of his hot face and her fresh one, before attenuating to her beauty, noticing first the smile. His nerves settled enough and studying her delicate features, he thought to himself that she could only have just passed her twentieth birthday.

"Yes, I'm okay I think," Kieran said, gradually getting to his feet more quickly than he needed to, and staggering. "Memorable, that's for sure!" he grinned as he said it, trying to make out it didn't hurt—*Not fucking cool*, he thought, annoyed and humiliated.

"We all trip every now and again." Her hand moved up to his forearm. "Personally, I thing tripping's good for you in certain circumstances. Gets all that pent up tension out of your system!"

A peculiar thing for her to say, he thought.

She held his eyes with hers, looking at him full frontally through his dilated irises, and onto the corrugated surface of his brain. He didn't understand what she was trying to get at, as disorientated as he was.

"Yes, I suppose so!" he agreed obtusely.

Agitated, he looked to the faces of the office staff to see their expressions, at the same time pressing creases from his trench coat. He was surprised as he glanced at each, that not one showed any emotion, either that of amusement or dismay. Strange. He tried to conclude whether this was a good or bad thing. No expression whatsoever which he imagined *would* be displayed by people having witnessed something so spectacular. *Anyway, they're not laughing sadistically*, he thought—that would be the worst-case scenario. A little more gathered, he visually prodded the specimen; no emotion—okay, a serious bunch of characters and ice to break.

"Got through the fog no problem and manage to trip at home base! Typical!" He chuckled as he said it, hoping for appreciative acknowledgement.

No one laughed that he noticed, but the young lady at his side distracted his attention from them, and holding his upper arm whispered, "Going to do some myself tonight, being a Friday and all, but that's another story, another me." With a fleeting, unexpected turn of character, she winked mischievously, let go and tapped him with her elbow, just as the serenity circulated through her face again.

Kieran agreed dumbly and laughed nervously (just in case she had *made a joke*), to show appreciation for her medicinal turn of phrase. Then realization of what she said hit and he warmed to her attempt to invite him in from the cold with her sassy vernacular. His heart rate responsively slowed.

Definitely more to my left, he thought.

"Great that you could make it here in one piece. That *is* the worst fog. We all had difficulty driving through that to get here, but you *are* here! You're Mr. Nichol, right?"

He noticed she held a clipboard. "Er, that's right, Kieran Nichol, that's K, I, E . . ." he was still mixed-up—she wasn't taking details, "I'm here to see Ms. M. Lock, the director. Your company might take me on as a graphic designer. Here's the letter asking me to attend an interview." He flipped open his briefcase and took out the letter to present to her. She focused on the letter and her smile diminished a little, as her eyes squinted slightly in concentration, roaming over the page.

The office was silent. For an age, the tense mood hung in the air as the young lady scrutinized the paper, almost as though she had before her the collected verdicts of the jury, and was about *herself* to make a final decision. Then Kieran looked to her gentle countenance, the youthful features, and felt relieved.

She was only the secretary—temporary hostess at the reception area, or at least this is what he thought.

She wouldn't be making any important decisions concerning his employment by the company. That would be in the hands of the director, who he would no doubt, in due course meet. As Kieran waited for the letter to return, he furtively glanced around the space.

The office was open plan, about the area of a tennis court but more square, with pale blue walls and brown carpet and large windows overlooking the surrounding cityscape. There were doors leading into two smaller offices along the wall through which he had entered Candlelight Ltd. so theatrically. One was in the far left corner, the other door, leading to a poky, Venetian blinded office, which for some unknown reason captivated his attention, was in the right corner.

On the opposite side from the office's entrance, and to the right, the view would normally be very dramatic, with Glebeton in its entirety being visible, along with all the neighbouring boroughs. That of course would be the case on a *clear day*. Outside, the fog was so thick almost to obscure from view the pigeons that hopped on the office's window ledges.

The complementary colours in the workspace were relaxing enough to the eye but the interior design was not really very different to that of office spaces in which Kieran had worked previously. There was all the paraphernalia one would expect to find in such a workplace. Rows of Formica topped desks with trays, stationary, computer keyboards and monitors, printers, photocopiers, colour copiers and a coffee machine—a modern office, functional but unremarkable in character.

Kieran looked out for the telltale equipment, a larger monitor, an A1 printer that might indicate the whereabouts in the office of his stationing. Perhaps they had decided, perhaps they hadn't. Maybe they would be flexible. All would be revealed . . .

The subtle and delicate smile returned and she handed the page back to Kieran, her eyes beaming as she did so.

"That's Ms. Lock's office over there," she said, pointing, with a more serious turn of facial expression.

Within the open plan space, in the far right corner from Kieran's point of view, beyond the office equipment strewn tables, he could see the director's office. It had already caught his eye before being described. It wavered as he looked to it through the convection-fan heated air, and seemed to him forbidding.

Home of the head honcho, he thought, trying to lighten his perception of what he saw, but he couldn't convince himself that just the closeness of workplace authority was the cause of the uncomfortable feeling. He couldn't see into the office—the heavily dusted maroon blinds were closed. The image of the *heavyweight matron* had disappeared from his mind, and now Kieran was increasingly intrigued as to how this salient woman might *really* appear, what her personality might be, how she would take to him. He questioned whether the job really was his.

But even though Kieran knew a degree of nervousness should be expected in this situation, he tried to realize the true source of his uneasiness, the enveloping disquiet with the elusive meaning.

Before he could consider further, the congenial young lady that had so far made him feel so relaxed, distracted him. "Sorry I haven't introduced myself—I'm

Gabriella. I'm in charge of promotion, but I'm also the human resources manager for Candlelight." She abbreviated the company title with the informality of the initiated.

Kieran was somehow pleased at discovering her actual station.

Gabriella continued, "It's okay, you won't need to see Ms, Lock today at least—she's away on business. Another very promising candidate visited last Friday, by coincidence. She already knew he had made a bona fide commitment to the company, and she was so enthused by him at his interview that she broke off early and dragged him away to the nerve center of the parent organization (of which Candlelight is a subsidiary). I expect she's settling him in to his new . . ." she hesitated and thoughtfully touched the front of her lips with an index finger, "office," she continued. "She's very occasionally here. I'll be responsible for your preliminary interview today." The curve of her sweet smile.

Once again, Kieran's nervous tension lifted with the sudden overture of her dulcet voice, this time gently resonating like birdsong in his ears.

"C'mon, I'll show you around," she said. "Let me get you a cup of tea—or would you prefer coffee?"

He didn't want to appear too relaxed; accepting hospitality from a senior member of staff might be misconstrued as a bit arrogant. He wanted to emphasize his aim to *serve* rather than to *be served*—"Er, well, no thank you. I think I'll miss on that. I'm not that thirsty."

"Oh, go on. Make yourself feel comfortable. I'm getting one for myself."

It was a nice offer, affirming her good nature, but made quite forcefully, he thought.

"Umm, okay. I'll have a coffee, please." Somehow he got the impression he should and that she would insist until he did.

"Milk and sugar?"

"I'll have milk and two sugars, thanks."

Kieran reevaluated his opinion of Gabriella. This office seraph was *overseeing* his settlement into Candlelight Ltd. With her putting forward an opinion to the mystery director, the matter was surely cut-and-dried. How could he fail to be employed with Gabriella's benevolent supervision during his suitability assessment for Candlelight Ltd., regardless of how ascetic the director might be?

He felt for once as though an angel was doting over him.

Chapter 13

The workers who had built the Devil's musical contraption and had seen it in action were rebelling, dashing the heads of their captors with their spades, slashing with their saws and sinking down their axes.

Satan was not concerned by their mutiny. They could escape from their immediate prison, but then where would they go? The access to and from this part of Hell was a transient one, requiring a special device made by Noctonomicus the Cyborg to reach. They could always steal one, but additionally the escape routes were under constant surveillance. It was possible for Satan to have them defended at the shortest notice.

The throne deck bastards connived in Satan's shadow, panicking with the latest developments. They were so jittery that they didn't trust Satan's broad smile. This was justified. His mood was as unpredictable as lottery numbers.

He temporarily calmed their nerves. "No need to fret, everybody! I found that a damn good show—for the while it lasted," his rasp tapered off with the last remark.

A modest, tight smile reappeared on his face. "Just the right place for the *new boy*, soon to arrive. Yes, a few minor revisions, and a general strengthening of the structure will be all that's required. Of course, the musicians will have to be up to scratch next time. Did that overzealous one have his head fly?"

"Yes, Satan, I made sure he was executed," sniveled Trollix Crabtree, with one hand holding in his dribbling brain.

They breathed out, relieved, and smiled as best they could at each other.

"Well done, all of you! You've excelled yourselves, you really have." Satan's smile and narrowed eyes were meant to convey warmth. "Yes, well done indeed . . ."

He looked at them all, standing quite prim considering their wretched physical condition.

"Thank you once again," he said. "And now . . . FUCK OFF!!!" The smile flicked off his face as once more it contorted in bitter hatred. He raised his trident, holding it like a jousting pole. His thorny, nodular fist squeezed hard on it, and a sharp ray of plasma flew from its bulbous butt. He aimed it at their feet, scorching them black as the plasma jet touched.

The fiery, walking excrement screamed and shouted, jumping overboard, crashing hard onto the semi-molten ground. As they rolled around in anguish over the earth, clutching their footsies, already some of the mutineering slaves had noticed them. The executives were away from Satan, and too preoccupied to notice the rabble, who sensed a chance to take revenge. Approaching the roly-poly servants of the Devil, they wielded their shovels, saws and axes.

Satan didn't worry about his "helping hands" as much as they worried about their feet. Being his servants didn't mean they were favoured, other than for their utility. He was effectively keeping them *on their toes.* He looked at them contemptuously as they tumbled about, and as the mob loomed.

"Move forward!" he snarled to the undercarriage of his throne deck. They strained to overcome its huge inertia—Woodlouse Man's solid black armour had deflected Satan's trident blast and he was still onboard, unmoving, along with Plingo Braintree, the master telepath, who Satan had deliberately avoided blasting. Gradually the throne carriage swayed forward.

Satan gave a token glance behind him to see that the grotty servants he had got rid of, like breadcrumbs from a tablecloth, were running from the angry slaves, running for their miserable lives.

The Devil growled to the alien crab, "Plingo, remind my *footmen*, once they sort themselves out, to crack on with the improvements to the *melody maker*."

"Yes, Lord Satan," said the crab sophisticatedly.

Chapter 14

Kieran held the white polystyrene cup in his hand, taking a sip here and there. It tasted a little off, but was drinkable.

Gabriella was holding her foam cup instead of the clipboard. "Okay Kieran, now as you were told in the letter, today will be a day of interview and discussion—*of sorts*. Having read your details (which are most impressive, I might add) and having checked your references, we're fairly confident that if you so choose, you can stay with us. That of course depending on how we all get on today."

Anxiety—his first impressions of the other staff were of unfriendliness. On the other hand, his and their relationship only had to be *civil*. Surely Gabriella would do the rest to get him in, just as long as they all got on, in at least a business-like way.

She said, "Tomorrow Ms. Lock will want to see you to make the final decision, before you're taken on formally . . ." she hesitated inexplicably, then recovered her thread, "but we'll have plenty of time together before then to familiarize and *prepare* ourselves. I can't foresee there being any problems though. Everyone here is nice enough and I know you're a pleasant fellow, so relax! Make yourself feel at home!" At this moment, there was a peculiar twinge in her smile, which made it appear less genuine to Kieran.

She continued, "We've been given express permission from Ms. Lock while she's stoking the fires at the corporation headquarters, so to speak, to get accustomed—we may be in each other's company for a while."

A few light creases appeared over her brow and her smile faded as she recalled, "Then again, maybe not. I believe she has plans to whisk you off to the holding company (for which our small office does the marketing) if you're accepted, that is." Almost to herself, she added, "It's within easy reach from here, these days . . ."

She refocused on Kieran. "Whatever, it's a welcome break from the grindstone for us, when we can spend time getting acquainted with someone like yourself."

Kieran thought it sounded too easy. It made him a tad suspicious. "Well that's nice to know," he responded, with a contrived politeness of manner. He didn't check over with her what she had said about his virtually certain employment, for fear of breaking that which wasn't broken, by trying to fix it. He decided to go with the pleasantly warm flow, for the moment in time.

She lifted her cup to her lips and sipped, keeping her eyes on him.

He had a discreet slurp from his own.

"So what's going to happen next?" he asked.

"Today, I'll give you brief details about us, where we've been, where we are, and where we believe we're going—as a marketing company under the auspices and control of the parent organization, and how you stand in relation to that."

"Okay, sounds fair enough."

"But I think firstly, we should make this day as informal as we possibly can. Our company ethos is of *putting people first*. That applies to those within the organization we are employed on behalf of and who we promote, as well as those within *our* small company. It extends to the members of the general public to whom we market the parent organization."

In all honesty Kieran didn't have a clue as to what the parent organization's line of business was. He knew that Candlelight Ltd. was the marketing body of this organization and that he would (if employed) be involved in the creation of promotional material for it. He had surmised that this was as much as he needed to know but now felt as though he should have done more research. Just a quick Internet check would have sufficed.

He only hoped that Gabriella would enlighten him before he faced interrogation from Ms. Lock. He didn't think that ignorance in this regard would cost him the job but not knowing the nitty gritty could put him in an awkward predicament.

Gabriella raised her voice, "So, without further ado, let me introduce you to the crew!" She animatedly gestured with a hand, to the people in question as she spoke.

They had been eavesdropping, but were on the verge of reengaging in their duties before being mentioned. They peeked from behind their computer monitors.

Kieran was a little perplexed that they hadn't displayed the same positivism when he arrived that Gabriella displayed. But *never mind,* he thought, in due course he would find out what they were about.

With an assertive but welcoming voice, she continued. "Okay guys, now this is Kieran, that's Kieran beginning K, I, E, by the way, and he's starting with us today—*maybe*." She cast a glance and smile to him. "So be nice to him!"

Despite probably being more than ten years younger than him, she was already beginning to, albeit unconsciously, make apparent her authority. She took firm control of the direction and tone of their dialogue. Kieran didn't mind this. He already felt comfortable with her as his guide.

"Stash your things over there for now, put your bag next to mine, Kieran," pointing at a coat stand in one corner, "and then ladies and gentlemen, let us proceed to the meeting room!" she gestured to the lucid but seemingly tranquilized bunch of people, directing them to the office with ultramarine blue, drawn blinds, to the left of the director's somber, drab looking office.

As Kieran moved toward the coat stand, they languidly rose from their seats. As they stood, he could see that there were five males and five females. They were a motley bunch, the casual dress code being exploited to the full, many looking as though they had just come off the street. They were ethnically diverse as well, not altogether surprising, considering they probably all originated from some part of racially mixed London.

He'd removed his coat, but Kieran still felt uncomfortable in the Casua-man suit he'd purchased the previous Saturday, especially for the interview. He'd already undone the top button of his shirt, which had been grazing his flaccid neck.

If they hadn't been at their computer stations, he would have thought from their manner that this lot was *indolent*. He wondered how it was with such a relaxed atmosphere, that this company was at the top of its game, according to the information they had sent him, at least.

He placed his trench coat on the stand, and the briefcase next to the *Aya Nappa, Summer of Love* duffel bag at the stand's base. He tossed the empty cup, as light as a dandelion, into the tin bin nearby.

He continued to eye them up as they shuffled through into the smaller office, as his superiority complex began to inflate. He wondered why the melancholia and the seeming lack of enthusiasm? Perhaps they were antisocial types, which would suit him just fine. Minimal interaction was what he wanted. And this would preclude office politics of the type he had previously experienced. His stomach just wouldn't hold up to more of the same. As well paid and as easy a ride as it could be, and with possibilities for career progression, meaning bigger bucks.

In the meeting room, the buoyant feeling in Kieran's head, which he first noticed just before entering Candlelight Ltd., amplified. It was like his skull was gradually being pumped full of helium. Kieran put it down to a new side effect of the damn pills he swallowed for his stomach.

The rectangular room was crammed with the defunct equipment that no longer had a place in the main office, which by all accounts, was the heart of a thriving business. While being quite an intimate sized room, the objects within it and its décor were actually quite distancing. Their unruly, cluttered arrangement made it feel as though at any moment one would be clumped on the head by a falling file of documents, or a hefty office calculator. The dissonant colour scheme, in contradiction to the main office space, would prohibit any normal person from feeling at ease in there for any length of time.

Dragging themselves chairs, the twelve people including Kieran, began to sit around the plastic topped tables, ranged end to end. The office filled with murmurings, as they conversed in pairs and threes. Kieran chatted about nothing in particular with his host.

Gabriella was of medium build with a fresh complexion and dark features. Her smile was something quite unusual. Its appearance made him feel so at ease that he relinquished all psychological barriers. He was aware of being completely receptive, at a deep, subliminal level, to her advice and guidance. This was very peculiar. He was never usually at such ease in the presence of virtual strangers. Of course, he was always *outwardly* polite and affable, but kept an attitude of distant suspicion, playing his cards close to his chest. This always made such introductions trying for him personally.

Gabriella broke off, keeping to her interview/ induction schedule. She stood at the end of the meeting room's long line of tables, readying herself for further discourse, briefly brushing her smart navy blue dress down to her knees and then primly straightening herself to a strong upright position.

Her eyes, most noticeable, had an arresting liquidity, a judicious quality, which invariably became the focal point for Kieran sitting close by, as he watched her intently, beginning her address.

"We're a very specialist office, as you well know, working to promote the interests of *The Company*, the parent organization directed by Ms. Lock (whose headquarters are down under). We've been working alongside them, and for them, for quite a number of years, in fact for as long as I can remember!" the response was gentle, dry laughter. "And we've always provided our client company with a first class, professional service . . ."

Had Kieran heard correctly that Ms. Lock was also the director of this larger corporation (apparently based in Australia)? If so, it was little wonder that her commitments today were elsewhere, they probably were most days. An international conglomerate would require her to travel extensively to the various sites, and attend meetings overseas.

She might not even be in the UK presently.

He was still none the wiser as to what business the proprietary company conducted. He only knew what small part *he* would have to play in all of it. Since leaving school he had always been one thing—a graphic designer—no more and no less. And after all, he had only to arrange and artistically present their literature, not write it. Anything that he didn't know but had to know, he could learn on the job.

Despite thinking this, Kieran was now kicking himself for not having done a little bit more homework about the company before applying for the position, at least to be double sure of getting past the interview.

He didn't even know the holding company's name.

Gabriella's silkily flowing report continued, "Candlelight Ltd., was originally conceived as the first port of call for outsiders. Really it's a shop front and marketing concern for our proprietor, to give those interested some simple information about it, without being confused by its esoteric complexities . . ."

Kieran was frustrated that she still had not revealed *The Company*'s title, but he expected that he satisfied Ms. Lock's selection criteria by applying before the ink on the interview letter she had sent him dried, almost certainly the critical factor.

Gabriella said to the gathering, "I would say, that all in all, Candlelight is a less hectic environment to work in—there are no idle hands at Ms. Lock's main establishment, *that* I know. But naturally (as most of you who have been here long enough can vouch), things get, how shall I put it, a *bit livelier* when she's on the premises, though those visits are rare . . ."

Kieran resigned himself to the probability that he would not be enlightened about the custom, or even title of *The Company*.

On the monitors around and in front of him was what appeared to be a picture puzzle, enticing the observer to figure out the hidden image contained within. It glided almost imperceptibly within the random pattern on the screen surface, but he couldn't pin it down. He didn't much care for those visual puzzles, and this one looked completely unsolveable. Maybe it was a red herring, and concealed no secret.

Kieran decided immediately that this wouldn't be the screen saver to grace *his* monitor when he started up with the company. He preferred the unfolding maze from the *standard selection* offered under the *screen display* menu.

But no matter where he looked, the radiosity of one of the multiple monitors caught at least the corners of his eyes and as if drawn by the static on the screen. His pupils migrated towards it and his attention would settle for a short while, before he would, with a little flinch, pull away from that annoying picture sliding about.

Considering the amount of time the image had thieved from him, he was irked that he had not worked out its secret.

Gabriella continued propagating the services of Candlelight Ltd., somehow managing to do so without giving any hint to Kieran as to what the major corporation's specialization was. He again became slightly anxious, as by what seemed to be pure fluke, she comprehensively summarized the nature and order of operations within Candlelight Ltd., with minimal reference to the business of the holding organization.

Then, looking around, he calmed himself as he unavoidably inhaled the emanation of someone's relaxed sphincter, which had become an unpleasantly monotonous feature during the address. Others twiddled their fingers, tilted back precariously on splaying, flexing chairs, or gently twanged polystyrene rulers at the vinyl tables' edges. They were an easygoing bunch. Or perhaps just disenchanted with their occupations.

She redirected attention to the newcomer, still none the wiser as to the value of *organization x* in the equation. "We'll meet in here later, so that we can remind ourselves of the parent corporation's achievements, and its expectations of staff, and to conclude Kieran's interview cum induction."

"But I'd like you now, to get to know each other . . ."

The introductory procedures were always the same. Even she, as outstanding in personality and appearance as she was, was bound to conform to them, ordained by the *powers that be*.

Kieran sighed quietly; *let's* get to know about these thrilling characters, *let's*. As reluctant as he was, he knew his employment depended on how they mixed, at this interview at least.

They seemed a trifle more appreciative and acknowledged him in a candid way, with smiles, nods, gentle hand waves, and the odd salute, without moving from their places.

Kieran realized it wasn't disinterest or hostility he perceived in their behaviour earlier, but more a *doubtfulness*, a skepticism naturally expressed through their body language, about the stranger that had walked into their midst. The effects of a relaxed office code were obvious in the staff's dress but also in their uncontrived manner.

"Now, what I'd like is for you to introduce yourselves to Kieran, in turn, one-on-one, and have an informal, intimate conversation with him. Over the course of the day I want you to really build an association, and give Kieran an insight into *The Company* and Candlelight.

"I'll decide the order in which you'll be sent in to chat, but in the meantime, you can return to your work."

They began to lift from their seats with that familiar sluggishness, and rambled toward the door, alongside which Gabriella was standing, like a shepherd herder taking a headcount of sheep returning to the pen.

Chapter 15

From the single file of those vacating the room, Gabriella made a selection, and after a brief exchange of words, the individual floppily made an about turn and approached Kieran.

He pulled the chair next to Kieran at the end of the long row of tables, and parked himself down, as Gabriella assumed a position standing between them.

She leaned towards them. "Hope you don't feel so much like the *new boy* now," she said to Kieran, placing another cup of coffee next to the computer monitor, displaying that exasperating puzzle.

"Yeah, so far so good." He didn't feel the need to say anymore, adopting a more casual attitude that was in keeping with the staff there—it might make bonding with them easier.

She rested a hand on Kieran's shoulder. "Now, I'll be close by if you need me for any reason, but for now I'll leave you two to acquaint yourselves."

Her hand remained for some moments after, a time lapse during which an enigmatic impression of maternal sympathy swathed him, in a way he did not question and had not experienced since being an infant. After its conveyance, with a caress she removed her hand. Kieran, in childlike, wide-eyed wonderment, looked at her. Suddenly endowed with a strange flowing grace, she seemed almost to glide to the doorway.

She went through out of sight. Kieran remained transfixed on the door.

The man alongside him shifted, distracting Kieran from his mystified thought. He swiftly became his frugal self again, wondering why he had let himself go to the extent he just had. Very illogical, and really, *very out of character,* he thought to himself, rubbing his cheekbone in bafflement as the man sitting next to him vied for his attention.

With Gabriella gone, suddenly the meeting room, steeped in junk, seemed to be closing in, and the floaty feeling in his head increased. Uneasily, he looked over the man sitting beside him.

"Here you are, dude—your kworfee. Or is it tea?"

The man pushed the polystyrene cup toward Kieran. Kieran wondered whether the cup was for himself, and why the man had called it "kworfee".

Then, "No, it's coffee. Thank you." He took a sip.

Of all the people Kieran had seen that morning, he was probably the most casually dressed, wearing scuffed cowboy boots and worn jeans. But the overall look was made slightly more formal by his bizarre decision to wear a navy blue v-neck sweater over a flare-collared shirt—with necklace tie. His shoulder length hair, bleached and tangled, moved uncannily as though it were a solid mass when he turned his head. He wore spectacles with chunky scarlet rims.

"Hi, I'm Fred Philadante, general dog's body really, any odd jobs that need doin' I'm the one they hassle—but I'm also the technical writer." He spoke in a lilting, pseudo-American accent.

"Oh right, I'm Kieran Nichol. You're a technical writer, are you?" Kieran inquired, in an attempt to seem keen about this fellow's plight. Then he realized *now* was the time to catch up on the homework he had not done. "And umm, what are you responsible for writing?"

"Well, all sorts really, mostly technical stuff as you might expect, my bein' the technical writer an' all. You know, the nitty-gritty, the nuts and bolts of it really. I've gotta be familiar with all that. Gotta be able to present it so that the ordinary public, Joe Bloggs on the street, can understand what it's all about. The details an' all."

"I see." Kieran felt his way carefully, not wanting to seem too ignorant about the business of *The Company*, which Candlelight Ltd. was a subsidiary of. He carefully measured his words. "And what would be the nature of your writing—what details in particular about the parent company are you describing?"

"Well, all sorts really. I don' jus' focus on one aspect, two or even three. I cover everythin'. They chuck everythin' at me. I have to chew it up, and spit it out in a way that is readily accessible and looks pretty to people on the outside of *The Company* and promotes it. Most read it and decide to investigate further. A few decide *The Company's* service ain't for them. I even do instructional stuff, for the administrative staff within the organization."

Fred had skirted around what should have been an answer to Kieran's indirect question. He eyed up Fred and drew the conclusion that he didn't look the type that *would* be offended by his ignorance. For that matter, none of the others Kieran had seen did either.

Well, okay then, thought Kieran, *I'll come clean and ask my question bluntly*, but before he could do so . . .

"Huh, goin' off on a slight tangent, I bought myself a new drum kit recently. Are you into drums?" he didn't wait for a reply, and continued, not in the least bit attentive. "Maybe not, but your into music, right? Huh, after all, who ain't?" He chuckled as he said it.

Kieran began shaking his head in disapproval, then stopped, not wanting to risk being disagreeable. He began to resume nodding. He didn't need to make the effort though, as he was to find out.

"Yeah, I play drums. Been playin' for quite some time, but this kit's damn fine! Yeah, and cheap too, set me back just eight hundred pounds and that ain't bad for a seven piece . . ."

Kieran continued nodding . . .

"Yeah, the double bass drum is somethin' else! It's always somethin' I've wanted. Got a Splash and China too. It's a comprehensive rock oriented kit, on a rack mounting. I forked out the little bit more for the extra two toms . . ."

He went on at length.

He displayed a considerable, youthful and vivacious gusto, which, even when considering he was talking about his own interests, disguised to a degree his mature years. But Kieran was not really sure about Fred. He exhibited all the attributes one would expect to find in a musician in your bog standard, American, stadium-rock band (which he made no bones about wanting to be).

All in all, this chap wasn't really the type Kieran had ever had the "pleasure" of sharing company with in the past, either voluntarily or at the behest of someone with the authority to make or break him (as Gabriella quite discreetly but undoubtedly was). Neither was he likely to have that "pleasure" in the future, unless Kieran was to sit next to him at Candlelight Ltd., or if he ever attended Wembley Stadium (though it was unlikely), to see the character play soft rock in rainbow coloured spandex.

Kieran didn't attempt to elucidate the image, because he didn't want to be thinking about, let alone talking to, Fred anymore. Nevertheless, he continued to make the effort to look attentive, knowing the onus was on him to be polite, especially on this, his first day.

"Yeah, been playin' drums for a good ten years now. Yeah, I'm in a band, 'Limp Rhino Horn'—it's a comedy name. Been goin' for three years already. Gonna break it big soon! Yeah, Limp Rhino Horn, watch out for us. We've already played some fairly big venues. Hell, we've played Glebeton Ice Rink twice! You might have seen us there? Maybe not, or you'd have already known me. But maybe you know of someone who has?" He paused, hoping for an affirmative response, a slightly tense expression on his face.

"Actually, no. I'm not from around here. I'm from Tewsbury. I don't watch live music," he said diplomatically (he rarely listened to *any* music), "and don't go ice skating either for that matter, but—"

Fred continued, "Yeah . . ."

Kieran sighed inwardly, and drank some more coffee. For a short while he allowed his mind to wander, leaving the nodding of his head at suitable intervals to his autopilot. But whenever Fred swung his head, as though to shake his rigid hair into place, Kieran, with slight head movements, looked around. Every so often, Kieran returned eye contact to Fred, in order to preserve the impression of being interested. He felt that he was doing okay. His distinct *lack* of interest in Fred's unfolding story went undetected.

There were computer monitors, tower units and smaller miscellany scattered over and under the tables at the timber-framed back wall, with a clutter of shelves above these, filled with clip files and document containers. Many had spilled onto the floor. They were yellowed and sported footprints. More computers jostled on the tables through the middle of the long office with that confounded puzzle on their monitors. The carpet was an olive green, the walls were a Prussian blue and the ceiling was discoloured white, with lights shining out of untiled squares in a series of diagonal formations, casting a uniform but cool, dull light, adding to the room's uninviting ambiance.

He looked around again. *Shithole*, thought Kieran.

But in his line of sight, straight in front of him, on the only wall that was relatively free of clutter, he noticed *the clock*.

What immediately struck him was that the time was wrong—quarter to twelve. But there was something else that made him return to it.

A substantial object, it was perhaps a foot and a half in diameter and *appeared* antique. He studied the clock face and body for a while at intervals, between reengaging with Fred (so that he would at least have the bare bones of his rambling).

The creamy clock face, circled by bold, crisp, black digits, firmly rested in the mahogany surround (*was* it mahogany, it could just as well have been coloured ABS, though this timepiece was not really evocative of post-war industrially mass produced plastic products—a bit more uncommon than that). He couldn't really place the clock in any period from its outward appearance, and he wasn't an antiques expert anyway, but nevertheless, *a timeless timepiece,* he thought in flippant, self-amusement.

Squinting, he began inspecting the case more closely and after a while, became absorbed by its intricately patterned surface, the irregularity of it, while at the same time appreciating a certain integrity it seemed to possess. Becoming more fascinated by the swells, protrusions and relief over its mottled surface, he looked for a recognizable composition but couldn't see one, though he knew there was an order, other than the final discipline of the clock's circular shape, imposing itself over the whole.

He was more fascinated by the detail within, and continued to concentrate on that. From his viewpoint, he was only capable of seeing the most superficial, but there was detail within detail, and then more detail, which was only initially hinted at by the overall flowing and undulating pattern. *A remarkable thing*, he thought in private awe.

He began to conjure from the seemingly random and abstract shapes a whole array of fantastic creatures—tigers, dragons, birds and people. No sooner did one image appear, when it would suddenly turn into something else, the only consistency being that everything he saw, writhing in that miniature maelstrom, was something from the natural, living world—plants, animals and people.

Then he diverted his attention away from the clock case, and onto the pearly clock face. His eyes rolled around its outer perimeter, like a steel ball on a roulette wheel, until jabbed by the prongs of the unadorned hands, as black as the moon's hidden side. He began to slide down the static second hand, with minute incremental movements of his eyeballs into the centre of the clock face, a vortex sucking the very soul from his primed, diluted, succumbing mind. Slowly, slowly, the ethereal fluid siphoned from his head, through miasmic IV tubes, spiraling into the nub of the clock, the supernatural fulcrum of the earthly orrery, as he barely conceived Fred, banging on about the studio session his band booked last Tuesday . . .

Chapter 16

On the Earth's twin, an alternative world, the highest mountain reverberated with the sound of bitter emptiness. The high winds, a million vacuous screams reaming the air of its substance, swirled up powder clouds of snow into the stratosphere, stretching out like a black, speckled blanket above the world.

Gleaming like the outside edge of an eclipse, the ebony cylinders grew on silvery stems from the very rock that was the mountain peak.

For a million years there had not been the merest sound, other than that of the frigid wind.

In the early sunrise, the behemoth stood silhouetted, his eight arms hanging down at his sides, veins like rumpled oil pipelines over his forearms.

For one hundred years more he stood motionless at his black and chrome machine. The clouds passed around the tract of his shoulders, and the ice crystals formed, following the direction of the vortices of wind about the boulderous features of his face.

The great countenance looked down through the clouds, through the thickening air, to the facsimile earth below.

In the kitchen, the Siamese was tossing its glow green plaything.

The blue, red and white candles were lit and in their Triple Goddess holders. The woman placed one to the left, one to the right and the red one, behind the activity, at the middle.

Leaning into the pantry, she flicked through the cellophane packets and small containers of herbs, oils and resins, on the shelf above the incense and charcoal, mugs and chalices, above the floor stacked with cast iron cauldrons.

Agrimony, alfalfa leaf, alkanet root, allspice. She picked out ingredient x, opened the resealable packet and let the small seeds flow onto a gilt tablespoon, whose contents she then poured into a soapstone mortar. She resealed the packet and replaced it in the collection.

Mandrake, marshmallow root, meadowsweet, mistletoe. She picked out ingredient y, opened the packet and a tablespoon of the ingredients she added to the mortar.

Witch hazel leaf, woodruff, wormwood, yarrow flower. She plucked out ingredient z and did the same.

She added twenty drops of jasmine oil and seated herself at the marble work surface.

With a firm grip on the pestle, she began grinding down the contents of the mortar.

Some fifteen minutes later the secret herbs were effectively blended. A little wisp of white smoke that smelled of almonds rose from the mortar. She patiently waited another five.

Donning her polythene gloves, she scooped up the mush with the spoon and placed it on a plain white china saucer. Holding a little *bolline*, she began shaping the small mound into a cube.

She conducted a curt wave of her wand, spelling the Greek alpha and omega over the dice (this ritual at least and one other, were of the utmost importance) and then fetched a brown paper bag from the pantry. She removed the empty jar labeled *Tykhon Y2K*.

Gathering the now brighter looking cube, she placed it in the glass jar, then took off her gloves and chucked them into the flip-top bin. She wrapped the lot in a brown paper bag and returned the jar to the dark, cool and *dry* pantry. At the same time she took out another brown paper bag with an identical jar, containing the cube she had made the day before. She blew out the candles.

Next, she ventured to the tricolour room. She opened a small wall cupboard and placed the inert glass jar—which contained the active, unstable, chemical compound—back in the dry darkness. After checking the dressing table's drawers, she double-checked that the vital components were at hand.

She beheld briefly, feeling a certain sourness, the A4 certificate on the wall above the bed.

Back in the kitchen, she moved the tools into the sink. From a jar in the fridge she hooked out a little pork sausage, and placed it in the center of a bed of catnip, in the feline's bowl. She fetched a stool, and settled down to develop her face.

The doorbell rang, like wind chimes in a hazy summer garden. Her Siamese looked up at her in expectation. The eyelashes were in place. She wiped her fingers of the glue on a Kleenex, and stuffed a few brass bangles and nail polish into an embroidered silk makeup box hurriedly. Then with her forearm, she pushed the lot up against the window cill. The mascara, foundation, lipstick—the whole toolkit, she left like uncapped painters oils at the easel of the looking glass, as she was caught up by the tight schedule of what was just another working day.

She would tidy later, after the day's *conversion*.

Her fingers were Vaseline, squeezed from a tube—long, thin and limber, and she pulled the sheer, white, flowery stockings up around her equally long, thin and supple legs, just below the groin. She allowed the long split dress to fall again, returning them to mysterious darkness. She pulled at the stretch cotton top so that her plentiful bosom was more revealed.

The doorbell's soft tinkle sounded again. Unfolding like the wings of a new moth, she elevated from her seat, and left the kitchen. Building momentum to a promenade, she moved to the front window. Standing a little away from it, just the touch of her carefully trimmed purple nails altered the net curtain enough to be able to see outside onto the gravel driveway. She looked keenly for the vehicle that would clue her up about who she would be dealing with, whether he would be worth the time and effort.

There was the gentleman's car, a sleek black BMW that met her approval. A silent nod. *I would like one of those*, she thought.

The wind whined within the infinite solitude. Another era passed.

The muscles on the torso and back of the giant being erupted, as it raised the lightning rods in each of its fists. Its arms fanned and steadied, a black scarab in the circle of the sun, in the dawn sky.

It sat poised, as time was suspended.

She turned and purposefully strode out of the room, ambling more legilly when the stained glass front door was in view, and through its glass a blurry man, her client. The figure in the doorway was at least her height, maybe five foot ten, and dressed in a suit.

She'd collected her heap of mail from beneath the letterbox that morning, as soon as the postman delivered it. As far out in the country as she was, there was no junk mail to be bothered with—just as well, so that she could be sure that what *had* arrived—her reverie over which, was not overstated. Moving as though in slow motion, her hand deftly flicked the door latch and she pulled the door slowly towards her, moving simultaneously to the perfect center of the doorframe. She stood straight-backed, waiting for his introduction.

Chapter 17

The man that stood before her in his pinstripes, stooping slightly, scratched and rubbed his hands together agitatedly. His brow and forehead were as animated as his fidgeting hands. There was a black briefcase on the floor between his legs.

She was pleased by first appearances, though not overly pleased. Lookers made her work easier to do, but this feature was not as important to her now as it once was.

With a nervous smile and laugh, "Eh, hello, I'm Mr. Skidmore." He nodded apologetically as he said it.

Their hands met and shook.

Shifting from one foot to the other, he said, "I phoned you a little earlier about . . . a meeting?" His nervous smile remained. He twitched his shoulders and his hands flurried. He put them in his pockets. There was barely visible perspiration, formed at his forehead, his mouth opened slightly in trepidation.

Enough time had lapsed. "Yes. Hello. I am Divinity Callisto . . . Yes, I do recall our conversation last night." Spoken like hot black chocolate pouring from a ladle. She gave him a faint smile, which flickered away like candlelight in a vacuum. It was sufficient for him at this time. "Come inside . . ." She stood to the side and beckoned him in with a long hand waving delicately on her willowy forearm.

He shifted awkwardly on his size tens a couple of times, crouched for his briefcase and walked inside, the look of discalm on his face slightly mellowing in the soft interior light. He looked around the entrance of the diviner's grotto with unease.

An imperceptible signal in the whistling winds. Electricity arced over the rocky knuckles and between the gripping fingers of its eight, mighty hands.

The superbeing came down upon the black and chrome machine, rattling the rims and smacking the heads, rumbling like landslides. Its eerily coordinated arms powered out a syncopated backbeat more precise than any earthly metronome.

The layers of air squashed and stretched under the sonorous onslaught, as the sun began to rise.

"ATRUBBATRUBBATRUBBATRUBB ATRUBBATRUBBATRUBBA . . ."

Miss Callisto shut the door and led him through, suspended above and gliding across the floor like a squid moving through deep water, wafting her scarf tail in the current of her slipstream, revealing endless, lissome legs through the darkness of her long dress as she walked.

They passed a large print of Diana the Huntress, doors coloured blue, green and yellow, the walls with painted, plaster-cast stars and moons, the tinkling, crystal chandelier, the finely woven rugs on the wall, laced with glinting silvery threads, and a pentagram tile above the golden braided curtain at the door frame into her "office".

They went inside, Mr. Skidmore knocking a silk and mirror-work pot with his awkward feet. He looked around, momentarily distracted from his concerns, without the nervous smile. He registered the pungent smell of potpourris in the warm, dry air. It made his nose run. Traffic fumes had been pouring into his car through the air conditioner during the long drive back from his place of employment in the city. It was strange that only now this interior environment should activate a response.

His eyes, traced with angry red capillaries, felt stung and tacky around the lids, the legacy of a day spent at a computer terminal, combined with lack of sleep, as much as the smog. But a relaxing glow leeched through the drawn blue curtains. It dappled the elaborately patterned carpet, its intense colours reduced in the dim light.

Tie-dyed drapes, like opaque spider's webs, filled the cornices and hung down, almost to floor level along the walls. Swarming between the languid folds of soft linen, there were small, simply framed paintings, with mostly abstract meaning—hard edged symbols, including a lotus flower, an earthen pot and simplified fruits and leaves.

He saw indecipherable images resembling company emblems and logos that had been shredded and put back together haphazardly, colours neutralized in the monotone light.

"ATRUBBATRUBBATRUBBATRUBB ATRUBBATRUBBATRUBBA ... "

Mr. Skidmore saw larger symbols, and images of deities of various mythologies from various countries. He was unfamiliar with most, but if he were more knowledgeable he would have recognized the pantheon of Greek gods, including Dionysus, god of parties, drunkenness and chaos, wearing a crown of ivy. Hades, king of the Underworld and god of the dead, with his three-headed dog Cerberus. And Poseidon, god of the sea, holding a trident, between the alcoves of the drapes.

And there was a collection of African artifacts, scattered randomly. From the Ivory Coast a gold shield. A Liberian fibre skirt. A Dan Spirit Mask, worn during ceremonial circumcisions of boys, of wood, cowry shells and metal.

He saw, but was ignorant of, the replica Yoruba panels, with images alluding to the gods Eshu and Ogun, carved from rosewood. A figure of Shango, God of Thunder. The small, replica Edo bronze altar, dedicated to the power of the *right hand*, and a wood and brass commemorative head of a dead chief, from the kingdom of Benin—all from Nigeria.

On the mantel, above the fireplace, were displays of hieroglyphic prints and statuary—sphinx, Egyptian gods and Pharaoh heads.

He saw pictures and figurines of Celtic, Roman, South American and other pagan deities.

"ATRUBBATRUBBATRUBBATRUBB ATRUBBATRUBBATRUBBA . . ."

She had squeezed a lot of expensive curios into a room of no more than moderate size, all happily coexisting. The effect was eclectic but harmonious—a tribute to diversity of spiritual convictions, even if misguided.

Mr. Skidmore attempted to adjust to the setting—a heady mixture of mythologies some people might have taken offense at, if they had not considered the woman's profession, or were more discerning in their spiritual beliefs. Mr. Skidmore wasn't particular in that sense, and felt no offense, the theme to him seeming more of spiritual liberalism (if there is such a thing and whether it was the intention of the owner to convey that impression, or not).

The adorned room also conveyed the impression of wealth, which implied the owner was doing good business, in turn suggesting an *accomplished* practitioner of the mystic arts (whether or not it was her intention to suggest that). But Mr. Skidmore didn't follow this thought process—there were so many other personal matters vying for his attention.

Near the wall, in relative darkness, on a round table covered in a substantial chintz cloth well beyond its edges, was the central focus. The business-end of the clairvoyant's service. He looked at it and then turned his gaze back to her.

The Drums, upturned Saturn Five rocket thrusters, suspended on a liquid silver gantry, resonated under the pounding, sending out a shimmering shockwave, traveling north, south, east and west.

"ATRUBBATRUBBATRUBB ATRUBBATRUBBATRUBBA . . ."

Miss Callisto stood to the side of the door for measured moments as he resettled into his new environment. Her balanced upper body was well defined beneath the slight, elasticized cotton top. Her arms were folded under her large breasts which revealed an expanse of cleavage, wispily covered by the scarf. One graceful leg slid through the split dress, her shapely ankle turning her foot on its pointed heel.

Her features were highlighted in the warm luminosity from the doorway, through the curtain's braids, the shadow on her face a cool blue. He perceived vaguely the narrow length of her subtle nose, meeting the fluted upper lip, and the pigment enhanced fine lips themselves, a sinuous line, glistening ruby. Her black lashed, cobalt blue eyes, were highlighted like gold crescent moons in the light from the room's entrance. The translucent skin seemed to blend into the surrounding colours like glass, and the rich black curlicues of hair, soft as sable, tumbled down below her slender shoulders, delineating the outlines of her flesh.

Knowing that deep within his head he was aware of her, she said, "Here we are, and already I am feeling your vibrations. How curious."

He raised a brow. "Yes, hmmm, here we are!" he placed his hands over his jacket pockets, smiling inanely, overdoing it. With a more staid expression but still overdoing it, "What did you mean about my vibrations?"

Again she kept him waiting, a high priestess conducting a formal ceremony. "You have strong vibrations. You are a thriving spiritual being, but my feeling is that you are not harnessing your considerable psychic strength. It goes unnoticed by you, and therefore goes to waste."

"I see . . ." was his response. He struggled to think of something with which to follow this up, but came up with nothing, his concern over his domestic problems conflicting with his social nature.

They stood at the doorway, beneath the image of the semi-naked, tumescent Osiris of Egyptian mythology.

"ATRUBBATRUBBATRUBB ATRUBBATRUBBATRUBBA . . ."

She watched him with the eyes of an owl looking down from the trusses of a barn. He was clutching his briefcase, smiling toothily and nodding nervously.

As she knew, keeping him waiting did nothing to make him feel at ease.

Then she said, "Please, Mr. Skidmore, take a seat." She pushed the back of his arm, gently urging him to move forward. He did so, shuffling on his feet inelegantly.

She could smell the perspiration as she stood closer to him.

He pulled out a chair from under the small round table, placed the briefcase to his right, next to the chair legs, undid his jacket button, and sat down. He shuffled the chair under himself, trying to find a position of comfort.

She moved around him, watching his back, and reached for the matches on the table. She lit the cylindrical stump of wax within the short candleholder, and the exotic paraphernalia nearby cast faint, warbling shadows on the floor and walls. She walked back around to face him.

In the candlelight she analyzed his face, as the warm glow danced over his features. Though he attempted to disguise it, the facade was racked with worry. Each muscle within it seemed to gravitate to the floor—his mouth turned down, his brows dragged downwards and his cheeks followed suit. Most obviously, beads of perspiration twinkled in the soft light, betraying his inner turmoil. He leaned forward tautly over the table.

She observed with reticence, her arms still folded under her breasts.

In the candlelight, his shuffling, hunched figure reflected in her midnight black irises. Finally she saw him settle down in his chair, as he continued rasping his hands together under the table, still ill at ease. She stood motionless, computing the distress signals emanating from the man, frequent as his exhalations of breath, and attenuated her plan of operation.

Mindful not to overextend the interlude, "Now, Mr. Skidmore, would you please make yourself comfortable. It is important that you release the tension within your physical self, so that your astral self can migrate freely and intermingle with mine, and vice versa." Miss Callisto skated over to the chair on the other side of the round table and sat down, herself becoming bathed in the flickering, weak light of the candle.

"Yes, Miss Callisto. I'll try to do that," he said as he shifted again in his chair.

A silent pause followed and Mr. Skidmore could hear his guide give a sigh, like a sled runner over snow.

"I'm detensioning myself now, Mr. Skidmore, I would like you to do the same," she said in a silkily firm way.

With her eyes closed, she released further long sighs and turned her palms, resting them on the table, facing upwards, the petite joints of her tapered digits touching the table cloth. She motioned him to exercise control of his breath with her hands, raising them at the wrist, moving her long, thin fingers in a fanning motion, and Mr. Skidmore felt them stroking him under his chin.

"Breath from the belly, raise and lower, raise and lower." Without looking, she expanded, "That's it. Keep doing that until you feel yourself claimed by relaxation, in, out, in, out . . . good."

But only nervousness provoked him to respond, "Okay, Miss Callisto, I will, but—"

"No need to speak, Mr. Skidmore, just breathe." She gave out another deep sigh as an example, then listened again to her entrusted's breathing. It was irregular and mildly wheezy. "Yes, that's right, in, out, in, out . . ."

Mr. Skidmore was distracted from his meditation by the Siamese that wandered in through the curtained door, moving more like a snake than a cat, with a little pork sausage in its clamped maws. It ventured under the table where they were seated, out of his view, and between the table's four legs. He felt the brush of the feline above his ankle, as Miss Callisto continued to gesture with her hands. Mr. Skidmore gave off some sighs in parrot fashion, in-between nose sniffles, to oblige the lady.

For a few minutes this preparation continued. Mr. Skidmore, not really feeling much less distressed, looked toward the object on the center of the table, seeing the light glimmer on its glass surface, and then raised his head to the unusual woman who would conduct the private investigation on his behalf.

As she knew it would be, his heart was palpitating just as it had been when he first arrived. Her fingers crept up like vines to the crystal ball, their points dinted on the surface and reflected over its curvature.

She asked, "Mr. Skidmore, now I would like you to tell me, in just a few words, what it is that you would like me to enquire about with the spirit guides." Her inhalation swished, as her eyes momentarily closed, waiting to absorb his request.

"Right, now, were do I start? Well, yes, I'm a married man, and I believe that my wife . . ." his voice quavered. Then he paused, with effort gathering himself, "I believe that my wife may be less than faithful—when I'm at work, you see . . ."

"Yes, go on."

He budged his chair and rocked on his seat a little. "I've tried everything. I tried the detective agencies—they couldn't give me anything concrete. Couldn't confirm what I suspect. You're my only hope to uncover her brazen infidelity!" he exclaimed.

"Please, Mr. Skidmore, be brief." She wondered why he needed her confirmation when he had formed his own opinion so solidly, and when a further push would plunge him into ruin.

"Tell me about my wife. I want my suspicions investigated—and confirmed. Tell me what she gets up to!" he nervously rustled his hands under the table as he said it, as droplets dribbled down his temples.

A pause of self-control, of collectedness, which exaggerated the feverishness of *his* utterances and hammered home to him his derangement. Then, "Mr. Skidmore. I would like you to know that I can only tell you what I see—I have to accept what I'm given. I cannot tell you what I myself have not received from the guides. They are the arbiters of hidden knowledge, and I am the vector by which they reach the world of men. They may choose to answer your questions or they may not. We shall see."

He swayed on his chair in dissatisfaction. "Please do what you can!" he said anxiously, almost pleading.

Her sled runner exhalation sliced snow, and the room was reclaimed by silent, melancholy candlelight.

He rubbed his hands and ground his teeth. Seconds, like years, passed.

Then, Minerva-like, she interrupted the torrid quietude.

"I see two people, together . . ." her eyes appeared energized, fixated on the crystal spheroid.

"Who are they? What are they doing?" he percolated.

A pause. He ground his teeth and rasped his hands.

"I see a male and a female . . ."

He clasped his hands and gritted his teeth.

"Who are they?" he asked, expecting something ominous.

"It is unclear . . ."

He waited for more. Nothing was forthcoming. Then, "What do you mean it's unclear? You—"

"They are together . . . *intimately* together . . ."

His eyes were boggling, and his face was flustered and wet.

"They are physically joined . . . copulating," she said in monotone.

"Aaaye? Wha', what do you mean . . . copulating?"

"I see them together, she perpendicular to he. Making sexual motions . . ."

He slammed his fists onto the table. "This is an outrage!" he bellowed, and sprung from his chair like a jack-in-the-box.

Not looking up from the ball's invisibly angular edges, making it more a Pandora's box, Miss Callisto strictly ordered, "Mr. Skidmore! You must try to keep control of your emotions. Your outbursts deter the spirit guides from furnishing the ball and thence myself, with the knowledge sought. Please be seated!"

He remained standing, as the air around the altar seemed to crackle with the drama unfolding.

"Mr. Skidmore, please sit down!" She raised her eyes from the globe, and stared at him unequivocally. He gradually sank down onto his seat.

"I will resume." She splayed her tendrilous fingers over the glass entity.

He was somewhat drained and stunned, blankly staring at her.

More languorous moments.

"I see the woman now . . ."

"Whu, what, what is she doing? What more . . ." he babbled feebly. He slumped forward, a pronounced roundness appearing in his shoulders.

Her steely talons clamped upon the crystal vole. "She is driving—the car is black as sin," she said wryly.

He said nothing, depleted.

She continued, "I see the manufacturer's emblem, above the rear bumper. It says B, M—I cannot see more . . ."

"It's my car . . . It's the BMW," he muttered, his head facing the table top. "I drive it normally. She's got me in the back whisking me to my funeral, I'll bet," he said with sardonic bitterness.

"I see very little else—the images are washing away, dissipating . . ."

He raised his head to her, his sweating face cleft with anguish.

"No, nothing else . . ." She paused but then said, "Oh, there is something. I see her lips. Yes, clearly. I see them . . . they are . . . smiling."

He broke down over the altar like a marionette whose strings had been cut. His head thumped the table surface.

"Nothing else," she said.

"Not to worry," his woeful voice was drenched with crying, "I know it all anyway . . ."

"ATRUBBATRUBBATRUBB ATRUBBATRUBBATRUBBA . . ."

In fact, he didn't know it all. Miss Callisto's clairvoyance had supposedly revealed two individuals (physical features not described) who could have been anybody. But in Skidmore's state of mind, of paranoid suspicion, the worst-case scenario was the one he settled for.

He was heaving and sweating profusely, beginning to resurface after the shock. The patch of moisture under his arms, she noticed (much to her annoyance), growing before her very eyes. She found so much perspiration very off-putting. He shook his head in agonized disbelief, absorbed in his thoughts. He said not a word.

She stood up from her chair, watching with a look of remoteness, seeing him squirm in mental anguish. She could visualize him running to cul-de-sacs, returning, running along another, returning. She knew of the contortions of his mind, its twisting, like a salt burned slug.

And she knew that there could be no relief for him, and that he would be open to suggestions.

Walking behind him, as he held his head in his hands, ostensibly not wanting to take any further part in the world, she calmly glided over to the fireplace, and stood at the bronze, phallic statue of Priapus.

With taciturn eyes, she watched his forlorn, soulless shell hunch over the table and listened to his sobbing.

He was thoroughly sucked dry, drained of his spirit.

If at that moment he had any semblance of awareness, he could have noticed. He didn't and so she permitted herself a smile.

She touched the sculpture's tip.

The supernatural being hacked a throaty gob, and spat—it fizzed through the air like ball lightning, down into the abyss.

He snarled and spun, changing tempo, lashing viciously at the hi-hat, then launching into a stuttered roll over the toms. All the while, the bass bulged and juddered under the relentless thumping.

He slashed the ride, which sizzled histrionically, then returned to a backbeat, undulating and rolling.

"ATRUBBATRUBBATRUBB ATRUBBATRUBBATRUBBA..."

She ruffled the silence. "Mr. Skidmore, I'm so sorry . . ." She stared at the back of his head. "I regret that what we were illuminated with was not what you were hoping for—but you asked me to divulge everything. Everything I was allowed to see, I passed on to you, as you requested."

She clocked no movement. This did not disconcert her.

"The guides do not regard a person's emotional condition. They do not judge the efficacy of insight on the basis of whether it will offend or appease. They simply reveal what it is required to know."

Still nothing.

Then, "The cheating bitch . . . how could she do it?" he burbled weakly through the tears, gradually lifting his head off the table.

"Mr. Skidmore, the spirit guides always reveal what is pertinent to a seeker's life, whether it is what the seeker would like to hear, or not. The guide's sentience is directed benevolently. May I advise you that what they have provided, if you react to it in the correct way, will be of benefit to you?"

He turned his racked face to her, with the tears rolling from his eyes and snot from his nose and demanded, "What positive can I derive from all that shit that was revealed, that has fallen on top of me? Tell me that!"

She waited for the reverberations to cease. "I can think of no way by which your wife's infidelity can be curbed, but—"

"Curbed? She's already done the dirty on me! You can't prevent damage if it's already been done!" he exclaimed.

"But maybe there is something else."

"What do you mean something else? Our relationship could never be the same again!"

She eyed him thoughtfully, cupping her chin in her limber fingers.

"That may be so, but there could be an alternative to repairing your marriage, which I agree, may be *beyond* repair."

His mouth opened and brow lowered, as he wondered what she meant. "And what, *pray tell*, might the alternative be?" He was still seated at the table.

She paused, seeming to be processing this idea in her mind for its viability, for the first time.

"Mr. Skidmore, you may or may not know, that practitioners of magick understand that everything on Mother Earth, and beyond also, should be respected. Everything possesses an energy (this being true of the animate and the inanimate) which is, in fact, a shared energy, which people can access for their benefit, when their own is low."

His perplexity precluded more tears from flowing.

She continued, "It appears to me, that what you need more than anything right this moment, is a rational frame of mind."

There was no way he could disagree.

She said, "You need to regain mental tranquility, this in order that you can reasonably decide what to do next—to be able to make an *effective* decision. The guides in their infinite wisdom planted within you the knowledge that you must act upon, *with wisdom.*"

He waited with bated breath for her to enlarge, rubbing the residue of tears on his shirt sleeves. She did so:

"Everything possesses an energy. Some energies can strengthen a person's life force, others can reduce it. Practitioners of magick know how to distinguish between entities, to select ones whose energies can be utilized, for the good of themselves and their fellow man."

"Right, and what bearance does all this have on the mess I'm in?" he ventured.

In her own time, "These energies are derived from objects, but equally, they can be derived from *places.* The energies in some environments, be they external, *or internal,* can be very beneficial. Time spent in such a location would enable you to regather your equilibrium."

She had not changed her position from at the side of the statue, as high as her waist. Neither had she altered her physical posture. Her demeanor had not changed from the time Mr. Skidmore had first arrived.

"I'm in no fit state to drive," he said brusquely. "I don't know whether I could make it back to the house, let alone Glastonbury—"

"No, Mr. Skidmore, I make no reference to Glastonbury, though great positive energies flow there—"

"You want me to set camp in the middle of Stonehenge tonight, is that it?"

"Mr. Skidmore, your flippancy offends me. I would like to help you, if at all possible."

"I'm sorry, I just feel so completely . . . hopeless." He lowered his aching head back into his hands.

Her irises distended, black as spades, greedily gathering in the meager light reflecting from his curled figure, a pork scratching, still somehow erect. She bathed a little longer in his sorrow, then pressed on.

"I know a place where we can go . . . a place nearby. There is great energy there. It will ease your pain . . . I am quite sure . . ." Her eyes bore into the back of his head.

"Where?" he groaned.

"Come with me."

His hands were still wrapped around his head. "Where?"

"Follow me!" meant to rouse him from his slumped position over the table.

He turned to her blearily, a glimmering of realization that he was moping in a relative stranger's house.

She said, "Please, let us rise up to the apex of the pyramid. That is where you will find peace of mind. The energies from the apex of the pyramid are greater than in any other part of a structure's geometry. Let us ascend and irradiate ourselves in the energy that is our bounty to exploit at such times of crisis. Let us go this instant."

"Good grief . . . Egypt?"

"No! Come with me upstairs!" Her voice beamed but there was no recognizable smile on her face.

Mr. Skidmore was flummoxed by her request, "Sorry—Miss Callisto—I don't quite know what you mean, but look, I really don't feel like continuing. I am most perturbed by your revelations, and—"

"It will be the solution to your problems, at least the immediate one. Don't hold back on this opportunity to right a wrong. Come with me to the apex!" She strode slowly towards him.

"Miss Callisto, this building is polygonal not pyramidical, how can it have an apex? I've heard enough already. I'll manage my own stress. Miss Callisto, you're too kind, and I am most touched by your concern, but I would be imposing on you—"

"You are concerned over trifles, when your own troubles weigh so heavily upon your shoulders. I am truly moved by your selflessness," she said convincingly. "It is not an imposition upon me, in any way. Come along, so that you can be repaired sooner . . ." She ignored his polygonal, pyramidical elucidation, and raised her sinuous arm to him.

He stood up, but didn't offer the crook of his arm. Instead he gave a gesticulation of exasperation with his arms—"But what can you do? You saw what's happening in my life. Aren't you powerless to change the course of my fate?"

"There are certain things that can be done, so that *you yourself* can change the course of it, as I explained." Becoming impatient, her outstretched hand was tensioning like a claw. She softened the effect, and diverted his attention. "It is not something I would usually do. It is not normally part of the service I give, but with my help it might be possible for you to alter the course of events. But only if you take advantage of my assistance."

He was on the borderline before acceptance, looking at her uncertainly.

"Miss Callisto, I don't know. You mean it really is not an inconvenience for you?

"Come, it would not be a burden upon me. Let us go to the upper room immediately before your spirit declines further. I feel partly responsible for your upset, being the conduit for the spirit guides, and know how to rescue your beleaguered heart. Give me your hand, I will lead you." She was aware of her hand gnarling again.

"Do you really mean it would not be a hassle for you?"

She struggled to prevent her outstretched hand from further stiffening and giving away her anger. She continued, "That is a fact. It is nothing that I would not do for a friend. I know you very well from our combination over the crystal globe. You are an admirable man, and I would like to do this for you out of friendship. Before you leave, I want you to think of me in the same way, a friend."

Mr. Skidmore stood, gazing at the ceiling, his arms floppily about his sides, pondering her proposition. It seemed very odd but on the balance of it, accepting could be no stranger than his decision to pay the clairvoyant a visit in the first place.

He volunteered his hand, looking at her pensively.

She reached with her hand, stiff as ash twigs, for his, which was slick with moisture.

She looked him in the eye for some seconds. Something black rustled behind her pupils and settled. She turned, her dress fanning out as she did so, and led him through the braided curtain doorway.

The Drum Demigod skipped a few beats, and then surged frenetically over the kit, which shivered like the wings of a fly. Arms one and two cracked out a press roll over the snare. Three and four tumbled over the toms. Five and six spackled the hi-hat, and seven and eight alternated between the ride and crash cymbals.

The percussion assumed a colour as it saturated the air, a distinct, rich red.

"ATRUBBATRUBBATRUBB ATRUBBATRUBBATRUBBA..."

Chapter 18

He held her hand and they ventured forth up the stairwell, within the oddly proportioned house. The downstairs "spiritual room" was so jumbled with mystical paraphernalia, that the stairway seemed to Mr. Skidmore (as conditioned by now as he was) under-decorated by comparison, even though there was sufficient adornment for most people's tastes. A blue and green diamond carpet, and pressed floral wallpaper, coloured white, was titivated at meter intervals with pictures—portraits of occultists; Aleister Crowley, Eliphas Levi, Guido von List, Marie Laveau and others. There were simple decorations on the first floor landing, a couple of Greek vases in the black figured style to the side of a door, with just a primer coat of paint over its surface.

She held his hand. The stairs and wooden floorboards were uncarpeted after the first floor landing. Just a portrait of a TV magician, Saul Daniels, on the way up.

He held onto her hand. On the second, items were stacked against a wall—an unopened box, half a metre high and wide, and objects hidden under bubble wrap, expanded polystyrene chips sprinkled around.

She was holding his hand. There was nothing at all on the third floor, apart, curiously, from a length of tinsel. The pink of the plaster afforded the only warmth.

The odd house was five storeys high, but the stairwell had felt chasmic to Mr. Skidmore. It had gradually tapered as they ascended. Without sound, apart from the creaking of the step's timbers, they climbed the last staircase.

Holding hands, they alighted on the top floor, at the final short landing, before the single room's entrance. They walked forward and entered within.

He was taken aback by the tricolour room. "My gosh! What is this place! Is this some sort of temple?" he said in befuddlement, releasing her hand, momentarily snatched from his worry. He wandered to the middle of the well-lit space, his face looking like a fly's staring at a car's windscreen, knocking something with one of his two left feet as he walked.

She quietly moved around and behind him, as he gawped at the spectacle, and turned the key in the lock.

"It just gets better," he said. "Are you running an Ancient Egypt fan club in here?" Everywhere within the incongruously asymmetrical attic, blue tacked to the oblique ceiling aspects, and walls, decked out in red, white and black, were memorabilia of Egyptian Pharaohs, ancient Egyptian mythology and the ancient Egyptian empire. The curtains, fully drawn, were striped the three colours, the bed was a bright red.

The walls themselves, barely glimpsed, seemed to be heaving under the weight of posters and prints, overlapping each other in places. There were even a few on the ceiling, a painted Egyptian flag decipherable on its facets.

Amongst the faces and figures, was a substantial bust of Nefertiti of polished granite—the Great Royal Wife (chief consort) of the Egyptian Pharaoh Akhenaten, wearing a crown. A gold-embellished, tomb-painting of a banquet scene, featuring dancing girls and musicians from the fourteenth century BC. A highly stylized painting from the tomb of Nebamun featuring his namesake, hunting fowl in a marsh, from 1500 BC—somehow acquired from a British collector.

Mr. Skidmore, without realizing it, was turning in his hand a bronze statuette of a falcon from 600 BC, in the Delta area of Egypt. Associated with the god Horus (indeed Horus was depicted as having a hawk's head), originally owned by a wealthy devotee of a cult that worshipped Horus, all those millennia ago.

The fire grate mantel he stood at was festooned with historic regal memorabilia; an aventurine figurine of an Egyptian noblewoman, wearing a black, painted diadem, with complex patterning in red and silver. She stood in elaborately pleated linen, rendered in the stone. There was an obsidian head of Osiris—one of the oldest gods for whom records had been found, who was a merciful judge over the dead and those who should be granted life. And a small Shabti statue in the form of a mummy, that had been taken from a tomb. The Egyptians believed that these would magically carry out any work they had to do in the "afterlife" (when they had died). And a version of King Tutankhamen's death mask, a Pharaoh who ruled Egypt from 1333 BC to 1324 BC, as part of the Eighteenth dynasty, whose life was cut short at eighteen years of age.

Miss Callisto materialized at Mr. Skidmore's side, and caressed the statuette from his slick hand, replacing it in its position on the mantel.

"Mr. Skidmore, do not be distracted by that which is only incidental. Remember the urgency of the matter. What this room contains should not take precedence over your dilemma—"

Realizing her close proximity, he, for a split second, analyzed her porcelain features. "It certainly doesn't, but the . . . loudness, for want of a better word, begs explanation," he said, looking to his surroundings once again.

As was her wont, she enigmatically withheld explanation, just intently looking at him, cradling her breasts under folded arms, as he breathed in the room.

He narrowed his focus, in a fleeting attempt to furnish his own mind with the significance.

He said, "What do you mean incidental, anyway? There's stuff everywhere. It looks like some kind of shrine in here!"

But the superficial pageantry, the primary coloured vibrancy, did nothing to lift his spirit. He bore in mind Miss Callisto's advise, to disregard that which was not relevant to his plight.

He resolved it all had some relevance to *her* but accepted that her policy of *keeping him in the dark* was well intentioned. It was of no significance to him. He became again completely submerged in misery.

Her gaze was fixed on him, chasmic depth in her eyes. She said again simply, "Do not be distracted by that which is incidental to you . . ."

He had the presence of mind to politely look back into her face.

She said, "The apex of the pyramid was our destination and we have arrived at that. Here the energies are strongest and will revive your depleted soul, but before that can happen, we must perform the necessary ritual . . . Do not be cynical—you will only undermine yourself. Give yourself over to me now, and I will put you to right."

He needed out of his well of grief, and could only accept the unlikely lifeline she was offering. He shrugged his shoulders in agreement.

Then he stiffened as something rebounded in his head. He repeated to her, "The building isn't pyramid shaped. This room isn't pyramid shaped either—the apex section of a pyramid is also a pyramid . . ." Before they started, he would ensure that this query, at least, would be answered.

She had prepared a response. "It is not a pyramid *as such*. That is simply my own terminology. It is the top—the apex, of this sacred building, and that is the main thing. It is close enough in shape to a pyramid—do not fret over trifling details."

She had never understood geometry in school.

Satisfied, he let sadness reclaim him.

"Come along now," she said, "we must make haste," and carefully reached for his elbow.

"ATRUBBATRUBBATRUBB ATRUBBATRUBBATRUBBA . . ."

In the middle of the room were two, narrow-seated stools.

"I know of the effectiveness of this room's power," she assured him, and sat him down on the walnut of one.

"The science is advanced and the custom may cause trepidation, but you need not concern yourself with my method. Just allow the experience to wash over you." Miss Callisto rested a reassuring hand on his back.

"The key is to relax. Do not, at any point, question what I do. Do not resist. This will only negate our efforts. Okay?"

His slumped shoulders shrugged. "Yeah, I suppose . . ."

She removed her silk scarf and his jacket, carefully placing them, folded, in the corner. She returned and positioned his arms over his thighs.

Divinity leaned down to face him, oddly close, displaying the recess of her cleavage. "Starting with some simple massage, to facilitate the flow of energy within you, and to allow the room's copious energies to permeate . . ." she said gently.

Facing him, she crouched, and placed her fingertips against his temples. He flinched at the sudden contact. She started motioning them in small circles, which grew larger, and fanned out over the whole side of his jaw and skull, disturbing his hair.

As though reading Braille, "Mr. Skidmore, it really is essential that you do not resist. I feel the tensed muscles—so tense, and it concerns me . . ." She migrated to his face, tracing the orbits around his eyeballs.

"If we are to make progress, it is imperative that you give over your body to my healing hands. It is key to success."

"I'm trying, Miss Callisto but I'm so upset, I just can't relax," he grumbled.

"You must let go!" she said with an urgency that made his eyes gape and his eyebrows rise above her fingers, in startlement.

"Do not physically oppose what you do not understand at this time. My methods are esoteric and will surprise, maybe shock you, but you must see beyond this unfamiliarity to the long-term benefits you will derive," she said, without releasing contact.

Mr. Skidmore yielded.

The depression within him was tinged with bemusement. He could see some logic in the requirement to *loosen up* though. For the first time, he noticed the smell of rose petal upon her body.

She stroked the back of his neck this time, with firm fingertips, from the nape to the base of his skull. This, for about five minutes.

At the perimeter of the vast expanse of his melancholy, there was faintly a pleasant feeling, but nothing to write home about.

She opened the loop of his tie to the limit, and undid his upper shirt.

Mr. Skidmore muttered something, and was raising his eyebrows and hands from his lap.

Divinity quickly quashed the uprising with a forefinger to her lips and a stern stare.

He abated.

She released the buttons to his navel and flicked open his shirt. She moved along his neck, expertly massaging it at the point where it met the shoulders.

She touched upon his chest, below the collarbone, kneading the ridge, then glided over his pectorals, feeling the springy dark hairs under acuitised fingertips. She lowered herself at the knees, and slid her hands over his stomach, over the contours of his abdominal muscles, pushing into his navel.

Divinity rose before him, her twin comet breasts streaking past his face. She stood pertly, then stooped a little, diving her hands through his collar, and moved her palms sensually over the undulations of his shoulder blades, down to the arch of his mid back, and then to the top of his shoulders again, her bosom skimming his forehead.

Clearly a trained masseuse, his initial skepticism about this degree of intimacy between them had vanished. Another five minutes later, and Mr. Skidmore had given himself over (almost) to her expert touch. He was even beginning to feel *at ease.*

She continued working on his chest and back.

Mr. Skidmore was becoming more aware now of her sexuality, as close to him as she was. The physical contact was reactivating something within him, which he did not resist. Her large pale breasts were appreciably at close quarters. Within her luxurious embrace, he rested his gooey eyes upon their cleavage.

Divinity gracefully flexed, and graduated to his lower back, not changing her position from in front of him. She motioned the sweep of her body to and fro, as she melted the stiffness away, but he was more aware of another sensation.

One of her knees, between his legs, pressed upon his private part, as she stretched over him. Of course, it was a coincidental feature of her technique, an absentminded misplacement of a limb. Nobody's perfect, he decided, but nevertheless, the rubbing felt sort of . . . *nice.*

143

Five minutes on, Divinity was cutting swathes through his despair. He began murmuring but would cough immediately after, to disguise the fact. His eyelids were closing every now and again, and she felt the muscles untangle completely.

He was warmed up, she thought, eying him as she physically cocooned him on the stool. It was slow progress, but nonetheless *was* progress. She decided to proceed to the next stage.

Divinity began more vigorously manipulating his body, which was in remission—her probing more forceful, rocking him on his seat.

Mr. Skidmore physically receded into oblivion.

All the while, the reanimation of his lunchbox area continued and intensified. It was all delightfully accidental, extraneous activity, and so he withheld protest.

He could feel a chuntering in his underpants, something rusted, creaking back into motion. It was surprising how sensual the inside of someone's knee could feel—then again, it belonged to the *divine* Miss Callisto.

He was sexually aroused, while at the same time consenting to her bona fide technique. The rubbing and kneading and nudging persisted.

Now, when Divinity leaned over him during the course of her massage, her breasts firmly pressed onto his face (all delightfully accidental, allegedly). He felt them rolling, like huge, warm ball bearings over his face.

She let him feel pangs of suffocation, and then released, allowing him to catch his breath in weak gasps, before returning to smother him again.

He was slowly becoming accustomed to her brand of pleasure.

He was very much aroused now and receptive to her charms. The crotch articulation continued—no accident, he was certain by now, but *who cares*, he thought, smiling idiotically, and spreading his legs wider.

His hair was in disarray, as Divinity continued buffeting his head with her humungous boobs, so vigorously that her slight, cleavage-revealing top could barely contain the voluptuous mounds of flesh.

Mr. Skidmore, completely compliant, was moaning between submersions, with dreamy pleasure.

The jostling of his hidden willy and her general attention to that area only increased, short of actually handling it. Now she slid her graceful leg between his, like a snooker cue over stubby, bridged fingers.

She smothered herself upon his rubescent facial features a few times more and then her headlights were showing—an assisted jailbreak, which Mr. Skidmore didn't argue over, even though somewhat shocked.

He was bewildered but delirious, unable to resist her advances, completely succumbing to her superior skills. A deep intake of breath, and his head lolled back, facing the heavens.

She didn't want to lose the moment, though there was little likelihood that he would refuse. She knelt between his legs, and opened the zipper, but didn't venture to loosen his belt. She had formed her hand into a scoop shape, and without fuss, reached into his parted fly. She swiftly levered against his knob.

For the first time, he fully appreciated the strength in those fingers, which had solidified like polished stone.

The superhuman drummer was so wildly animated that his head and upper body were the only features that could have been tracked by the human eye.

Beyond his shoulders and below his waist was just a motion blur, as demigod and machine married in perfect harmony.

He looked upwards to the sun at its zenith, and he and his musical chariot levitated above the apex of the mountain.

The deity and deific creation hung in midair like a second satellite over the Earth, looking especially effulgent.

Then, in the pulse of a flea's heart, he stopped to statue stillness, so that the sudden silence seemed more violent than the precedent cacophony.

Still looking to the sun, he held out his eight arms to their limit. Fork lightning issued from them, splitting the crystal daylight.

The UFO gradually descended, gently as a feather, to the mountain's summit.

He resumed.

"ATRUBBATRUBBATRUBB
ATRUBBATRUBBATRUBBA . . ."

Chapter 19

It jumped out, as though spring loaded.

The look of startlement redoubled on Mr. Skidmore's face.

Divinity viewed the member objectively. It teetered semi-rigidly, a chrysalis poking through tufty fronds, awaiting the metamorphic catalization that she would instigate.

She considered her next action; rather droopy, she thought—as a pasty draught excluder, propped against a door. She was somewhat affronted by the quality but decided that clearly, the long-term lack of use had caused the supply to be redirected away from his intimate area. But at least there was something to work with, a starting point . . .

He looked in amazement at the proceedings. He stammered something, feigning a protest, which melted away like a knob of butter on hot toast.

Divinity fondled his *cojones*, she let them roll like jumbo jumping-beans in her spidery hands. At that moment she decided it was no longer necessary to cast her eyes to his face, to glean his propensity, being quite sure that he had not *had it* in a very long time. Instead she fixated on the semi-erect pecker . . .

Gripping it at its base where it rooted into the crotch, her elongated fingers formed a firm tourniquet around the shaft.

Mr. Skidmore looked down, and gasped, on the edge between stupefaction and acceptance of this bold erotic act.

Slowly, methodically, she began to masterfully massage. He settled down nicely, hypnotized by her foreplay, and his gasping grew louder in concurrence, presence of mind vanishing like an ice cube in a microwave oven. All his attention was focused on the vision of lust, realized.

As she proceeded to stimulate—with what Mr. Skidmore believed was an unprecedented dexterity—a tactile sensation, that was something he had not ever before experienced, the willy stiffened like a developing tree, from a sapling to a solid trunk. The tip inflated above her white knuckles, Humpty Dumpty-like, atop the wall.

"ATRUBBATRUBBATRUBB ATRUBBATRUBBATRUBBA . . ."

She led him by the *giggle stick* to the double bed, and made him lie down. He did so willingly, without the least resistance. She undressed in front of him. She was wearing no underwear.

Her naked, alabaster figure made him gibber some incongruous, appreciative profanity. He saw her shapely hips lilt illicitly, under a wasp waist. In perfect balance above, her voluminous breasts undulated like hot wax in a matmos.

She sashayed over to him, and resumed her stimulative procedure.

Mr. Skidmore gasped louder, as though he was being dipped into a bucket of iced water on a lolly stick. He looked down at the extraordinary sight, and the smarting eyes in his head rolled to whiteness, as he irresistibly lost all tension in his limbs. His elbows gave way under him, and he collapsed back onto the bed, as she toiled at the vertex of his hairy V legs, doing things to him, exercising him by such methods, that he could not begin to comprehend, either in their devising, or in their execution. Electricity seemed to flow through her fingertips. Up, down and around, down, up and around.

Because he had never experienced such a delicacy before, he was unable to understand this talent. Her magical touch seemed more like a *divine power*.

The resulting sensation was something pleasurably alien to him, plunged as he was into a midnight carnival, in a sensual foreign land. Every now and again he hoisted his head from off the abundant scarlet bed covers to view the mirage, but could not decide whether what he saw was the life giving substance he had been thirsting for in the arid desert of his bed, or the demise of his moral integrity.

His striated pectorals spasmed, pulling the enormous beams of his arms, as his lightning wielding hands thrashed over the drumheads of solid energy.

More coordinated than any Billy Cobham, even improved by a factor of one thousand, more meticulous than a Gene Kruppa, to the power of a hundred, his time keeping more perfect than any vibrating crystal.

Manifold arms, writhing like atomic particles about a nucleus, counted down the intervals between, and duration of all physical processes on this particular planet.

His timing was absolute, because time originated within him.

"ATRUBBATRUBBATRUBB ATRUBBATRUBBATRUBBA . . ."

Divinity Callisto could sense his intoxication without seeing his face with her eyes. She had an infallible method for elucidating the changes taking place within her subject.

Next stage: She unbuckled his belt and pulled down his trousers as best she could. In his inebriated state, the strength and coordination had gone from his body, and she had to struggle to remove the trousers from under his buttocks, which squashed her hands and forearms as she yanked. It made her look a touch less elegant than she would have liked, but he was too far-gone to have noticed this hiccup. She rolled them over his knobble knees and ankles.

Mr. Skidmore struggled to lift his back from off the bed, and propped himself upon his elbows. He examined what was occurring. He could see her lowering. He felt her voluptuous black hair brush over his upper thighs.

She reckoned the frog, awaiting the transforming kiss of a princess, and went down upon him, as if it were a popsicle.

It was nothing short of miraculous, he thought, that she could get its entirety into her mouth, without gagging.

Mr. Skidmore winced, as tears, partly of pain, partly of rare pleasure, welled in his eyes as he felt himself inside her mouth. His prick was so enlarged now that he could feel the rush of an ocean within it. He collapsed again.

It lasted a short eternity and then she gave him respite. She raised herself off his sweaty body—a cobra from a humid basket, and swayed, surveying the scene, before rising and waltzing off, to where, he did not know.

Craning, he could see—a good third larger than it had ever been before. He almost felt a second heartbeat emanate from it. He wondered what manner of witchery was this, which could cause his member to become so greatly enhanced!

Mr. Skidmore dimly tried but then acquiesced. He was not in the mood to analyze that, or the feeling that something was amiss, perhaps his soul. Instead he waited for the return of the sexual high priestess.

Seeing that he was paralyzed in sexual bliss, Divinity had determined the moment was right to call upon the services of her friend, Tykhon Y2K.

She was at the small wall cupboard and took out the brown paper bag, inside which was the little glass jar containing the chemical substance. The next stage would be critical, time being of the essence.

Divinity moved stealthily to the dressing table to her right, keeping her back to her client, and took out the jar. She could see the gentleman in the reflection in the mirror above the table. With haste, she twisted off the plastic top.

She tipped the jar slightly over a porcelain dish on the dresser, and with a pair of antique, solid silver sugar tongs, placed the cube onto the center. In form it was a little dice, not unlike a cube of snooker cue chalk, but more porous, and with a mild, lime-green self-illumination.

With a gold filigree teaspoon, keeping the dice steady in the tongs, Divinity scraped at one corner, which crumbled like semi-set plaster, much of it clinging to the spoon. Some of the curiously magnetic powder flew onto the dish. She scraped off some more.

The remains of the cube, she plopped back in the container. Its short shelf life prohibited mass manufacture, consequently there was presently just one other of its kind in the jar downstairs in the pantry. She sealed it and returned it to the brown paper bag.

A quick glance at the mirror revealed that the partially naked man had still not come around, but was breathing more steadily. His erection was intact.

She opened a drawer below her with her left hand, and picked out the white box—of female condoms.

Quickly, Divinity opened and pulled out the plastic-foil-wrapped appendage and with her tapered fingertips, sheared the covering. She took out the accessory, like an oversize *after eight* from its packet.

She extended the device, which resembled a small, transparent, plastic sock, and delicately fitted her fingers inside, careful not to tear the thin material. Then Divinity pushed it inside out.

She lowered the femadom over the little green mound on the center of the dish, and pushed into it, with her rubber-covered thumbs. The chemical compound clung to the inside of the tactile plastic device, like iron filings to a magnet. She smothered her rubbery thumbs over the powder some more, so that the whole of the inside was thickly covered with the granules.

"aahhuh . . . aahhuh . . . aahhuh . . . Miss Callisto—
Divinity . . . what are you doing? . . . aahhuh . . .
aahhuh . . . aahhuh . . ."

She said nothing in reply, just glancing into the
mirror to gauge the condition of his boner.

She continued preparing the rubber appendage.
With great care she gently turned the femadom
inside-out, so that the powder-covered interior sunk
through the ringed mouth.

Another look in the mirror confirmed that the man
was still oblivious to proceedings—but the erection
seemed fine.

But now he did have his head turned towards her,
which made her slightly uneasy—if he latched onto
her activities, suspicion could be invoked, which could
jeopardize the whole operation. Divinity could not
allow the prone man to escape from her view now, as
he regained his composure. She looked in the mirror,
sussing his response to her behaviour.

In the very least, the next procedure would be the
most unglamorous to perform. *Whatever*—she would
have to go ahead. She worried about the erection—it
was time critical now.

She held closed the rubber, chemical sock by its
mouth-ring and scrunched it up in her right hand.
She noticed his head yaw a little. When his eyes left
her figure, in a single swift motion, she inserted the
femadom inside her. *Voila.*

Miss Callisto looked to the man who had driven
her to such ignominy to attain her goal, and inwardly
frowned. The bane of her life, the accoutrement of the
penis—and yet supposedly its owner. The detachment
with which she had viewed the man, whose brain she

153

would completely wash, became a certain degree of contempt.

With the device tucked away, she made her move towards him. It felt uncomfortable, but being the professional that she was, she didn't let *him* know.

Divinity stood over the man, lying spread-eagled.

She had manipulated it so well that it was still sufficiently rigid. Nevertheless, all told, he had been hard work.

She eyed it, like a tawny owl about to dive for a field mouse.

Quickly, Divinity slid over his pelvis and eased him in. She sunk down upon his manhood, stretching the rubbery device hard over him.

Mr. Skidmore screwed up his face, trying to contain the effects of the unusual, *questionable* pleasure. For an age, she swiveled, gyrated and squeezed, in that order, he all the while gasping and yelping, gasping and yelping, watching her marvelous breasts shake in slow motion. It was a unique experience, somewhat excruciatingly abrasive, but at the same time masochistically pleasurable.

Divinity leaned forward—time for the *coup de grace*. As he looked at her stupidly, she grabbed the tongue of his tie, while with the other hand, she grabbed the knot. She jerked the neckerchief tight around his neck, and used it as a grab handle, slamming herself upon him, powering up and down with her thighs.

The willy was simply overwhelmed—a royal mail post box in the eye of a tornado. She gained in momentum, completely swallowing his member within her, squashing the creased femadom upon his boner, like an uneaten sausage between heaped crockery, and all the while pulling his tie tighter and tighter.

The veins bulged in his neck, and he gagged in dismay. His arms and legs flapped about uselessly, hardly controlled by a fading brain.

Mr. Skidmore, on the verge of passing out, asked himself whether this was really *enjoyment*.

It was too much for him. Semi-conscious, he convulsed (as though given a defibrillator shock), once, twice, three and four times, and then *pop went the weasel*. Cannon balls shot from his throbbing, rubber-capped, knob.

A moment of stillness followed the climactic scene of adulterous, "casual" (!!!!!!!) sex.

Divinity elevated herself off him, a mantis over the husk of a beetle.

The ceremony was performed. She was pleased with the result. His prick was buckling like a limp salami, the chemical residue over it, sherbet on a well-licked lollypop. Already she could see the faint green tinting over the whole, and the tinge of green around the tip's rim.

Still observing it wane, she finally gave a curt, decisive nod of satisfaction, at which it toppled like the bombed shell of a building.

Quintuple, quadruple, triple and double strokes rattled out over the snare, fast as machinegun fire, and flams over the burgeoning floor tom, throbbing like a sick Brontosaur.

The god's sweat steamed from his dense leather skin, forming thin clouds in the supercooled air about his eventful anatomy, generating and governing the symphony.

"*. . . Ratatat-tat, ratatat, CHUD, CHUD, CHUD, Ratatat-tat, ratatat, CHUD, CHUD, CHUD . . .*"

Half an hour had passed since their detachment.

"What will you do to me next?" Mr. Skidmore asked with a desiccated voice. "I don't know if I could take any more of this . . . how can I put it, *recreational* procreation . . ."

"Believe me, fella, not much more." Miss Callisto's tone was suddenly steelier, "Which is just as well, because playtime's over."

There was some dead air as he tried to gather the mental energy to figure her out. He was able to open his eyes and maneuver his head in her direction.

She was fully dressed, her back to him, tidying the wall cupboard.

He bumbled on, "You sound a little different to me . . . Is that a cockney accent you speak with? I didn't notice that before . . ."

"What's it to you?"

But his was a coherent question. She had lived in Shoreditch for some seven years and the vernacular had rubbed off on her. She made no further effort to disguise the fact, having accomplished her aim.

In the drowsy fog, he felt bemusement. "What do you mean, *What's it to me*? Why the sudden hostility? Didn't we just make love?"

"Make love? *You're 'avin a laarf*! I don't believe in the thing. Make love!" Miss Callisto cackled coarsely, not caring to offend Mr. Skidmore's sensibilities. "Make love indeed!" and her sardonic laughter reverberated in his ears for a couple more minutes.

Some of the life force had filtered back into him, and he was able to interject, "If that wasn't love, then what was it?" he demanded indignantly.

"That, *me old china*, was a transaction. *It was trade*," she said, matter-of-factly.

A look of disbelief on his face, "I don't understand, what do you mean by *trade*?"

She said cagily, "I gave you your heart's desire, and in return, you shall give something to me . . ."

The expressed puzzlement was confined to his tapered brows and mouth alone. The rest of him was immobile. "What is that? What is it I'm going to give you?"

Mr. Skidmore still lay prone, exhausted, on the bed, with his member exposed.

She didn't answer him. Instead she busily tidied the dressing table, as though their intimate encounter had never happened.

He hoisted his head to face the soreness. "Hey, wait a minute, what's that green powder on my willy?"

"Oh, that's just a sex aid," Miss Callisto said casually, not diverting herself from her cleanup.

He suddenly realized its condition. "It hardly felt like you were using one. It looks wrecked and seems to be . . . glowing somewhat!" Mr. Skidmore was beginning to feel a little sick inside. "Surely that was lovemaking . . . don't pervert our experience together—" he winged.

Miss Callisto intervened, "*Do me a favour*! You've got it all wrong." She made no attempt to hide her annoyance as she said it, and turned to him, the warmth having completely disappeared from her body, dressed and very distant. She speared his gonads. "It was *your lust* and *my business acumen . . .*" Her grave features told him of her sincerity, and his heart sank within him. She put the box of femadoms into the drawer.

There was a telling pause as Mr. Skidmore reflected on his crime, which she ended, jabbing proceedings forward with a needle.

"Look, you've overstayed your welcome—I'd like you to leave," Miss Callisto stated categorically.

"What, what do you mean . . . leave?"

She was adjusting her hair now, not bothering to give him her attention.

"Get yerself dressed and go."

The shocked puzzlement forced him up from the bed onto his elbows. "But we just had intercourse—you want me to . . . leave?"

"Don't you speak English?" she asked sharply, making him jolt. "Get your gear back on and get out, or I'll chuck you out as you are!" she said, scowling at him now.

He struggled off the bed with his dead arms and legs, not having been able to come to terms with the dirty feeling inside him.

She observed him hopping drunkenly, as he pulled on his trousers.

"Hurry up or I'll call the police!"

"Okay, okay, I'm hurrying!"

She watched him stagger about, her stony face conveying no friendliness towards him, unsoftened by the wafting scarf about her neck. When she saw he was sufficiently collected to be able to mobilize, she unlocked the door, urged him out and followed him downstairs.

Passing her "office", she poked, "Don't forget your briefcase!"

He stumbled in and leaned over with a creaky back, dropping his jacket as he grabbed the briefcase's handle. She waited at the braided curtain door, having a good mind to go in and finish him off there and then, kick him over onto the floor as he teetered, and then in the teeth, but refrained from delaying his exit from her property.

"Right, you all set?" she asked rhetorically as she snappily gesticulated with an arm for him to leave the room.

"But the payment . . . how much do I owe you?"

"Forget it, it was on the house," she said, pointing to the door.

"Look," his rosy, sweating face turned to her in consternation as he struggled to the front door. "There's a chemistry between us . . . Surely that didn't pass you by—escape your attention?"

Miss Callisto held it open. "Chemistry had something to do with it, but it's not any that'll be of benefit to you. Now run along!"

He didn't run—he couldn't. He floundered out, totally ungratified and debased by the *Big Stupid Sex*.

The Drum Demigod's eight mighty levers pummeled the rhythmatron, pulsing out beats of percussive blood, as the musculature over his diaphragm transferred, like tectonic plates over the Twin-Earth's surface, at its birth.

Water flowed like lava from his pitted skin, a patchwork hide, denser than iron a metre thick.

It was an irrevocable description, a colour decree, ranging from pink-tinged white, to blackish brown. It creased and folded, containing the exploding brawn—a powerhouse of unimaginable magnitude.

"*. . . Ratatat-tat, ratatat, CHUD, CHUD, CHUD, Ratatat-tat, ratatat, CHUD, CHUD, CHUD . . .*"

Chapter 20

Satisfied that the day had been productive, that night, lying on her bed, she reflected, looking at the certificate on the wall above her, amongst the many other items adorning the walls of the tricolour room. She stared at it with mixed feelings.

Shoreditch Secretarial College

Career Secretary Diploma

C115285 Chantal Callisto

Unit	Grade
Work Ethics: Security & Confidentiality	Distinction
Written & Spoken English	Distinction
Handling Mail	Distinction
Communications Skills	Distinction
Filing Duties	Distinction
Management of Time	Distinction
Relationship with Clients	Distinction
Graphs Tables and Charts	Distinction
Handling Petty Cash and Stock Control	Distinction
Health and Safety at Work	Fail
Personal Career Development	Distinction
Preparing Reports and Meetings	Distinction

This student has qualified for the above award with Distinction.

Date of Award   July 1997

Until her latest venture, it had been the only real achievement in Chantal Callisto's life. In the blink of an eye, the essential outcome of that achievement flitted through her mind.

There she was, kneeling before the managing director, performing what he had requested—her job depended on it.

He wasn't dictating a letter or asking her to prepare a report. His utterances, "Yes, that's very good, very satisfactory," was not in commendation of her services as a PA—more a spontaneous regard for her oral technique, as their flesh melded moistly.

He hadn't even washed that morning.

In his office, behind drawn blinds, he had listed Chantal's revised job requirements—of a more sexual nature.

When she refused to accept the new terms of her contract, the corpulent managing director, his jowls wobbling on his reddened face, vociferously reminded her of her lowly position—a newcomer on the job market, without credibility—on the verge of being sacked, and if she was, certainly without a reference to present to a future employer (for whom she would have to contrive a reason for her dismissal).

He gave Chantal the ultimatum, and she erred on the side of her career, obliging his voracious sexual appetite (which was in evidence even at her first and only interview, where she could almost feel him fondle her well-covered breasts with his puffy eyes, as he smacked his chops).

She had heard statesmen say that one should never give in to terrorism. But she had. Her gamble didn't pay off.

Six months on, she was still required to satisfy his sexual proclivity, he with no intention of allowing his geisha to fly away. Chantal was quite sick, but with no possibility of a reference if she left, she endured for another two. She resigned from the company, with nothing to show for her previous eight months "service", the MD having written to say that she had been officially dismissed for general incompetence and a lack of aptitude for the job. He added that she should not approach him for the all-important reference.

Deluded by her experience, she left the profession for good.

Omniscience guided the operation of the battery.

His fists bombed down upon the mechanical extension of his being.

A rim shot and a gunfight broke out over the snare—two, three, four arms pressed upon it, piercing sound splitting the atoms of the rarified air.

Million-year-old ice splintered off nearby glaciers and clattered down the mountain faces, and rocks the size of houses showered from the mountaintop. The bass drum boomed out, like a howitzer.

". . . Ratatat-tat, ratatat, CHUD, CHUD, CHUD, Ratatat-tat, ratatat, CHUD, CHUD, CHUD . . ."

She squirmed inside and changed her focus, looking around the tricolour room at the various glitzy images.

She had since a young age been fascinated by the last Egyptian Pharaoh, Cleopatra, who represented herself as the reincarnation of the goddess Isis—the patron of nature and magic and mother of Horus, the god of war. The Pharaohs were her children seated on the throne that she provided. That initial interest led Chantal to become fixated and then obsessive about the Ancient Egyptian civilization and especially the female Pharaohs—Sobekneferu, Hatshepsut and Peseshet.

Chantal had seen Cleopatra as an inspirational example of how a woman could transcend above the traditional stereotype of what a woman *is* and *can be*. Cleopatra most obviously flouted this rule—the embodiment of power—the reincarnation of a goddess, no less, in a world which nowadays men, from their conception, seek to monopolize.

In the Egyptian polytheistic religion (which people today would say was paganism), Chantal saw a Utopian institution, where women were as equally entitled to power as men. Many female goddesses including Isis, Hut and Hathor bore testimony to this fact. And this belief system pervaded ancient Egyptian society, where there was balance in gender roles and where both genders were considered equal in society. And they didn't just have power in the workplace, but total, supreme power.

And so she celebrated the Egyptian pantheonistic religion and the nation that resulted under the historic ruler-ship of the Pharaohs of ancient Egypt—the opulent, exotic backdrop for their time in power. She voraciously read their life stories, sometimes scandalous but always glamorous, and exciting and the halcyon days when their civilization was the most advanced and sophisticated, those glorious days, a bygone age, a better time.

After her experience at the office, Chantal reviewed her conception of the woman's apparent power within the ruler-ship with a degree of acrid amusement.

She had been so naïve.

While she had always known that a glass ceiling was in place, round about knee height for career-minded women, she had thought that the women of ancient Egypt generally and those with executive power, were an undying paragon of a woman's unlimited potential.

But then, in the final analysis, Cleopatra was defeated in battle by Octavian, the Roman emperor and male military dictator of an empire that did not permit its women to vote or hold any political office. They were apron wearing stay-at-homes—cooking, sweeping floors and bearing babies.

So now, Auntie Cleo's legacy in Egypt is a vestigial one. As powerful as she was, as bejeweled as she was and as seductively attractive as she was—now a bit of a clotheshorse and nothing else.

Her nation was conquered and she committed suicide.

So no fairy-tale queendom and no fairy-tale queen.

"ATRUBBATRUBBATRUBB ATRUBBATRUBBATRUBBA . . ."

She formulated a revised notion of how men had always exerted their will upon, shaped and "enlightened" the ancient world, to the exclusion of, and while excluding women, and were now doing the same, only in a more "politically correct" way.

Very much embittered by the way the system worked, she vowed, one day, to take revenge on the man who had sexually exploited her and robbed her of a career. At that moment, he symbolized the oppressive monopoly of power males had over the world.

She devised a scheme, and set about the preparatory task to avenge herself.

From an early age, long before her interest in ancient Egypt, she had been intrigued by herbology and later became absorbed in this recreational pursuit passed on by her mother. Even before her teens, she had an insight into every plant, seed, berry and root that grew in the fields and forests of Nottingham. In her youth, she learned the herbal cultivation, and preparation methods for healing poultices, fomentations and compresses, aromatherapy and cosmetics. Chantal had considerable natural intellect, in particular directions.

She was so engrossed in the subject of herbology that she even considered it as a career, then deciding that a clerical job would be more likely attainable, and better paid.

In the somewhat smaller kitchen of a previous Shoreditch address, driven by a hatred of men (and one in particular), Chantal Callisto began experimenting with herb combinations, testing the formulations on mice from a local pet shop. Early efforts produced no results (at least, not the results desired).

Then a breakthrough, when one mouse gradually developed the classic symptoms—a faintly luminous green coloration over its entirety, lethargy, and wasting of the tissues. Much to her disappointment, it eventually died. However, she had arrived at the prototype, which she refined to get the same combination of symptoms, without the mortality. After much vexation, "divine" inspiration and a lot of chemical trials, she had developed what she now referred to as *Tykhon Y2K*.

There was no natural antidote that she was aware of, or that she had got around to concocting.

She returned to the managing director's office, discreetly carrying in a handbag a jar of Tykhon, a female condom and the other items—not for a work recommendation but to offer him her service—one last sexual favour. She had changed address after inventing Tykhon. She left his office without passing on her new address details.

It would be a humiliating, debilitating and *lasting* reminder of their association.

Soon after the visit to her former boss's office, she became aware of a recurring dream of a squealing pig, sometimes a rat or some other ungracious, creepy crawly, nursing its injured penis.

Invariably, the chance meetings in the dream state resulted in her reacting violently towards the filthy creature, to immediately lash out at the degenerate thing. Naturally, when awake, she assumed the rodent with the gammy phallus was an abstract representation of her former employer. The dream persisted, and she thought nothing of it, other than that it was her mind reminding her of the condition her former boss would presently be in.

Then, out of the blue, her emancipated lesbian friend, Hilda, rang. She had such a severe demeanor that the boss had been dissuaded from making the run of the mill sexual advances towards her. Hilda had remained with the company, albeit resentfully, for the decent salary she was earning.

She, with great satisfaction, told Chantal that the MD had had a psychotic breakdown. Preceding it, he would accost employees, and then inanely babble about recurring dreams of being molested by a ghastly witch. He had become so disturbed that he was resigning from the company. Before doing so, though an emotional wreck, he had set up a female to become the new director.

Chantal was amazed by this development. Did Tykhon Y2K have anything to do with his mental demise? It would cause embarrassment and sexual dysfunction, but alone would not have caused such complete psychological devastation. There was something else.

It clicked. She understood who the dream creature was—more than just a representation of somebody—it was a person appearing to her *in reality* (or at least, the reality of dreams).

That night, in the dream, she set upon the pig with double the gusto.

Divinity had made her chance incursion into the world of psychic phenomena. She realized that there was a certain link between individuals, transcending beyond the physical limitations of distance and barriers.

The psychic meetings only ever occurred in the dream state. She began analyzing her dreams to try to uncover whether there were any other re-acquaintances occurring with people she might know. There weren't any that were obvious to her. But the dreams of her former employer became no less frequent, and her reaction toward him no less savage.

The causal connection between Tykhon Y2K and the dream encounters with her ex-boss became clear.

Tykhon Y2K had (as she had designed it to do) ravaged his genitalia, turned it a glowing green. This debilitating ignominy inevitably caused the man to ponder over, and curse, their association, during which he acquired this affliction. It played upon his mind all the time, day and night. And the more he thought of *the bitch that turned his willy green*, the more he appeared to Chantal Callisto at night in the dreams.

The man's intense interest in her seemed to cause his psychic instatement in her head. Perhaps now he knew who his dream oppressor was—which would bring Miss Callisto *even more* to the forefront of his mind.

It was clear to Chantal that he was not able to break free of the vicious cycle.

"ATRUBBATRUBBATRUBB ATRUBBATRUBBATRUBBA . . ."

She put all the ingredients into the cauldron of her mind, stirred and allowed to stand. It mingled in the pot and clarified over the following couple of years while on the dole.

The disempowered Pharaoh/Queen.

Male sexual aggression—their worldwide domination and the empires they forged.

Her physical beauty, herb craft expertise and psychic experience.

She reviewed the resultant brew, and brainstormed a new career plan. She envisaged a money-spinning venture—a scheme to *win big*, combining her life discoveries, passions and natural abilities. And one that would satisfy her desire for payback on men.

Chantal Callisto's business would be rooted in her finalized beliefs.

That women relied on the patronage of men for material advancement: Males underestimated females—their physical inferiority having somehow become an intellectual one. This enforced their dependency and status as sex objects.

The dominion males always had over the world, most obviously manifested in the form of empires. Empires were primarily male concerns and were attained as a result of male physical aggression. They were acquired by force—superior military strength, and maintained with the same—a marauding, raping action upon the world.

The male phallus symbolized this action—a sword-like appendage, thrusting into the virginal world, corrupting it. Penetrating through international boundaries, inseminating nations with its rules, culture, laws and values.

The jigsaw came together. By her guile—a feminine attribute—Miss Callisto would secure the penis as *her* sword, with which to generate her own empire of slave men, and wield the phallus as *her* scepter, with which to rule over it. She herself would be the queen, or New Pharaoh, reinstated as the almighty sovereign.

She steeped herself in the subject her business would, *superficially*, be based upon—she had decided on that of clairvoyance and mediumship almost on the result of a coin toss (it was either the mediumship or plumbing). Chantal visited the professionals in the trade (little did they know of her intention to subvert their honourable profession and code of ethics), bought the specialist books and borrowed them from the College of Psychic Studies. She read the classic texts in the British Museum, Reading Room. Then she began to make the purchases of the essential hocus-pocus equipment for her workplace.

Now, at age thirty-two, after three successful months of free enterprise, Chantal was engrossed in her new line of work in the guise of Divinity Callisto—bogus spiritual medium, phony clairvoyant, seductress and self-proclaimed militant, women's liberationist.

The furious powerplay was an omen of trouble coming for anything with a bucket to kick.

Some had more to worry about than others.

It was the precursor of death and consequential regeneration for an observer with flowery thinking.

Mostly, the Drum Demigod just liked to beat the hell out of his drums.

His blood was up, and he just couldn't stop.

The rest of the universe couldn't help but listen to the countdown. This might be the forerunner of their own Judgment Day.

He bit his lip and buried himself deeper in his kit, as all life on the parallel world—Earth's twin—wondered if their card had been pulled.

"ATRUBBATRUBBATRUBB ATRUBBATRUBBATRUBBA . . ."

Chapter 21

She always selected male clients that would be suitable. When men phoned her to arrange an appointment, she would make the indirect enquiry as to their professional status—"Can you attend on a weekday, between nine and five o'clock (my usual working hours)?"

If they could, they were likely unemployed. Before ending conversation, Divinity took their number. She would call them back, and postpone the appointment (normally due to having a sudden, fake illness of some sort), saying she would be in touch when "better".

If Miss Callisto suspected the man on the phone *was* employed, she kept him hanging on the line, engaged in meandering conversation, during which she collated as much information as possible about his work circumstance.

Again, if she felt he was a low earner, she would terminate their association. Miss Callisto desired *high-earning* professionals.

She simply told females they had dialed the wrong number.

The selection process relied to a degree on guesswork, but she was normally accurate in her choices.

"ATRUBBATRUBBATRUBB ATRUBBATRUBBATRUBBA . . ."

In the beginning, Miss Callisto derived a great deal of pleasure from gratuitously tormenting the men she had collected in her dreams. In the night she would physically abuse them out of spite.

Of late, even though she still found the sadism element of their dusky meetings pleasurable, she was starting to find that the money she was laundering from them was becoming more of an aphrodisiac, and was becoming her primary focus.

Miss Callisto's nocturnal forays into the dream state had become more coordinated. She was more measured in the violence she applied to her captives, so that they would not become confused. It was used only as a means to harvest wealth from them.

In the ruse of Divinity Callisto, Mystic and Fortuneteller, she was satisfied that she was taking the potency from men, and transferring it to womendom, on a daily (or nightly) basis. It was a symbolic transfer of power for women at large, but it was procurement of real, tangible power for her own benefit.

As the business was becoming more successful, her ambitions became more defined. She saw how she could become the uber-monarch or Super-Pharaoh and build an empire to rival the first great empire of the Egyptians or any other empire that existed or had existed.

It would require a lot of hard work but she was determined to fulfill her objectives. With the acquired money, Miss Callisto moved to her latest, roomier premises in Surrey, on the edge of London, Britain's business and trade center (where there would be no shortage of the professionals she sought). She stocked her estate with the necessary exotic, mystical paraphernalia, which made her con-act more believable. She took driving lessons (after the first lesson, the male instructor unsurprisingly taught her free of charge), passed her test and bought a car—necessary for her more hectic lifestyle. She had spent a small fortune, but she considered it to be an investment. She upped the number of clients she was seeing from one every two days, to one every day.

She would colonize mankind in the name of woman, but financially for the exultation of herself.

Tucked in her bed in the tricolour room, Divinity settled her eyes on the painting of Pharaoh Cleopatra handing the "Sa" amulet, symbolizing protection, to a suppliant slave. She liked the detail of her coronet and sumptuous dress and the man bowing, but thought the inclusion of the Sa absurd.

With a supple arm, Miss Callisto reached behind her, under the mattress, and pulled out the "Green Mamba" plastic dildo. It was a little tacky but more realistic in shape than any sacred, facsimile phallus she had ever seen. She held her *tool of civilization* tightly to her chest, and fell asleep.

In the landscape of her dream there was a sunset in a black sky. Below it, the thick, green woods. She strolled towards the trees and examined their drill. Standing erect to attention, just the way she liked it—that is, all except one. A newcomer to the ranks, she scrutinized it. Rather sloppy, she thought, branches oddly shooting from its lower trunk and the foliage over the whole, less than the rich green she expected from her troop. It leaned at a slight angle to the others, which made her especially cross.

Clearly it would require disciplining. She held out her right hand, and a hatchet appeared. She glared at the tree, with narrowed eyes and a furrowed brow, moving closer. She wound up the axe far behind her back, and swung. It sunk into the trunk as though it were marzipan. Red blood spouted from the split bark. The silent woods were suddenly filled with the shrill of the tree's scream.

Divinity took no prisoners.

In the morning, she performed a general tidy and cleanup of her premises, and completed the sundry chores. She had deliberated over whether she could arrange for some male butlers to do such work, but decided that she wouldn't stand their physical presence. Miss Callisto only associated with men in the first place in order to recruit them for her Empire. Once captive, her only dealings with them were on the astral plane.

Divinity checked her mail, as soon as the postman delivered it. From the little pile at her front door she picked up one manila and one white envelope. She opened the white.

A Mr. S. Boateng signed the cheque for the sum of one thousand, five hundred pounds. Very satisfactory, apart from the fact that it reminded her that he had missed the previous month's payment. She would have to get onto him about it.

She opened the manila. Mr. C. Slater had paid her one thousand pounds for the month, plus an additional two hundred pounds, Miss Callisto presumed as a further safeguard, to protect himself from her wrath. *How very generous*, she thought.

In fact, when she opened and inspected the many envelopes in the heap, she found that over half of the cheques were overpayments. This was much to her satisfaction. Chasing up non—and under-payers afforded some morbid pleasure, but was becoming increasingly difficult as her Empire expanded. But when Miss Callisto *did* catch up with the dodgers, she was wickedly vicious.

The sun was coming down fast.

His eightfold arms hung in midair as he twiddled the rods of lightning, crackling in his hands. He looked down balefully through the clouds, scanning the surface below. He stopped twirling, and closed his satellite dish eyes. Time stood still.

He exposed his eyes to the subzero air again, and plummeted onto the sound machine. A sonic boom burst outward.

"THHHHOOOOOOOOOOOOOOO OOOOOOOOOOOOOOMMMM."

Sometimes payments would cease because the subject had gone gaga—snapped under the harsh regimen Miss Callisto imposed upon him. Not all her captives successfully made the transition to slavery. In these cases, harder beatings only made the disoriented manservant less likely to perform his duties. She would back off until he recovered his faculties, so that she could return him to servitude. If the serf was irreparably damaged, then the most Miss Callisto could derive from him was as an object on which to relieve her stress in various ways.

There were no covering letters included in any of the envelopes, which is what she had requested. Miss Callisto wasn't one to stand on ceremony in matters of money. Some names were missing from the pile, but she expected the outstanding payments to arrive within the course of the next few days. She had decreed that payments be made within the first week of each calendar month.

The client that Divinity was expecting today would arrive in the evening. To her chagrin, before then she would have to visit the city to do the shopping for essential groceries. She also needed to resupply her pantry with jasmine oil, chamomile flower and passionflower. Divinity would have to go in her old Volkswagen. The new car would be delivered tomorrow, by her new, obliging client. *A pity*, she thought, she would have liked it that day but some things couldn't be rushed.

After that, she would need to make some more Tykhon and conduct the other necessary preparations.

Warheads arced up through the sheets of cloud, their fiery contrails setting aglow the mountainsides.

Down below there were famines and pestilences and great floods.

The Drum Demigod gazed impassively into infinity as his arms whirled about him.

"ATRUBBATRUBBATRUBB ATRUBBATRUBBATRUBBA . . ."

That evening the man arrived, a few minutes late, and introduced himself as Mr. Skeptikos.

Miss Callisto took him into her office to soften him up in the usual way, but soon realized that it wouldn't be necessary. He appeared to forget the reason for their meeting, and rapidly became a professor of anatomy. All he did, with a very poor attempt to conceal his enthusiasm, was study her hips and bust. She went with the flow, cleverly encouraging his eagerness, and then straightforwardly offered the more special service.

Before long she had whisked him up to the tricolour room and they set about it, hammer and tongs. Obviously, her special *sex aids* came into play.

In fact, Divinity often found it that easy.

Half an hour later, he was still exhausted (as they always were afterwards) but disturbed by a flagging aspect of his own anatomy.

He questioned Miss Callisto about the matter. "What have you done to it? It looks . . . different!"

"What do you mean different?" She was preoccupied with the tidying of the wall cupboard.

"Well, it could be my eyes but it looks sort of greener!" said the stark naked man.

"Oh that. That was the green lubricant gel I used," she lied, not bothered to explain the details of the herb formulation that would make him her possession. "I made it myself."

Incredulity over his face, "What do you mean lubricant? It felt more like gravel! It looks more like gravel! And why's my willy all crumpled?"

"You over exerted yourself and that's what happens," she said unemotionally.

He pondered, "It's never happened before. Most peculiar—but then, it was rather intense."

At that moment, Miss Callisto's Siamese entered through the narrow opening in the door—she hadn't locked it. It simply wasn't necessary with as keen a customer as Mr. Skeptikos.

It was a cat that moved in a winding fashion. Its paws were large and padded, dangling at the bony legs. It brushed against the lower tresses of the silk garment Miss Callisto had put on, after her calculated fling.

"Ubasti, there you are!" she said, bending towards the cat at her heels.

"Who's Ubasti?" Mr. Skeptikos asked, fumbling from his reposed posture for his underpants to the side of the bed.

"Ubasti cat." She picked up the feline and cradled it in her arms.

"After the goddess Ubasti?" he enquired, yanking on the pants.

Her lashy eyes flicked onto him. "How'd you know that?"

"I teach my kids about ancient Egypt. I'm a history teacher—"

"That, I already know." she remarked. "Not all that high an earner," she said, as an aside.

"For that matter, what's with all the Egyptian royalty and military pictures on the walls? It reminds me of my recent holiday to Cairo. Like some sort of museum," Mr. Skeptikos said loftily, forgetting his earlier fornication.

She had been to Cairo many times, when she hadn't been broke. "It's my tribute to Pharaoh and Empire," she said proudly, stroking the head of the cat in her arms.

Miss Callisto looked to the row of curtained windows. "I am in the process of creating my own. I am the ruler—you are my latest conquest . . ."

"Are you on something? Run it by me again, in English."

"By the ritual, I've secured your penis as my tool, with which to civilize you and other men. And also to exploit you."

He paused, then went along with the "jest". "But that makes no sense . . . If you exploit, you yourself are uncivilized," he retorted.

Still looking at some far off thing, "Pigs are less civilized. We make efforts to civilize them—and then we *eat* them," Miss Callisto returned coldly.

"You what? You mean I'm a pig?" He had the strength to prop himself upon the bed.

Dispassionately, "A male chauvinist pig."

"Missus, that is very insulting!" Mr. Skeptikos said indignantly, his eyes protruding.

"Miss actually—would you have adulterated a married woman?"

"No!" he said—but *she* had adulterated a *married man*.

Struggling to rise from the bed, "You're off your rocker, Miss Callisto."

The cat was smiling in her arms. "You've overstayed you're welcome, I'd like you to leave."

"Gladly!" he said, offended.

She watched him struggle pathetically to get dressed, and followed him out.

After traversing down the stairwell and along the corridor, with not a word passing between them, he had second thoughts about leaving on such bad terms. After all, she *was* such a fine-looking lady. Perhaps he was being a little hasty—he might want to pay her another visit (when he had recouped his energy) in the not too distant future.

"Miss Callisto, that was a wonderful psychic reading. How much do I owe you for your kind services?" he asked smarmily.

She held open the door, Ubasti in her other arm.

"Nothing. Just leave," she said, not revealing the hatred she felt toward him in her body language.

Hoitily, he insisted, "But surely, a token payment is in order. I was so much impressed by your sooth-saying technique. I feel I must visit you again sometime—"

"As I said, you've overstayed your welcome, *you filthy beggar*, get out of my house."

His face became an exclamation mark; he took a step back in shock.

"You're mad!" he said looking at her, not penetrating a millimeter beyond the epidermis of her porcelain skin. He stumbled out the exit. On the doorstep he turned and looked again to her in bewilderment.

"Sling yer hook!" she said and slammed the door. "*I'll sort you out tonight,*" she added, with a whispy smile.

The summoned ICBMs, a fair drizzle now, detonated far below the clouds.

One of his swarming arms decelerated, lowered and curled.

He outstretched the great dais of his hand.

"ATRUBBATRUBBATRUBB
ATRUBBATRUBBATRUBBA . . ."

The next morning Miss Callisto felt good, very at ease, having completely dispersed her sadistic lustfulness during the nighttime.

She did the household chores and the expected item was delivered through her letterbox. In the padded manila envelope were the keys. Divinity opened the front door and to her delight, there it was—the ebony black BMW she had fallen for, the moment she had set her eyes on it. Its strong, muscular angularity simply turned her on.

The rest of the mail arrived and she hurriedly gathered the cheques.

Divinity's appointment with the client for the day was in the late evening. There would be plenty of time for preparation. Until then she would indulge herself with the vehicle. After setting the answer machine and shutting up shop, Miss Callisto drove around Surrey for the rest of the day, stopping here and there to pick wild herbs from the grassy verges and woodlands she often frequented.

While his other arms swirled over the kit, the flash of lightning was balanced on one steady palm. It altered, crackling and twisting, as though germinating, and began to gain in opacity and harden, forming the body of a dragonfly as large as the demigod's hand, from its heel at the wrist to his fingertips.

Wings began to creep out at right angles to the creature's body. There were four but seemed as two, being fused together while the blood entered transparent veins—two frozen, oval pools, glittering in the twilight. They jutted out perpendicular to the huge body of the insect—a thick, long, semi-patinated, bronze bar. The bulbous head of the creature, its compound eyes, dazzled in Technicolor.

The Drum Demigod was pleased with what he saw, and lilted his hand so that the giant insect caught the rays of the evening sun, rustling and shining like a pink-gold rood, reflecting in the water bound planets that were the demigod's eyes.

He brought the hand to his lips and blew. The dragonfly flew, like a vaunted spear, westwards.

"ATRUBBATRUBBATRUBB
ATRUBBATRUBBATRUBBA . . ."

Chapter 22

The man, with a mind as tranquil and clear as deep spring water, stood at the façade of Miss Callisto's expansive, geometrically awkward property, reflecting on his reason for the visit. A suburban Victorian five-storey detached—to his eye, rather a brooding and forbidding looking building in the twilight. Behind it, a shadowy vista of rolling, tree-cloaked hills. He took in a couple of deeper breaths of the pure air. He checked his watch. *Duty calls,* he thought, and walked steadily forward.

The dragonfly shot through the air like a stealth helicopter under rocket propulsion. As it flashed in the highest skies, it was reducing in size by a man's lifespan every hour. The same it lost in length, wingspan and girth, it gained in density, acquiring a gravity that was its own. The dragonfly flew, looking like a spark through a scratched lens, and became the size and appearance and speed of a particle of light. Now the Earth moved, gently jostled by the creature's gravity, towards it.

"ATRUBBATRUBBATRUBB ATRUBBATRUBBATRUBBA . . ."

Everything was in order and precisely at eight o'clock the man who had the previous day telephoned to arrange the meeting arrived.

Divinity looked through the window but no car was visible, which puzzled her.

She answered the door.

"Good evening, madam. Mr. Goddelijk. Pleased to meet your acquaintance." He offered a bony hand.

He looked more like Mr. Magoo, she thought.

Miss Callisto was a little put off by the man's appearance but knew he worked in quite a propitious profession as a doctor. It was very modest of him to omit his title of doctor. She expected him to be a high earner.

She showed no disdain towards his appearance, but didn't shake his hand either.

"Good evening. I am Miss Callisto." She ghosted to the side of the door, inviting him in.

The wiry, old man prodded forward, his light coloured jeans and shirt swaddling about him. He tapped the floor in front of him with a hickory cane. Mr. Goddelijk stood beside her and looked up, humbly awaiting her instruction.

She looked down over him, glancing off his shiny, bald pate, through the round-rimmed, thick-lensed spectacles, into his black dotted eyes. A long moment passed as they peered into each other.

She broke off. "Follow me," she said, turning, the silk negligee wafting around her. They walked through the corridors. She had to adjust her cadence to accommodate his slow, stooped gait.

They reached the braided curtain doorway of the mezzanine. Divinity requested he enter.

She sat him down at the table, his baggy pale clothing draping over the chair as he did so. He placed the cane on the floor alongside.

She lit the candle. The light glimmered off his lenses and the little ankh pendant, revealed through his shirt, unbuttoned down to his mid sternum.

Divinity cut through the air, laden with incense, "What can I do for you, Mr. Goddelijk?" She had asked all the essential questions regarding professional status during his interview over the phone, but hadn't enquired as to the nature of his call.

He lowered a hand away from the white moustache he was tweaking. "I'm here because of a very concerning matter, Miss Callisto."

"Oh really. And what is that?" she asked, still standing, folding her arms under her breasts.

The candlelight deepened the furrows in his gaunt face. "As I recall we discussed," he said astutely, "I am a doctor working at the psychiatric ward of the Tewsbury Hospital."

"Well really," she said, but no inflection in her voice signaled surprise. "Should I address you as Doctor?"

"No, Mr. is fine. Miss Callisto, I've been a psychiatrist for over thirty-five years. In that time I've dealt with people who have all types of mental illness—manic depression, bipolar disorder, schizophrenia, delusional states, paranoia and so on." His face very grave, he looked to his hands, crossed on the tabletop. "It is often the case that people suffering from mental illness have common experiences—suffer from similar delusions. For instance, many schizophrenics claim that they are Superman or have been abducted by aliens." He

187

brought his hand up to his spectacles, and pushed the frame up the ridge of his nose.

"I see," she said, standing at the doorway.

"This commonality of experience is well known in my profession. We see it a lot."

"And what has that to do with your visit, Mr. Goddelijk?" she asked, smoothly, without intonation.

"Miss Callisto, in the last three weeks, we have received into our care two individuals who have strikingly similar symptoms. Both were professionals. Both had psychotic breakdowns; one was passed on to us by a GP, the other by police authorities." He swiped the top of his shiny head with the palm of a hand. "That in itself is not extraordinary, but when they were assigned as my patients, I performed an investigation into their condition."

"Yes . . ." Divinity wondered what this was leading to.

He continued in earnest, "Their dialogue was garbled, it was difficult to extract anything that would give an insight into their illness, but I discovered that both suffered from delusions of being persecuted, at night, while dreaming. Both claimed that a hideous gorgon was tormenting them terribly."

She delayed her response slightly too long. "Yes, I see." He was onto her. *Of course*, she thought, *it was bound to happen eventually.* Even her mind control over them, through constant threatening, couldn't prevent it. Nevertheless, she hadn't anticipated it. But how much credence would he give to her victims' mad ranting? Her mind raced. Was the Tykhon she used on them traceable in their system? If so, the authorities would conduct a forensic investigation of her premises to find it, and then she would be looking at prison.

He looked steadily at her. "Miss Callisto, both men claim the witch in their dreams is you."

Her eyelashes fluttered. "How remarkable, Mr. Goddelijk," she said, bracing herself against panic.

"Yes, indeed. Though I cannot prove whether or not the two have previously met (they claim not to have), perhaps to fabricate their shared experience, it is a very intriguing accusation," he said, bringing his hand back to his moustache.

"Very intriguing, Mr. Goddelijk." *But what do you know of their green penises?*

With measured words, he continued. "But, even that is not the most uncanny feature of their illness. When I first met them, I was surprised that both had an obsessive preoccupation with their genitalia. Most unusual. Both expounded the same experience, of their sex organ glowing green in the dark, and having become shrivelled. They spoke so gravely of this feature of their condition, that it brought to my mind the withered albatross the cursed mariner in Coleridge's poem wore about his neck.

"I asked a nurse to inspect their private parts. He promptly confirmed their claims, and I immediately sent them, under nurse escort, to be examined by a physician at the Microbiology & Immunology department of the hospital. It presently has custody of the two." He pinched his upper lip, moving against the white bristles of his moustache.

Divinity felt her legs becoming flimsy, almost unable to carry her weight.

Apparently unaware of her inner turmoil, Mr. Goddelijk said, "Preliminary examinations indicate that the injuries they suffer from have not been physically inflicted, as they claim. There are no unnatural toxins in their system. It appears, so far, not to be a viral or bacterial disease." His bushy eyebrows raised above the round lenses. "I myself suspect the cause of the extraordinary physical symptoms to be a psychosomatic one, linked to their mental derangement."

"Gosh. How dreadful for them." She was relieved that nothing of Tykhon Y2K was traced in their bodies.

"Yes. Naturally, at present, they are in special care at the hospital. I am told of any developments. I visit them every two days to study their condition." His fingers migrated from the moustache, to his chin. He rubbed it pensively.

"I am sure that the Microbiology & Immunology department will get to the bottom of their illness, Mr. Goddelijk."

"Oh, I am sure. But Miss Callisto, I cannot possibly take seriously their incrimination of you, the wild accusation that their condition, physical and mental, is rooted in a sexual involvement they had with you. I find that utterly ridiculous."

"It certainly is a very colourful flight of fancy, Mr. Goddelijk."

"Indeed. For that reason, Miss Callisto, I decided to visit you informally, out of hours, so that I could confirm you do not know the two, and eliminate you immediately from any investigation into their condition other consultants would otherwise trouble you with."

"That was very thoughtful of you," she said.

He turned his skinny body on the chair and put a hand in a trouser pocket. He pulled out two portrait photographs with names written in biro. He handed them to her.

"Miss Callisto, these are the two patients. Have you ever met either of them?" He watched her cannily.

She scanned them briefly. "I have never seen them in my life, Mr. Goddelijk."

"That is what I expected you would say, Miss Callisto. That's the matter settled."

She passed back the photos, and he returned them to his pocket—but the matter *wasn't* settled as far as he was concerned.

"Well, I am sorry to have bothered you, Miss Callisto, but thank you for your time and cooperation." He uncoiled from his lean hunch over the table, beginning to rise.

"Mr. Goddelijk, it was not a problem, please, remain seated." She quickly moved her elegant carriage over to him and bade him not to leave, gesturing with her down turned palms.

He wondered why the sudden urgency in her manner. "Miss Callisto—"

"Mr. Goddelijk, before you leave, won't you please have a cup of tea. I most enjoy sharing in the company of someone as eminent as yourself." She had a sudden idea to retaliate without the risk of collateral damage, against the little man who had given her such a fright.

"Well, I—"

"Please, a cup of tea and some biscuits. It is a long drive back to the city, a nibble would sustain you on your journey." Miss Callisto's irises filled with black as she watched him. She leaned over the half standing,

191

ancient man, who appeared even craggier in the candlelight.

He sank back down. "I don't live in the city, but a cup of tea would be . . . reviving—"

"There we are then," she said calmly, her black lashed eyes fixed on his face. "Sit comfortably, Mr. Goddelijk, and I'll be right back." With that, she spirited out of the room.

In the kitchen, Divinity took a tin kettle and a rectangular, chromed tea tray from the cupboard under the sink and placed it on the marble work surface to the side of the sink. She filled the kettle with water, and placed it on the stove to boil. From the pantry she fetched a packet of chamomile, and put it on the marble work surface. From a wall cupboard, Divinity took a couple of white china teacups, and put them on the tray. She waited for the water to bubble.

That was *damned close*. It seemed that the organic substances in Tykhon were undetectably active, but even so, if enough of her workforce became unmanageable and approached the authorities, a thorough investigation of her building and activities would inevitably result.

She would have to postpone her recruitment drive—make do with the slaves in her service, and be more perceptive of their mental health. Miss Callisto couldn't allow any others to incriminate her through insanity.

She would have to remove the green colour feature from the symptoms of poisoning. That would mean a lot of further experimenting with the Tykhon herb formulation, but perhaps would be the solution. The medical profession would assume the symptoms of escapees to be nothing more than a naturally occurring impotency, or lack of sex drive. They'd suspect nothing more, and just give the lunatics Viagra—not that it would do them any good.

Steam began pouring from the spout of the kettle. Divinity snapped open the chamomile packet, lifted the teapot lid and poured in the loose leaves. She returned the lid.

The steam was a jet. She turned off the hob and poured the infusion. From a carton she took from the fridge, she poured the milk, then picked a teaspoon from a drawer and stirred.

Divinity returned to the pantry to collect the brown paper bag, and removed the jar. She twisted off its top. From a box in a drawer, she took a disposable plastic glove and put it on. She overturned the jar, and the cube of Tykhon Y2K fell into her palm. Holding it above one teacup, she squeezed. The faintly fluorescent cube crumbled, half into the cup. The other half clung to her glove. She removed the glove and flung it into the bin.

She stirred his cup until it appeared normal, and placed the teaspoon on the tray next to it. She took another teaspoon for herself from the drawer.

Finally from a head high cupboard, Divinity gathered the sugar and biscuits. A half dozen of the shortbread she placed to the side of his cup. On the other side, by his spoon she placed a few cubes of sugar. She smirked in self-satisfaction at this last touch. A spoonful of sugar helps the medicine go down.

Balancing the laden tray, with an elegant stride she returned to the vestibule.

A new rod of lightning emerged, fizzling from his fingertip.

He reformed the hand to a fist, and swung the colossal hammerhead back into the synchronous array of arms.

"ATRUBBATRUBBATRUBB
ATRUBBATRUBBATRUBBA . . ."

The small, thin, bespectacled man was still seated at the table, in the moody candlelight. "Ah, Miss Callisto—that's wonderful," he said as she placed the tea tray on the tablecloth of the small round table.

Divinity swiftly collected her "simpler" cup of tea, and moved to the chair on the opposite side of the table to him. She graciously folded herself down. She looked at him over the crystal orb, and took a sip from her cup . . .

Mr. Goddelijk plopped a sugar cube into his bevy and stirred. He fingered a biscuit and dunked it in the tea, letting it seep in. He lifted it to his white whiskered lip and bit.

There was a peculiar tension in the air, as though both were at the table over a chessboard rather than cups of tea. But she was close to *checkmating* him.

She interrupted the silence. "Mr. Goddelijk, I misunderstood our telephone conversation. I thought you lived in the city."

"No, Miss Callisto, not at all. Even so, I've come quite a distance."

"And how did you get here? I saw no car outside when I invited you in." She took another sip of tea.

"Car? Not a chance. I don't believe in them—grimy, polluting things. I walked." He finished the biscuit and cogitated. Then toyed with another shortbread.

She assumed he had walked from the stop for grimy polluting buses a couple of miles away, instead. She took another sip. The cup to her mouth, "It must be very difficult living without a car, having to travel into the city to your place of work, and then back in the evening."

The shortbread was dipped up to his finger. "Oh, it's not so bad. The exercise is a good thing, and I believe in simple, self-sufficiency. I couldn't base my life on those unreliable machines—couldn't depend on them." He swallowed the sodden biscuit.

"They're a utility to make life easier, Mr. Goddelijk."

"Supposedly, Miss Callisto, but to rely on the car is to neglect your body, which is your most valuable utility. And purposeful physical exertion is good for the mind as well, you know."

Her glare toward him was obfuscated by the ellipse of her teacup's brim.

He lifted his cup to his mouth and drank. He gulped. "Ah, splendid—a very distinctive taste."

"I am glad it meets your fancy, Mr. Goddelijk."

"It certainly does." He took another gulp.

Now his fists crashed down like meteors.

Dying suns, exploding, highlighted his composition.

The impacts blended into one humungous drone of solid sound.

The unrelenting violence thrummed the planet below the mountain, causing damage, shattering crystal glassware and skulls alike.

"BAAAAAAAAARROOOOOOOOOOO OOOOOOOOOOOOOOOOMMMMMM."

Chapter 23

The normal method was out of the question with two of her AWOL slaves mouthing off at Tewsbury Hospital. If the doctor described his meeting with her and his symptoms (glowing green penis et al) with the staff there, *before* she was able to get a chokehold on his mind, she would be in trouble. No, Miss Callisto couldn't have done that.

Instead, the educated gentleman would be her property by another method. He would have a phosphorescent green intestine inside his scrawny belly, but neither he nor anybody else would know about that. His manhood would be as proud as ever, but he would have lifelong constipation instead. And his enlarged brain would be in her jar, because even though he would know she was responsible, there would be no way the soon-to-be nutty professor would be able to persuade anyone to believe his pie-in-the-sky story, when Tykhon was undetectable in the body. Miss Callisto pictured Mr. Goddelijk with a syringe up his arse, being given one of what would be the daily enemas.

The suddenly ingested, mega dose of Tykhon Y2K was affecting his brain, too.

"Did you know it's my own recipe?" she said, keenly watching him falter on his chair.

To which he responded semiconsciously, "Most invigoratiiiiiinnng," slumping over onto the tray on the table, as the cup toppled out of his hand, spilling a few drops over the carpet.

Divinity would have loved to procure him in the usual way, as attached as she was to the ritualistic element of initiation—*to crush his little maggot between her thighs*—but it wasn't a possibility, as clued up about her method as Mr. Goddelijk was. That was a shame, she thought. The Woody Allen types were sometimes the most satisfying.

Ironically, she would still have to wait for him to come around (though that wouldn't be long), before chucking him out, just as with the others.

Miss Callisto had risen and was standing behind him, teacup in hand. She picked up his dropped cup in her other. She looked within.

There was something in the bottom, which plucked at her curiosity. Lowering her lashes like dark moth wings, in the light of the candle she looked at the residue of the beverage, that had formed in vaguely luminous eddies and tresses on the bottom of the small china teacup, under the influence of *chaos*.

Divinity had difficulty in extrapolating the significance of these patterns.

Among the grains of tealeaves and Tykhon, like particles of earth deposited by ants, she perceived the outline of a horizontal crescent. She moved from one point on the crescent to its other, noticing that a stem was bedded in the curve's underside. She joined the brown-green dots of the stem up, tracing along the length of the stippled pole. It ended in an area of more heavily layered granules, like a glimmering mountain.

Was it a veiled lady, holding high above her an oddly shaped parasol? Was it an elongated flag atop a long pole, spiked into the side of a mountain peak?

There wasn't much call for tasseography, she found (and her superficial skills were only gained as cover for her real agenda), but finally Miss Callisto computed the cup's readout. It was the scythe and hooded figure of the *Grim Reaper*. *How apt,* she thought. The death of Goddelijk's mind, his old life, and the start of the new one in her shadow.

She put the cup upside down on the mantel, next to the framed picture of Set, god of storms, the desert and chaos. Then there was something else she had to do—it had been annoying her from the time she first saw him. Miss Callisto slithered her long narrow hand under his loose shirt collar, and pinched the fine chain that held the ankh pendant around his neck. The links sheared easily between the tips of her icy fingertips.

"Looks like your good luck has run out now, Mr. Goddelijk," she said. She took a sip of tea.

His sticks of white, pale blue and pink lightning careened off the volcanic heads, rims and other metal alloys that formed the acoustic mega structure. Sparks of brilliant energy shimmered off its surfaces.

Then his nuclear powered arms froze in mid swing.

Clouds of perspiration rose, spiraling about him.

Another minute and Mr. Goddelijk was beginning to revive.

Miss Callisto was keen to get his carcass out of her sight. She would have to do it diplomatically though.

She didn't assume he suspected her yet, but if her tone suddenly changed, he would. Then the indicting story he could give to the authorities in his rational state would have far more plausibility than his patient's. As his physical symptoms developed, she would depend on her nocturnal prowess to gradually assume control over his thinking and gain his suppliancy. Until then she would tread carefully.

"Mr. Goddelijk, are you all right?" Miss Callisto asked, while budging him from his slouched position over the tray on the table.

She stood up again and drank another thimbleful, watching him labour to lift himself off the table surface. "Mr. Goddelijk, what's wrong?" she spoke in his direction. She leaned toward him as he bobbed and swayed to look "caringly" into his eyes. "What's wrong? Are you okay? Are you okay?"

He began to gather his senses. "Tea . . . aftertaste . . . most peculiar," he muttered to himself.

"Mr. Goddelijk, I'm relieved you're okay—you had me so worried." she said with fake concern but casually swirling the contents of her teacup beneath her bosom.

He twisted his torso as his triceps, like sperm whales beneath his skin, drove down his arms, plunging his fists upon the design of his mind's eye.

A thundercrack rumbled around the mountain's apex.

It was the kid brother of Armageddon.

"BAAAAAACHOOOOOOOOOOOOOO OOOOOOOOOOOOOOOOMMMMMM."

He brought up his fingertips and wiped his eyes under his glasses. "Everything seems to be intact . . . Miss Callisto." They began to focus again. One of the lenses of his spectacles had been scraped on the edge of the chrome tea tray.

"I was so worried about your nodding off so unexpectedly," she said, underplaying the importance of his blackout.

"Yes, very strange . . . I'll have my blood checked for diabetes tomorrow," he said, only tilting slightly on his chair now.

She added, "The doctor knows best," quite flippantly, he thought.

He had recovered sufficient of his considerable intelligence.

He wondered why she had not called an ambulance. At the center of the whirlpool of his thoughts, somehow a plan bobbed up.

"Well, everything seems to be in working order. A bit of outside air will refresh me, Miss Callisto. I think I'll be setting off," he said, to test her response.

Her eyelashes parted further in feigned surprise. "Mr. Goddelijk, would that be wise? So soon?" The briefest pause, then, "Well, if you think that is what you should do . . ." She took a sip of tea.

He felt disgust but then wondered. He began turning awkwardly on his chair. "Yes, I think so, Miss Callisto."

"Shall I call a taxi for you?" she tested.

"No, I'll be quite all right, the walk will recover my circulation," at which he stooped forward, reaching for his walking stick.

"Here, let me do that for you," she offered. She crouched by him as he leaned forward on his chair, her cup of tea in her left hand, underneath his arched frame.

Mr. Goddelijk, still a little unsteady, pitched. The thin, severed chain dangled through the loose folds of his shirt. Only one of the ends clung barely to his neck, as the little pendant slid down the swinging chain on its loose, circular link. It plunked into her china teacup as she picked up his cane.

Miss Callisto passed it to him, making sure he grabbed the crook, and helped him rise to his feet. The creaky tripod of his legs and cane stabilized. She moved around him, and with her free hand, took hold of his arm. Very slowly, they moved forward.

His body warped, pulling up his titanic arms, suspended in the stratosphere, kilometers above his head.

He mustered himself for the final cataclysmic assault.

They dropped down catastrophically.

"VVVAAAAAAAAADOOOOOOOOOO OOOOOOOOOOOOOMMMMMMMM."

A million megatons pulverized the iron horse. The air trembled and gathered, densifying into a scintillating shock wave, before rushing outwards from the mountain's base.

It passed over the earth, obliterating almost everything in its path.

The setting sun sacrificed itself in a final, brilliant flare, to glorify the demigod.

They walked back through the corridors, and Mr. Goddelijk became relatively firmer in his steps.

It was his intention, once he was off her property, to be in touch with the police, for now he knew of her deception—not that she realized.

Are all experiences we have, of our own choice? Are all the encounters we have, accidental? Are all the talents we have, of ourselves, or given? Are all the meetings we have, chance? Or are all these occurrences governed by a preternatural "arranger, causer, governor"?

In Goddelijk, Divinity had met her match—and her nemesis. For he too, among those rare in society, had kindled within himself—*or had been given*, the gift of a psychic ability—the ability to perceive information the normal senses could not, through extrasensory perception.

He knew of her psychic tyranny because (also without her realization) he had a developed psychic ability himself and in the short time he had been acquainted with her, in dreams and in her presence, had sensed in *her* the ability and experienced sinister overtones from her core being. Even from his association with the two at the hospital, he had intuitively sensed they were telling the truth.

As the saying goes, "There's always someone better than you."

Of course, she was a scammer, false spiritual medium and con-artist clairvoyant. He had, over the years, spent enough time with genuine ones that had on many occasions provided him an important service, to know the difference. And they, in fact, revealed to him his latent psychic ability and instructed him on its development. Now its full value was apparent, as uncomfortably, disturbingly, he removed the onion skin layers of her psyche.

"Divinity" indeed. A misnomer if ever there was one! A title meant to deceive her "clients" into believing she were some kind of goddess. Mr. Goddelijk knew for sure, that she was instead some sort of fiendish witch!

Eventually they were at the front door of her mansion.

Holding her china teacup delicately between forefinger and thumb, she stylishly swigged the last of her beverage. "Well, here we are Mr. Goddelijk, it's been a sheer delight to have met you," reinforcing the apparent success of her fraud with a marked friendliness.

"Likewise, Miss Callisto. Sorry for inconveniencing you with my collapse a little earlier. Most unexpected occurrence."

"Oh, not at all. I'm just thankful your lightheadedness passed so quickly." She released his arm, and motioned to the door handle. "As you say, Mr. Goddelijk, I'm sure the walk in the fresh air will put paid to your dizzy spell completely . . . *Kaff, kaff, kaff.*" She paused. Her hand came off the doorknob and cupped her mouth.

"You have a cough, Miss Callisto!"

"*Kaff, kaff.* It is nothing. Just a passing thing. Be fine in a moment . . . *Kaff.*" Her eyes were watering but she returned to the handle and opened the door halfway.

"*KAFF, KAFF, KAFF,* oh dear! *KAFF, KAFF, KAFF.*"

There was genuine concern on his wrinkled face, as he looked up to her. "Miss Callisto, that is more than just a trifling fad!"

The china cup dropped, shattering on the checkered tiles, as both of her hands fell upon her gaping mouth again, "*KAFF, KAFF, KAFF, KAFF, KAFF.*" She folded at her waist, gasping desperately for air, "*KAFF, KAFF, KAFF,*" her shocking eyes watering onto the black and white floor.

He dropped his stick and gripped her at the wrists, elevating her head as he pulled them up and away from her face—no obstructions in her gaping mouth. His mind focused—clearly her windpipe was obstructed!

As fast as he was able, Mr. Goddelijk hobbled around her, so that he was facing her bent back. He quickly gave her five sharp smacks between the shoulder blades, with a firm right hand.

"*KAFF, KAFF, KAFF, KAFF, KAFF, KAFF.*"

It made no difference. He looked in her mouth—nothing had dislodged.

Mascara was rolling from her eyelids, with the profuse tears. "*KAFF, KAFF, KAFF.*"

Behind her again, he hugged her around the abdomen and tugged hard five times.

No results with the Heimlich maneuver.

"*KAFF, KAFF, Kaff, kaff, kaff.*" She melted towards the floor, losing consciousness.

He kneeled astride her thighs and placed his hand over hand, onto her upper abdomen. Another five thrusts.

At the fifth, something shot from her mouth, ricocheting off the door and wall, tinkling onto the enameled tiling.

He ignored it. The small, skeletal man laboured over her buxom figure in repose. He expertly administered mouth-to-mouth ventilation and external chest compression. But his kiss didn't bring her to life. Miss Callisto was gone.

Distressed and fatigued, Mr. Goddelijk cradled her head, and looked onto her visage.

Her thin lips appeared ruby red, but beneath the lipstick he knew they were cyanosed blue. Black tears left streaks, from her staring eyes, down her face.

Not letting Divinity go, with his other hand he picked up the culprit. It had bounced over the floor, and was resting by the door ajar. He viewed it on his palm, grimly astonished that something smaller than an almond could induce death in a young, healthy individual.

The tiny gold ankh seemed to wink at him as he lilted his hand in the warm light. It was ironic that this "key of life" had resulted in Callisto's death.

A small, perfectly white mouse chased the tale of a terrified cat along the corridor and out the doorway.

Then Mr. Goddelijk wryly reminded himself that even seemingly innocuous bitter almonds contain cyanide.

Bones like granite columns crunched in their sockets, as he began decreasing the massive momentum of his megalithic limbs.

A glance over the marimba, a cheeky inflexion in the rhythm, rounded off his solo—it burst like a blood filled barrel.

Finally, the massive bending moments about the monstrous joints of his limbs steadied. The conflicting forces reached equilibrium. He gently lowered his arms, the subterranean tunnels of veins, bulging in their flesh.

He surveyed the world, a thousand miles below. He was an impetuous demigod and didn't suffer scoundrels or fools.

He had blown them all away.

Satisfied that virtually everything had been destroyed, he called it a day.

Chapter 24

The Drum Demigod now rested in a state of relative stillness and reverie. Something was not as it should be though. He had been so absorbed, carried away, enraptured even, by the bloodcurdling drum composition that flowed from his being, that he had put the plight of the people below secondary in his concerns. That they had all been annihilated was merely incidental to his murderous, musical meditation.

Now he knew there would be a consequence to such reckless conduct. It was all well and good that he liked his beats, but as sinful as the humans were, it was perhaps a little brash that he had decided, on a rhythmic whim, to waste them all. Perhaps he should have given them another chance to repent.

The Creator of All Things (including himself) had summoned him in order to Judge. Soon he would know and then experience his fate.

His fellow demigods suggested that, in the least, his preternatural, uncouthly rowdy kit could be confiscated and even worse he himself might be relegated to the more lowly rank of mortal human. Maybe without even a sense of rhythm . . . and cack-handed to boot.

Because, all empires, all demigods and indeed the whole universe, is at the feet of the One True God, who governs all experiences and all existences. He has the power to give and to take away, like a rattle given to and then taken from a child.

Chapter 25

Kieran came back, vaguely, to consciousness. He tipped over the second, half-empty cup of coffee on the desk before him, but didn't care as his hand rested in the brown puddle, his shirtsleeve soaking it up.

It was the coffee and the fantastical clock which caused his foray into the world of "Divinity Callisto". Though dazed, he was quite sure of that.

His head, feeling like a blimp wanting to break free of gravity, somehow from the clock regained ballast. Some of his awareness was returned by it, syringed back into his brain, so that he could appreciate the gravelly sounds emitted by—*Terry Lee*, now sitting next to him in the office.

"Well, by the late 70s I was already known by many in Newcastle by the affectionate nickname *KungMeister*, an indication the impact my skills were having on the local community," he said, his facial expression exceptionally serious. He wore a red, toweling headband around his forehead, the likes of which were popular with the old-timer tennis players of the 70s (McEnroe, Borg, to name the most famous).

He continued, unworried by this fact. "Yes, I was the proprietor and teacher of the travelling kung fu clinic, 'Kung Fu Master—Travelling Trainer.'"

Kieran's head couldn't decide whether it wanted to be *in* or *out* of consciousness and he struggled to focus on Terry Lee's exceptionally serious face, talking about his exceptionally serious topic. As Kieran stared, Terry's face faded away like it was marsh gas, and so instead he tried to focus on the bobbing red strip of his headband.

That too, soon vaporized, so that Kieran had only the deep intonations of the kung fu master's wise voice to hold on to.

It only lulled him sooner, back into the welcoming, if spindly, arms of the swirling, ecosystem of a clock, like he were a big baby levitating back into its circular womb, tugged by the umbilical cord into its centre.

Chapter 26

Sun and blue sky had been forecast for the mid-July weekend and as the hazy, lazy day unwound into noon, it appeared that the expectations of the population, at least in Surrey, would be fulfilled. It was seaside weather by most people's reckoning but for Trudy and Richard Pritchard, the coast was over twenty miles away and as partial as Richard was to skinny dip on a sunny day, the thought of the possibility didn't even occur in his dormant, marinating brain.

As much as the suggestion, at least to venture beyond the confines of number 7 Smeed Street, would have excited Mrs. Pritchard, Richard wasn't disposed to such exertion at this particular moment in time, quite satisfied instead to ride the heat wave on the "*Bentin's* Surrey" towel, (which he had taken from one of the chalets a couple of years back) positioned centrally on the lawn in his garden of earthly delights. Occasionally a fragment of recollected thought would flit back to him, reviving the adventure. A memorable two weeks indeed: meeting such challenges from time to time was really quite character forming, he thought.

Richard had been lying mostly on his front, virtually motionless on the long grass for some two and a half hours, just allowing the occasional thoughts to settle on his mind like butterflies. His back was reddening, *almost* comfortably—at least the sensation that he knew of as "the reddening" felt bearable and confirmed that changes were taking place, perhaps in some places more than others.

A negative thought, concerning the distinct lack of TLC conferred by his wife, nudged as he reflected, rubbing the small mounds of fat on his lower back, feeling a less pleasant, prickly sensation. He craned his head around to see the trouble spots—Trudy had such rough, undextrous hands, little wonder the hillocks were a deeper shade of pink.

The bottle of lotion was just visible to him through the thickness of the grass. There it was next to the radio cassette recorder, next to the deckchair.

Instead of reaching for it, he huffed in dissatisfaction and reached to the discomfort zones, in an attempt to smudge the sun lotion onto the missed areas on his back, from the adjacent areas. Failing, he huffed again and got on all fours, lazily reaching for the bottle of sunblock, two feet away. Perhaps all this would not have been necessary, he thought, if he had offered to rub *her* back with the stuff too. Anyway, he had persuaded her, in a way he thought of as gentle, that she needed to drop her son off, so there was no chance of her joining him on this sunbathing excursion.

His front, he could do himself.

Sitting cross-legged on the towel, he twisted off the top, placed it on the adjacent grass. He squished the butterscotch liquid into his palm, while surveying his surroundings.

The rectangular garden was approximately seven by fourteen meters, and three quarters covered by the unkempt grass—a lot of grass that he resolved was beyond the ability of the hover mower to crop (as erratic in its functioning as it was, he told himself). It was stationed engagingly in the open shed doorway, apparently by chance (or more likely as a hint from Trudy to get mowing!). He calculated, if his mental arithmetic was correct (and it was not bad when he made the effort), that this meant the garden's area was about one hundred meters square.

He massaged the oil into the light brown frizz between and then over, his breasts, or rather, pectorals, as some dribbled, following the contours of his belly, into his navel and beyond.

That meant that there was—dividing by four and multiplying by three—an area of approximately seventy-five meters squared of overgrown grass to be mowed; a veritable savannah! He would have to explain his discovery to Trudy, and settle the matter to abstain from mowing, finally, later on.

Just as the liquid exited his belly button onto the high pubic hairs below it, he dammed the flow with the edge of his left hand, as his right continued to massage the abundant loose flesh on his upper arms. He smothered the lotion in his left hand, over his face, around the sides of his nose, moving concentrically toward it, then pinching and twisting the chunky, rugged feature. Then back out over the loose skin of his cheeks, pushing into them with his fingers, up to the smooth forehead, pushing away the long burnt umber streaks of hair to the sides, and following through with pinches and palm swipes of his flabby lower jaw and neck, hearing the rasp of the hair around his sideburns and stubble recede as the lotion lubricated.

After completion of this task, satisfied that he was now uniformly covered, he turned his gaze yet further, wincing his brownish-bluish, mildly inflamed eyes in discomfort, as he saw the straggle of dull green wires that were the much argued about blackberry bush. Richard winced his eyes further, to creased slits, as he thought about grappling with the bush as tall as himself and better armed.

They did not have hedge clippers. Gloves were essential and he had not yet got around to buying them. Why did she want to get rid of it anyway? She could trim it and have a garden feature *and* it partially covered the grouting in the brickwork she had made a mess of.

But of course not. She wanted him to *plant flowers* there and around the place, make life difficult for everyone. Besides, why not capitalize on nature's bounty, a valuable source of vitamin C in the garden. He wondered whether she knew how to make blackberry pie. Perhaps she could crush the berries and make juice.

Then casting his gaze east, he could perceive in the other shaded corner, the dull green of the nettle bushes—and wondered whether Trudy had ever made nettle soup. Perhaps it could be snipped and tweaked into a feature—perhaps not. His acute wince returned as he excused himself again for not having clippers and gloves.

Before any major operation, it was necessary to plan—to foresee possible problems in implementing an operation, and anything that might hinder it. After a whole five minutes of consideration, alas, it seemed that these grand designs would never progress beyond the drawing board.

Satisfied that he had made the effort, in wistful resignation, he set about resting his back carefully on the towel, his front becoming the solar panel that would power further digital watch revelations of his fairly dormant brain. Two hours should do it, he thought, bearing in mind that his skin had only (after his recent sunbathing sessions), to darken a shade more, for the result wanted. Closing his eyes, he drifted into the bright red sun rays as they filtered through his eyelids.

A couple of hours on his slow boat in the sun, Richard was awakened. He was still lying on his back but he turned his head, folding his arms behind it, so that it was facing the shortest of the three walls enclosing the scrub-land that was his garden. Looking at the top edge, he followed the line from one end, which met his house, to the other, where it met the higher far wall, to which Trudy had applied her skills at grouting to very visible effect (quite unsuccessfully as far as Richard was concerned).

A light smirk appeared on Richard's full lips, as he anticipated the cheap, delectable thrill. Yes, over recent days, there had been no shortage of them, and it made Richard's mouth water, metaphorically speaking. He waited expectantly, in the mood of one in the audience before the start of the play, but not hearing anything more, he gently closed his eyelids once again, feeling a touch ungratified, even as the little smirk lingered on his face.

Then those mellifluous tones once more, at least, they were that to Richard; the falsetto and the baritone murmurings, faintly audible, but gradually growing in sonority.

Ah yes, they approach! he thought. His piggy eyes reflexively opened and his five-foot-eleven body quivered, as he tried to shift it slightly, so that he would be comfortable for the show he more than half expected, based on the happenings over the last few days. With his hands still behind his head as he lay, he felt he was as at ease as he could be. There was the possibility of an incident here. There was potential.

The faint dialogue he could hear was punctuated irregularly by a click-clack of high heels on ceramic. Momentarily, he raised his head off the palms of his hands, just so that he could witness his diminutive wife, framed in the kitchen window, overlooking his garden, and was pleased that she would be there to share the moment, to partake in the experience.

Not that she would derive any pleasure from it—he knew she wouldn't. Even so, he looked forward to replaying and analyzing the play, that night, savoring every detail with her.

Yes, there she was with her yellow dish washing gloves up to her elbows, with her dishwater blond hair in a bob behind her head—a familiar site around these parts. There she was, engrossed in some household chore which she felt was necessary to tackle, which Richard undoubtedly thought was not.

Richard conceded that the heap of soiled crockery, visible to him above the window cill, *was* worthy of someone's attention—hers, it appeared—but without giving this concession too much thought, he decided that she just didn't know, she hadn't a clue, *that woman*, as to how she should prioritize time for odd jobs around the house. For that matter, he was in no doubt that she hadn't the foggiest idea about what were worthwhile tasks to undertake—what was a job that needed doing in the *first* place.

"That woman 'tsk' 'tsk'," he mentally verbalized. "She makes work for herself where there isn't any!"

Lowering his gaze from the window, to his tiptoes, to his Bermuda shorts, he noticed the bottle top sized stain on the left pocket, and made a mental note to tell her that she would have to do them by hand—that oily ooze was a killer to remove.

All this reflection and conference with himself diverted his attention from what was to be the main attraction, and yes, the voices were still wafting on the summer breeze from the patio doorway of the newly occupied house next door. They could, though faint, be discerned by his ears now. He quickly refocused his attention as the smirk reappeared, wider than before.

"Look here, you bumhead! . . . out there and . . . those effing plants! . . ."

Smack, thump . . . slap.

He could vaguely hear the woman's distant booming voice continue—" . . . three coats not two! . . . idiot! . . ." It went on, ". . . much too long! . . . I said . . . light coats! . . . dripping . . ."

Thump. Then the male voice, in a high pitch, interjected, "Acch! . . . don't . . . hitting me there! . . . big bruise there . . . already! . . ."

Thump.

The gravure of the female voice once again, ". . . shift your skinny butt! . . . just do it . . . fucking-idiot-bumhead! . . . through asking you nicely! . . ."

It was a good one already! Richard's belly wobbled, despite his attempt to muffle his laughter. He clenched his teeth to restrain an outburst, and instead, his head pressurized and reddened. He raised his head to see if Trudy had cottoned on to the free show that had begun. Improbable, he thought, her being indoors. True enough, she had not noticed anything above the sploshing of water and clattering of plates in front of her—but she would, he would make sure of that.

Then there was a swishing sound and staccato rattle of water droplets on foliage, which signaled to Richard the man next door's movement in the direction of center stage, and into his, and Trudy's (if she would care to look up from her confounded plates for just a moment) view.

He twisted his head so that it was facing the short wall again, having recovered his composure, and waited.

The swishing sound continued, and told Richard the whereabouts of the character carrying the water hose—occasionally there was a sputtering sound, and fine mist would ghost over Richard's head. He could see the water shooting from the hose above the wall as the man neared, the aerial stream. The man (who had not yet noticed Richard lying on his back on the center of the lawn, due to his being so solemnly fixated on his task), himself followed. He briskly shook the hose from left to right, not missing a single petal on a single thirsty flower.

Then as he neared the center of his lawn, Richard observed his head lolling along and above the short, stony, viney wall, finally within his view. At this point the man took his gaze off the soil, flowers and grass, and glanced over the wall at Richard.

Immediately Richard closed his eyes to make it seem as though he was asleep, expecting that the man, who was now on the other side of the wall nearest him, would not have noticed Richard's being awake and in a condition to engage in polite conviviality.

It seemed he hadn't, as the continuing tic-tacking of water under pressure, vigorously applied over the crisp leaves, testified.

Richard much preferred at this time not to get involved in a friendly exchange. He was too much hoping that the show would not leave the road just yet, not when it seemed the two star players were only just beginning to settle into the roles that he had mentally typecast them in, their most likely role for now and the future! He relished the prospect of their being his and Trudy's neighbours, and the perpetual scapegoats they would become for him.

For now, he would disguise his acute attention to the proceedings, so that these stars would not shy away from his camera, capturing every nuance of their behaviour. He might engage in polite chat after but not before the event. He didn't want to be too obtrusive—it would dampen the chemical reaction between the couple that he had predicted would take place shortly.

And besides, he wanted a topic of conversation he could casually introduce, to refer to instead, when Trudy would subtly put forward her own agenda, later that night. He needed the forthcoming incident so that he would be able to change the subject—this time he hoped with more subtlety than he had used on a previous night.

She hadn't noticed the man in the neighbouring garden this time but Richard determined to himself, with the smirk on his face, that he would make her notice at the right moment (if she had not herself), by way of an interview with the stars, *after* their performance. She would enjoy that, he thought facetiously.

The sploshing sounds grew slightly fainter, as the man gradually edged his way up the lawn, from side to side, meticulously watering every blade of the crew-cut grass. The rattle of water against stone alerted Richard that the man had reached the far wall of his garden, and was most probably dousing the rich variety of alpines over his rockery, at the corner where their shared wall intersected the far wall.

Richard, with his eyes open again (and the smirk), mused over the tiered stone creation, the rockery, its construction spanning just eight hot days—some feat, with no assistance and no knowledge of how to build such a garden feature. *The boy did well!* Richard thought, and continued to wait passively for the inevitable incident that would enliven the situation.

The man was covering the far wall, moving from his left to right, and finally, Richard calculated, had reached the furthest corner from his viewpoint. No doubt, the faintly audible sound was him watering the pink roses, the last of the perfectly colour coordinated bloomers along the soil strip, adjacent to the far wall. They were an impressive collection by anyone's standard—even Richard had to agree (though reluctantly), mostly planted in the space of six weeks, slightly less than the length of time the man and his lady friend had occupied the house.

Richard put the fact quickly out of his mind, as he reverted back to relishing the prospect of an incident, that had so consistently ensued on previous occasions when the chap set foot in the garden.

The swooshing sound suddenly became a sputter and then just as suddenly stopped. The man was out of Richard's visual range but Richard, in his mind's eye, saw him winding the hose around his forearm while inspecting the rather luxuriant fruits of his toil, with a discerning eye (in fact he had also planted an apple tree at the far wall, perpendicular to his house).

After a minute, Richard predicted that he was reaching the center of the lawn again, faint noises giving away his position. Slowly, slowly, the hose winding, winding, winding like an anaconda, ensuring his compliance with her every wish.

Then the boom of distant thunder . . .

"What have you done! . . . idiot! . . . told you . . . not the roses!"

The rumble grew louder as the source came nearer.

"I clearly told you, just the hardier plants! I clearly said don't touch the delicate ones. You've drowned the roses, fucking idiot! You've shocked the sunburned petals off them, you burk! I clearly told you, the grass, rockery, trees and hedgerow! If those flowers are damaged, I'm gonna damage your stupid bumhead!"

Richard, not being able to contain his laughter, did as much as he could by muffling it, but let it splurt out as she spoke, knowing that her deep resonant voice would obscure his sniggering in private jubilation. His subdued chuckles continued as her voice grew yet louder, and he visualized her strident thrust toward the man with the hose—a grassbound lorry about to squash an insignificant hedgehog.

Richard quickly stole a glance at the window which still framed Trudy in its center, who still had her head down in the sink, the pile of crockery not appearing that much smaller, and closed his eyes, even as the vocal sounds of master and slave were certainly loud enough to stir anyone from a daydream.

"No, I must insist!" the man said. "I must insist this time. You have to allow me to explain before you lay a finger on—"

Chud.

"Aaach!"

"Don't argue with me when you know you're in the wrong! You've been pratting about all day, and when you finally get around to doing the job, you get it completely wrong. You can't follow simple instructions, can you? Can you?"

A plaintive murmur, "Stop pinching me, aaach! I can explain if you'll—"

"Oh shut up! Everything I've asked you to do today you've bungled! You can't get anything right, can you? Well, can you?"

"Look, I aaach!"

"Oh shut up! You're such a fucking idiot!"

"Will you stop? Mr. Pritchard can hear us," he said timidly, despite his struggle to gain some control.

A sudden hush descended over the dialogue as Richard gritted his teeth harder in a desperate attempt to hold back what would otherwise have been bellows of laughter. He was conscious of the muscles in his jaw bunching, and his thorax slightly shuddering, trying to counter the irresistible pressure of the canned laughter.

He was unsure whether they had noticed his straining as he tried to appear as though he was sleeping, but of course, they would be suspicious. The murmurs continued as they cogitated, Richard all the while keeping his teeth firmly clenched as his tummy quivered—he hoped unnoticeably.

The pair had so often been caught in the act, in their portrayal of master and servant, in full view of Richard, but for some reason, at this late stage, they felt abashed about the fact. Richard had noticed their becoming more wary.

Even though animal instinct ultimately took control of them, they were at least now *trying* to have some reserve; were now, with a sudden spark of awareness, beginning to realize the requirement to appear to be civilized, just for the sake of disallowing Richard his pleasure.

Would they ever get their act together completely? Richard dearly hoped not. Would they ever be a partnership like his and Trudy's? *No way*, he thought.

There was another marked difference in recent episodes in the series, compared with earlier ones, namely Emlyn's attempts to control his voice, to restrain natural facial expressions of fear and pain, in general, control his body language under the torrents of threat and abuse, hurled at him day in and day out.

He was doing a reasonable job.

Richard supposed that this was his idea of grace under pressure. Perhaps he thought of it as being quintessentially English—stiff upper lip, and all that. But then the man was Welsh. Nevertheless, thought Richard, it takes a hard man *not* to display emotion, redden with embarrassment, blanche with fear or yowl in pain when kicked in the shin, as Richard had seen Juliet do to him regularly in previous weeks.

Emlyn was not a hard man, Richard was sure, and for that reason was quite satisfied that the show would go on, for his—and Trudy's—viewing pleasure.

Chapter 27

For some reason or another, on their arrival at number 9 Smeed Street, Emlyn's other half, Juliet, would launch at her partner in reckless abandon, with such an intense savagery that Richard made the assumption they must have previously resided in some secluded habitat. Or some residence which was completely detached from what they would consider to be the interference of neighbors. He mused that it might have been a bungalow with a sizable surrounding garden, like a small island in the sea (he excluded the "Paradise" aspect from the comparison), or maybe some out-of-the-way farm. Someplace that was off the beaten path, that was for sure.

It was a minor mystery.

Anyway, old habits die hard! Richard could rely on their providing him with entertainment in the same way he could expect Trudy to trouble him with a request to do some tedious, fiddly job around the home, for as long as it took the odd couple next door to get used to their new, and undoubtedly more bijou, abode.

The murmuring had stopped. Richard had successfully wrestled his shaking diaphragm back to a motionless state, and he felt prepared for any eventuality.

He braced himself and . . .

"Hello there, Mr. Pritchard!" Her thick Brummy voice made him feel as though she was standing above him.

"What a fine day we're having today. Another."

Richard had hoped she would be less inclined to draw him into conversation if he appeared asleep, but suspicious of him as she was, she had no qualms about waking him from his apparent catnap.

He responded, "Oh, hello there, Mrs. Scott," they were not yet on first name terms but, ". . . or can I call you Juliet? Yeah, isn't it a lovely one—*again*. I was just having a light snooze, didn't notice you there!"

She stood at the short wall separating their gardens, both her hands atop the brickwork and vines, her heavy breasts hanging pendulously, almost touching the top of the wall. She leaned over into his garden and looked him straight in the eye. Richard had his head propped up now, under his right hand and held his left as though to salute the substantial figure, but was rather shielding his eyes from the sunlight streaming into them. Even as he greeted her he did not flinch from his position, lying on his back, feigning drowsiness. He could see that she was dressed in a white frock with a blobby floral pattern, brightly coloured.

"Yes, just isn't it a lovely day . . ." She watched Richard with inquisitive eyes, that appeared as much to be leering at him, although it was only gentle leering, if there is such a thing, and if she were leering at all—it was hard to tell. She was semi-silhouetted and the abrasive rays of the sun were beaming into his eyes.

"My Emlyn is just watering the garden plants . . ." her beady eyes squinted, "before there's a hose pipe ban. The plants must be gasping in this heat!"

With the reference to him, Emlyn appeared, and awkwardly stood next to his wife.

"Oh, hello there, Mr. Pritchard."

"All right, Emlyn! Just call me Richard."

"Richard. I hope I didn't disturb you with the spraying water?"

"No, Emlyn, that wasn't a problem, didn't notice it."

Emlyn, though trying not to be, stood nervously, holding the hosepipe in his right hand, the nozzle flopping and dribbling over his knuckles, while the coil of the hose was wrapped around his bruised left forearm. Standing upright to his full height, which Richard guessed was about five foot eight, he was still shorter than Juliet, resting her arms on the wall. He was a slim fellow, which made her physically seem all the more powerful, as thick boned as she was.

Before Emlyn had parted his lips to say another word, she quite abruptly wedged between the men, "I was just telling Emlyn that he shouldn't water the flowers because of their delicacy, wasn't I, Emlyn? The cold water just shocks the sun struck petals. It's harmful for the plants, I believe. I did explain this to him, but he just went ahead watering everything . . ."

"Oh dear . . . is that so . . ." commiserated Richard, only half convincingly and knowing that her gardening knowledge was one based on wild superstition.

Although the slapstick was over for the time being, he still derived pleasure from Emlyn's anxious demeanor and stared lengthily at Emlyn's pronounced hairstyle—lank black hair, limp over his ears, with a strongly defined center parting, slightly asymmetrical and untidy due to the slap or slaps it had been dealt. He was dressed in unremarkable, casual summer wear, but this did not tone down (at least in Richard's eyes) the comical combined appearance of the couple, which reminded him of a lewd seaside postcard he had once seen, the image recalled from the recesses of his inner head. "I never knew that cold, tap water could harm flowers in hot weather," said Richard.

"Yes, it's a fact," she said in error, casting a stern glance at Emlyn to her right, a glance that seemed to project knives and he flinching, as though stabbed by them.

"My father, who was a keen gardener, used to tell me . . . they're not hardy like evergreens, you know, those plants with hard, waxy leaves."

"Oh, I see, right," responded Richard casually, still lying on his back, with the edge of one hand over his brow, shading his eyes and his arm folded behind and propping up his head. "Well I never," he said, knowing that her father's gardening knowledge was also one based on wild superstition.

A pause followed, both the characters looking at him, her rather interrogatively. Richard *had* to turn again to the kitchen window, and seeing Trudy bearing a frown, looking out at them all, felt a special pleasure, that of having the footnote, something to make reference to, to substantiate the documentary story he was to tell her later on. It would be the truth, whole and nothing but. After all, he was not a *liar*.

Then, "Oh well, better get back to the housework—there's so much to do. See you again, Richard!" Juliet's sarcasm undisguised by the obviously forced smile.

Richard, with a contrived expression of seriousness, replied simply, "Okay then, see you again, Juliet!" not really caring about her barbed comment, having the roll of film safely in his hand, as it were.

"See you later, Richard," said Emlyn, following the lead.

"Yep, see you, Emlyn," whereupon both Emlyn and Juliet went their separate ways, he shuffling off into the small greenhouse on the other side of the garden, sliding shut the door, in audible jerks, behind him, she, regally in the direction of the shaded patio.

Blissfully sated after the feast of entertainment, which had exceeded his expectations, Richard glanced at Trudy one more time to see her glumly looking out of the window and seeming even smaller than her five foot one, then lowered his head again and nodded off, while counting limp hose-holding Emlyns.

He awoke, and looking at his watch saw that it was 3:30 p.m.—he had been sunbathing for over two and a half hours. The front of his body, facing the sun, had assumed the degree of reddish, soon-to-be tan he wanted and he rose carefully off the blanket.

He stood up, his belly still distended from the roast lunch Trudy had prepared for him earlier, which he had galumphed down. The expanding, flatulent gases of digestion in his duodenum given an extra energy by the summer heat, imparted a marked, convex shape to his belly. He pulled back his shoulders and stretched the ligaments in his legs, as the weak blood flow drained down from his head and body, and struggled through the narrow turnstiles of his knees, on towards his calves and toe tips, temporarily rendering him giddy.

He peeked over the short wall, into the garden next door. The *garden drone* Emlyn was not there and so

Richard took a closer look to see what he had been up to recently.

The garden on the whole was an impressive achievement (completed since Emlyn's arrival just over six weeks earlier), Richard had to admit to himself.

Along the side of the walls, variegated and evergreen shrubs were planted in a carefully thought out sequence, separated by vivid, blooming, flowering plants. There was the greenhouse, at the further of the parallel sidewalls of the garden, the tomatoes squeezed against the panes, next to which and above the height of the greenhouse was the apple tree, its branches laden with russet-red apples.

He felt a faint itch, becoming more distinct over a region of his back, to which a sprinkling of ill-fated ants and perhaps the odd small beetle had become glutinously squashed, in the evaporating ooze.

He continued his mental commentary: Emlyn had, *in next to no time*, also set up the timber frame shed and then there was the red, block-paving of the patio, on which were carefully positioned planters filled with annuals. Against the façade of the residence, at the corner near the short wall, the two healthy looking birches resided.

The itch persisted, Richard putting the irksome sensation down to Trudy's half-arsed attempt to cover his limp back with the sunblock earlier that day. Clearly, the raucous sun had made its effects felt on those less well protected portions of his back.

He resumed: of all the work that Emlyn had invested in the garden, the small rockery, covered with miniature flowering plants and alpines, had turned out to be the most impressive feature of all. Of course, a large portion of the overall garden had *already been planted.* But even so, that thin man, who looked as though he would struggle lifting a garden gnome, had, in perhaps five weeks, with just his two hands, built that rockery, set up that shed, dug the soil and planted those flowers. The end result was striking, juxtaposed as it was with Richard's bedraggled garden.

But no sooner had the feeling of humble admiration, reluctant though it was, caught hold of him, than he quickly corrected himself with the reasoning of a realist, as he saw it—a practically minded man. After all, he thought to himself, nobody *lives* in the garden. Keeping one like Emlyn's through the seasons was such a labour-intensive activity and though the end result which Richard beheld did (as hesitant as he was to admit to himself) appeal, the labour required to keep it looking like it did was not warranted. Better to keep it simple, he conjectured. Better to not bother with a garden at all.

He ambled over to the end of his garden, following the small wall, stopping before the forbidding nettle straggle heaped miserably in the corner, so that he could get closer to the rockery next-door that Emlyn had assembled with his blood, sweat and private tears.

Richard dearly hoped that the collection of rocks and plants would not appear so proud on closer inspection. He tentatively challenged previous opinions he had formed about Emlyn's hardworking nature and about his creation being something he, Richard Pritchard, himself did not have the know-how to do, the strength and stamina to make, the enthusiastic energy to construct and the ability to overcome his laziness to get up and attempt.

Despite dismissing Emlyn's handiwork as best he could, these lucid conclusions he had just a short while before, without conscious deliberation reached, niggled uncomfortably at his mind.

He flinched and reached snappily behind his upper back, unable to scrape at the spot where a coagulating ant, in its death throes, injected him with a pinhead dose of formic acid.

Richard scrutinized carefully at close quarters. He could see that Emlyn had stabilized the underlying stones with gravel, and that rather than the rocks, which were as large as the wheelbarrow he would have carried them in, being just piled up carelessly, they had been positioned in a way that would have been time consuming and demanding of much physical effort, in what was basically two roughly shaped pyramids, the tiers of stone comprising which, however, being almost exactly level. Emlyn was a painstaking fellow.

There was evidence here and there that Emlyn had used cement to further stabilize the construct.

In short, it was a proper job, thought Richard—no short cuts had been taken, no sloppy workmanship, and no skimping on the materials required, to save time, effort and money.

So, next, Richard summarized: Emlyn's rockery was the three tiers, which from a distance appeared essentially to be within two piles of rock, though this would no doubt have been an insulting description if heard by Emlyn's ears. Of course it would have. It was a simplification, but Richard mentally asserted, not an *oversimplification* of Emlyn's achievement.

It certainly did stand up to close attention and this made Richard lower his brow in a frown. He would have liked to pick the piles of rock, and they *were* just grassy piles of rock, he thought indignantly, apart, one way or another. He did not want to admire Emlyn, be in awe of his achievement—those of a *driven slave,* after all.

Yes, a slave compelled by the lash to do what he did, under instruction, under duress, with a mind too dulled by constant chastisement to even comprehend the finished results of all his toil. He was not creative. He was not naturally hard working. He was just a poor, henpecked sod. Yes, thought Richard. That's Emlyn, sandwiched between a bed of nails and an enormous sack of potatoes named Juliet.

Yes, he was just some sort of programmable android, no, a stress toy, no, he was an unsigned cheque, no, he was her *but-rag.* Yes, he was all of those things! In fact, those silly tufts of scrub on top of that pile of stones were him, Richard went on to surmise, bound as they were to those cold, hard, unforgiving, nutrient deficient rocks. No wonder they were the smallest of all the garden's plants. Richard wagered they would not last a month—they would just frazzle and expire, starved of all their vitality. Those scrubs, no, *weeds,* were him.

The trace of discontent lifted from his face but Richard continued to stare. He mentally drifted in the warm air and sun rays. The heaps of rock melded slowly in the shimmering heat of the afternoon, almost liquefying before his eyes, the alpines wavering and swirling in the rocky fluid and congealing into the shape of . . . Emlyn—there was Emlyn, stark naked, balancing with difficulty as though standing on a trampoline, or an inflatable castle, no, he was standing between two enormous breasts, seeming as though their undulations, their cataclysmic quivering would cause them, like two leaning jellyscrapers, to topple and squash him. There he was, sweating and toiling, red from his exertions in the shadow of the pink shifting boulders.

Richard focused harder. For delightful moments Emlyn sloshed and pushed, like Samson straining at the two pillars, only for Emlyn, two gigantic mounds of flesh, seeming at any moment as though he would be drowned in their top-heavy massiveness, like a punctured lido flung about by twin cellulite tsunamis, finally to be swallowed in their crashing collapse.

He was facing what would be the face of the heaving giant, his wiry arms holding the clashing bosoms at bay, the scrawny sinews of his back like knotted ropes in tension, his clenched, pale buttocks and skinny legs bending and stretching as he rode the wavy, fleshen surf. His head shook on top of his immobilized upper body, with the superhuman effort and his lank hairdo flip-flopped from one side to the other.

He turned his head and his pitiful grimace confronted Richard—a face red and contorted in anguish. He stared at him, whimpering and pleading, even though exactly what he was saying, Richard could not hear, and therefore could not fathom the meaning of.

Of course, he thought, it's an automatic response—the drowning man reflex, and Emlyn was clearly in danger of being drowned. Yes, that was obviously the reason. But after five minutes of observing the tossing cork that was Emlyn, Richard changed his mind, he seemed to be asking for more than just help. Emlyn's blurting seemed as much to be a statement or proposal, as a cry for help. But at least, the pleas *were* directed at *him*.

Or so he thought. It began to feel to Richard as though Emlyn was in fact looking *through* him, in a queer sort of way, yes he was looking beyond Richard, behind him, to whom, Richard did not know.

Then Emlyn seemed to be more in danger of being crushed by a cascade of rock, a landslide or avalanche as Richard saw him acquire clothing, it was mountaineering clothing; boots, rucksack, oxygen cylinder, helmet and all, waving a little pickaxe before him as he (Richard thought ill advisedly) went forth along the shingle and snow-covered sides, between two mighty and forbidding mountains.

In contrast, he seemed resolute now, in the altered role, walking briskly and proceeding up the mountainside more or less in a straight line, but moving around some of the larger rocks, continuing into the distance, without hesitations, on the grueling ascent towards the summit.

Richard traced what would be his route along the great trek, up between the snow-capped, cloud-covered twin peaks, perhaps never to return. He had heard that the descent on mountaineering ventures was often more perilous than the ascent. Would Emlyn conquer the mountain, or would the mountain conquer him? Silly question, he thought, witnessing Emlyn's stick body bow under the weight of his mountain equipment.

He felt a shiver down his spine, not of grave concern for Emlyn's fate but because the frigid air was biting into his body. Then he remembered it was thirty-four degrees centigrade and broke away from the daydream.

Richard was satisfied that his neighbour was becoming sufficiently relegated. He was shorter in height and now he was lower in Richard's league of manliness. With a sense of assurance that the rockery, and with it, the troublesome priest, had been dispatched in the appropriate way, he turned about, his hands held together behind his back, and strolled toward the kitchen door facing the garden.

Chapter 28

Relieved to be in the shade, he walked through the recently tidied kitchen. Trudy was no longer there working at the sink. He opened the fridge-freezer and stooped while holding the door to see if his hidden treasures were not moved. To his relief he saw the cans, eight or so, on the glass bottom shelf, undisturbed below the shelves of lettuces, tomatoes, tins of various sorts and other grocery items one might find in the average family fridge.

Stooping over further, feeling his rubbery pot belly fold upon itself, he pulled away a can from the plastic packaging, cracked it open, and held it to his mouth, pouring, his eyes closed to indulge more deeply in the sensory pleasure. After five or six consecutive gulps, he gasped in satisfaction, and walked to the storage cupboard.

Inspecting the bottom shelf of that, he was pleasantly surprised to find another sixteen cans of lager stacked in the small space, and promptly gathered a pack of four for transportation back to the refrigerator. He continued to swig the can's contents, holding it up to his mouth with his right hand, the fresh cans in the other, and then shoved the lukewarm replenishments into the bottom shelf of the fridge with the rest of the lager, simultaneously releasing a long, cascading burp.

He felt self-satisfied that he had the foresight to stock up so well for what could otherwise have been the worst-case scenario. As it turned out, he pondered, it was the best for a lager drinker, as he was savouring the final bitter drops of fluid on his palette. A beer in the sun was as pleasurable, as much of a lifesaver, as a vodka in the Siberian wastes. The picture that formed in his mind reminded him of the predicament he had earlier imagined Emlyn to be in, trekking up the hard, frozen mountainside. Richard chuckled to himself, hearing his laughs resonate in the cool, silent kitchen air and clenched his can holding fist, crumpling it, before tossing it into the open topped, recently emptied, waste disposal bin.

He flexed his red forehead and blinked his eyes hard, in an effort to loosen the sun induced, stiff, gritty feeling in them, then leaned over floppily onto the crumbless, unsmeared work surface, the sweat and residual sunblock that had not already evaporated from his forearms and belly depositing visibly on the Formica top. He shifted his tingling, semi-naked body to get as much surface contact on the smooth, cool top, with his head eventually resting on his hands, placed over the surface.

There he stood hunched over, allowing the heat to dissipate from his lethargic body, for some five minutes, not thinking about anything in particular. The kitchen air began to acquire a subtle hint of the same smell usually confined to Richard's armpits, with his careless realization, as he rolled his torso stickily over the surface.

Somewhat cooler, he struggled away from his slouched attitude, turned around and looked at the rack of dishes and cutlery he had seen Trudy scrubbing an hour or so before. "Well, I suppose there's no requirement to dry and put them away," he thought to himself. "Not in this weather."

He would have liked to find fault in the degree of rigour evident in Trudy's execution of the day's domestic activities, but no, there were no indications of work shyness from the appearance of the kitchen space, as much as he was hoping there would be.

His glazed pink eyes ogled the white crockery, in two neat stacks, with the long, narrow, perforated metal container betwixt them. Richard rubbed the corn coloured stubble on his chin in contemplation, staring out of the window with the sunlight beaming through, looking out onto the desolate garden. Dissatisfied, he averted his gaze towards the cloudless, illuminated blue sky, the sun just out of view.

The thing about Trudy, thought Richard, was that she didn't have a job. A job, he reflected, implied *paid* employment, a trade between two parties, of work provided in exchange for a salary—work required by someone to be completed—*real, valuable* work. There was little wonder in Richard's mind why Trudy was able to do, to even consider as being worthwhile activities, the sundry, humdrum, tedious chores which he himself had long since decided that, by their nature, did not merit the labour inherent in their undertaking. No, these were what he considered to be trivial activities, labour intensive but ultimately unrewarding, and that Trudy undertook them meant that in some way, her mentality was skewed.

His hand, gently scratching the side of his bristly face, migrated towards his bulbous, oddly proportioned nose, as an index finger penetrated the fleshy nostril. It twiddled and hooked out a sizeable, semi-gelatinous nugget of mucous. He lowered his eyes, cockeyed as they scrutinized the glob on his index finger, centimeters away, like an upturned exclamation mark. He revolved it, to appreciate its profiles from every angle.

Richard had decided that he would devote *his* energy to enterprises that would bear fruit in an appreciable, impressive way—challenges that in so doing, would raise his self-esteem, not demean him in the way Trudy wanted to demean him, by her constant nagging of him (though he had to subliminally admit, more like, *advice* to him), to do those piddling, sweeping, scrubbing, bobajob "*duties*".

Granted, he was *redundant*, presently on the dole and therefore couldn't be the breadwinner he wanted to be, but that didn't mean she should constantly buzz around him like a "Tinker Bell", wanting him to waste his time doing those sorts of activities a Tinker Bell is preoccupied with.

He began rolling and shaping the nasal, jelly-carbuncle between his forefinger and thumb. At first it disintegrated into an uneven smear but it began to take on the desired spherical shape, as Richard persevered with his expert modeling techniques, extracting the moisture with and adding dirt from, his fingertips, to reduce its stickiness.

It had a lot to do with state of mind. Her state of mind was one with a marked degree of subconscious guilt, thought Richard. She was a self-taught hairdresser and in the past, before having her son, had always had difficulty in finding employment.

Now that was *so sad*, he thought, but it really was the woman's own responsibility to get trained, to get an education, *if* she had the mental capacity to do so. Anyway, Richard did not care, either way. The point he was trying to reiterate to himself, to reassure himself with, was that Trudy *had* to, she *had* to somehow make herself feel useful. She was *not able*, perhaps did not have the cerebral equipment, to make a recognizable contribution to society, in the way *he* could, through paid employment—the payment vouching for the worth of such work (even though he was presently unemployed, claiming handouts).

She was not able to do a proper job resulting in what could truly be called achievement. No, she had to somehow convince herself she was of use, by engaging in activities that were unfulfilling, pointless, unrewarding, by his learned standards. This made her feel useful.

Richard viewed the end result. The little black ball, half its original size, was ready to fly. For moments, he held the concentrated spot of nose dirt between thumb and forefinger, beholding the end product. Then, overcoming his attachment, he lowered the hand from his face, holding it out in front of him, winding up his finger to give it a good flicking.

If she wanted to be that way, he wouldn't stop her—live and let live. But no, he *would not* be dragged down to her level of desperation. He was not desperate. He would resist her attempt to infect his mind. Yes, she was afflicted with a condition of mind, alien to his own, but potentially contagious.

At the same time he felt a degree of pity for the *poor soul* with *no sense of self-worth*.

Like the hammer to the ball bearing on a pinball table, his index finger met the ball of dirtiness full on, and projected it into the air. Richard tried to follow its trajectory but it moved like a jumping flea, and was too fast for his eye.

It skittered and rested amongst the crockery that Trudy had carefully washed and that he would possibly eat off later—*if* his darling wife were returning before nightfall.

He turned away slightly more energetically, walked back over to the fridge, fished out another can of lager and swiftly pulled open the widget—the can's gasping exhalation pleasing to his ears. He guzzled some more, perhaps a third of the can, and sauntered off into the living room of his domicile.

The air was cooler still and pleasantly fragrant of lavender. Trudy had left her mark in here also. Every item of furniture in the correct place, the vacuum cleaned carpet, the coffee table's high reflectivity, which duplicated his can of beer when he placed it on the surface. He collapsed on the armchair and fumbled along its side, without looking at what he was doing, for the TV guide in the magazine rack. He couldn't find anything of interest in the listings. Instead he dredged up two or three women's weekly magazines. No paparazzi photographs of semi-nude celebrities, so he quickly stuffed the mags back into the rack. Leaning forward, he picked up the remote control from the coffee table to turn on the TV, then let it fall back, and magnetically reattached his hand to the can of lager on the table. He swiftly pulled it toward his agape beer hole. Richard watched without noticing what was on his screen for a few minutes and then supposed as to the whereabouts of his "sweetheart" Trudy.

He stared into open space for a few seconds, feeling exhausted from over-relaxation, letting his abdomen prolapse. Before long there were bubble and squeak noises within. He seesawed to his left, lifting his right buttock from the armchair's seat. He let off a lengthy fart.

Just before his "calling" to sunbathe, he had reminded her of the imperative requirement to drop off their son, Jacob, at her parents'. He had stressed that it was a good idea due to the fact that they would be house/garden bound all day long. On the other hand, her parents would no doubt be enjoying the great outdoors, valuing every one of the last granules of the sands of time still there for them, representing their time remaining on the planet. They would be cramming in the adventure (if a day at the seaside could be described as an adventure, he thought sarcastically). Anyway, the boy was so full of beans that Richard felt it would be in both their interests to offload (or as he put it, suitably accommodate) him with her parents. They at least liked to have him around, as boisterous as he was. For them he was a tonic—an adrenalin injection. It was logistical efficacy to combine the acidity of infancy with the alkalinity of age, to arrive at the perfect, neutral compound. They needed to be socially adjusted as much as the boy—all old people did in Richard's opinion, putting two cans of lager in one carrier bag. They, at least, liked to have Jacob around. Richard did not really dislike the kid's company either, but well, he thought, the boy *was* likable, but so hyperactive and demanding with it.

With the strength of a pond skater breaking free of water tension, he strained to lift himself up off the armchair, then teetering like a skittle butted by a bowling ball, managed, just, to stand upright. He walked over to the bookshelf next to the TV stand.

Richard had been insisting, in the way that he insisted every weekend, that Jacob would be better off with them, since he himself (as he stated every weekend) had no plans for the weekend, nothing *exciting,* at least. Richard corroborated his reason with the threadbare excuse that the car's gastroturbine was too osmotically sensitive and was therefore (the recurring problem reared its ugly head), flatulatedly out of sync.

Her expression was one of puzzlement at this, but she didn't probe to any great depth, to any length, with any degree of enthusiasm. She just sort of seemed, well, resigned instead, much to his satisfaction.

Nowadays, Trudy reluctantly yielded to his requests to have the boy transported (she had before equated it to the transport of an item of livestock), wherever, whenever there was the opportunity (as seen through Richard's eyes), to send him wherever, whenever: his *real* father's house, a friend's, cousin's, or Trudy's parents'. Richard wanted the house quiet, and his coaxing was for Trudy's benefit also.

Trudy couldn't drive. She and Jacob would have caught the bus to get to her parents'. Richard wondered why her parents couldn't have collected the boy by car themselves, then reconciled himself to the unpopular opinion they had of himself. They hadn't been near the house in five months.

He removed a few of the substantial tomes from the top shelf—the shelf he'd decided a seven-year-old could not reach, to reveal a row of video cassettes stacked neatly, side by side, in concordance with the rest of the room's presentation.

Although she never complained about the boy's behaviour (she would always contradict Richard, encouraging the child and involving herself in play), at age seven, he really needed to be more disciplined, thought Richard. Disciplined enough not to spill drinks, not to leave things lying around the place for someone else to tidy up, and not to speak out of turn—when in his presence. Yes, as much as he enjoyed the short chap being around, it was a pleasant relief—*for them both*, when the boy was away from the house, he conjectured.

He raised the aforementioned index finger and pointed to the spines of the cassette cases, as he lopsidedly looked at the titles; The Crudkickers US Tour 2001, Death by Whisky, Immortal Infant of the Damned, Tungsten Tank, Dark Angels of Untimely Death . . .

In addition, it freed up time for Trudy to be able to do those household jobs, which she considered to be so important. And besides, he thought, the onus was on the boy's *true father* to take his fair share of the responsibility of looking after the boy. Why should Trudy do all the cooking, the looking closely after him, the taking him to school and so on. He could understand that she was devoted to the boy, that these duties were a labour of love, but Richard, from his objective viewpoint, could see that the boy was too taxing on her mental—and physical—resources and they were very important to her also, he thought. She needed to be fit in body—that is, to be able to do her odd jobs and suchlike, so that she could be fit in spirit.

He winced his eyes to lubricate away the remaining inflammation and pinched the cassette out from the line up, reading the back side of the case in a way evocative of a wine taster reading the label of an unexpected *amontillado*.

By encouraging her to send the boy away, he was relieving her of what, because of her subjectivity, she was not able to realize herself, that the boy was a burden on her. Richard loved the youngster as much as she did, bless his freckles, but he knew how to detach himself, to act *rationally*, *unemotionally*, in hers and *the boy's* interest, without the degree of sentimentality which so often fogged Trudy's own decision-making surrounding issues relating to Jacob.

Satisfied, he walked over to the video cassette deck under the TV and inserted. Returning to his seat, he reached for the video remote control and turned on.

No, on such issues, Richard was the practically minded realist, emotionally detached enough to be able to make those decisions, which at first instances appear cruel, but turn out beneficent. That was him. *Of course*, when he saw the boy's face, the blond flattop and those big blue eyes, he understood why Trudy was so fond of him. But Richard could break away from the temptations of mollycoddling a child, the deception of those childlike features, that really cried out for alternative treatment.

Better to have the foresight to appreciate the advantages of treating a boy like a man when it was appropriate, when the child was truly ready, rather than wait for the superficial, insubstantial signal of physical appearances. Some children, despite their diminutive size, were early starters on the road to adulthood and Jacob, in Richard's opinion, was one of those precocious kids . . .

Richard picked the can of lager from off the coffee table and slurped the remainder that tinkled within it. He watched the TV with detachment as the long, mousy haired, bearded lead singer, with a desperately serious facial expression, sang in a slightly tuneful way into his microphone. He wore a papal mitre atop his head and a white cassock, which denoted him as a pontiff-type, somewhat out of the norm; his vestments had been drizzled with facsimile blood and were as soiled as any butcher's apron. Around his neck a weighty inverted crucifix swung over his bared chest, featuring a meager draggle of hair and atop his crosier, which doubled as a mic, was a little, silver, devil-wizard head.

He extended the logic of his attitude toward the boy. *Indeed*, Richard knew what was good for the child's development, like a stern but kindly master, sending a child away to summer school, or knowing the advantages of packing the child off to a boarding school. If he had the finances, he would do that, he mused. As things were, the more the child was away from himself and his mother, the more his character would develop to maturity in these, his formative years . . .

On either side of the lead singer who fancied himself as the pope, were the fat lead and bass guitarists, contrastingly garbed in the traditional heavy metal regalia; black leather jackets and trousers, studded belts, wristlets, codpieces et al. As they headbanged, their long hair whipping up the sweaty air, they pushed out crunchy, reverberating power chords and base accompaniment, somewhat at odds with the papal gurneying of the lead singer. The drummer had been consigned to the background, banging away, entombed within his twenty-piece kit, swallowed up in the dry-ice mist.

He continued to extend his reasoning: *And further*, he debated with himself, not only was it good to nurture a degree of self-sufficiency within the kid by sending him here, there and everywhere, away from them, *but of course*, this was also the justification, *the explanation* for his constant reprimanding of the *little tyke*. *No wonder* Richard was always shouting at him—it was his natural wisdom taking control of his actions.

His wisdom was so sublime, so intrinsic to his nature that he, without even realizing it, would scold the boy (for the most apparently insubstantial reasons according to Trudy); for being in the living room while Richard was watching his videos, for leaving his comics around the house, for asking him stupid, pointless questions for no other reason than to annoy him.

Richard lowered one brow and grinned—he liked what he was hearing. He couldn't quite make out the meaning of the lyric, which didn't seem to have any relation to the lead singer's appearance—the band's song and look seemed eclectic and confused. There were a lot of mixed messages going on. But he was turned on by the brutal riffs and the chorus, sung with a more vehement gusto, as the lead singer heaved off his overturned crucifix and pressed it into the camera lens.

"Back again, I told you so!"
"You double crossed, now I'll punch your ear!"
"I'll slap your face, make it glow!"
"On my return, you will know fear!"

"Gonna bust your bones bro!"
"The grass you grow you gotta mow!"
"What you reap is what you sowwwww!" The last line growled in histrionic fury.

On these occasions, Richard would invariably fly into a red (*wisdom induced*) rage, whereby he would impart to the boy valuable life experiences, *preparatory* experiences of what to expect from that element of society, perhaps friends, colleagues at work, maybe even eventually a wife, with an extremely vicious, volatile (or at least irksome) temperament. Thanks to these elements, society was always biting its own arse in a cannibalistic, masochistic way, he thought.

Such experiences as these, that Richard was furnishing the boy with, would stand him in good stead for the future. To be emotionally resilient enough to be able to absorb such torrid, vehement references to himself would be an invaluable attribute. That was Richard's gift to the boy.

Oh yes! Too good! So irreverent, so profane, *so subversive!*

He couldn't get enough of those satanic verses and waited keenly for the band's next track.

Of course, he always knew what Jacob's safe limit was—he knew how much the fellow could handle, but at the same time he would marvel at how much (*wisdom induced*) contemptuous criticism the boy could carry on his narrow childish shoulders, without cracking. No doubt his influence on the boy was leaving a permanent, positive mark.

The lead singer reappeared in formal heavy-metal dress, this time straining and grimacing at his mic from the outset, in a rendition of a recent top thirty hit of theirs, a variation of the generic *pink torpedo, flesh tuxedo* song, that Richard was very familiar with.

He would desensitize the boy further, would remove the delicacy of his personality, which in rough-tough society (and society was throughout, rough and tough, he interjected) resulted in the downfall of so many. Jacob would instead be a survivor!

Yeah, that's it! he thought, releasing a rumbustuous burp of triumph. He would be a winner in the world of work in the way Richard was himself—when *he* last worked.

What a lucky boy he was to have Richard as a father figure! It was wonderful, the way providence worked! That this small, fragile, helpless boy could have (albeit not the father that conceived him but) a powerful, practical and above all wise father figure to look up to, to be molded by. He was a *surrogate*, but of far greater importance to the boy than his true father could ever be, who, Richard concluded, was a complete waster.

The boy would have no weaknesses. The way Richard was shaping the child's character was the result of being in perfect harmony, perfectly attuned to the boy's mentality. Richard would continue to work spontaneously and intuitively with him—would continue to *swear at* and *insult* the young lad, continue to send him packing to anybody who was prepared to have him.

The lead singer was fondling a busty blond, a whole foot taller than himself, apparent even as they reclined over the bonnet of a scarlet Ferrari Testarossa.

"You like talk!"
"I like pork!"
"Let's meet for dinner!"
"Pop a cork!"
"You'll wanna winna inya!"
"You sent for the dorkkkkkk!"

Richard's regime amounted to a virtuous cycle for himself and the boy. A symbiosis, whereby he would gain satisfaction by imparting unto him the preparatory lessons for manhood and would consequently witness the boy's personal development, thanks to his inspired fits of rage. These occurred so naturally, without his conscious deliberation. Concurrently, the boy's psychological constitution would be toughened. He would eventually be a man fit for the society they lived in.

He crushed the can and flicked it onto the carpet, as his brain continued to storm. He had not finished there—he would like to go *yet further*, fired by his sense of duty towards Jacob, he didn't want to hold back. He wanted to let his creative imagination run riot for, over, the boy. The bounds of his concepts were yet broader. Their relationship was such a beautiful thing that sometimes Richard wanted to give Jacob *other gifts* from the repertory of his inventive mind. He did not want to refrain from using any device by which he could accelerate the child's progress to manhood. Oh, he would have so liked, so often, to give the child an old-fashioned slap, or thump, or kick, in (*wisdom induced*) anger . . .

Unfortunately for the boy, Trudy intervened on the few occasions Richard had deployed such techniques. She was so ignorant, too misguidedly sentimental, to appreciate the value of Richard's guiding touch on him. It was really (if she could develop insight into their relationship), the touch of reassurance in disguise. That firm hand was there to steady, to stabilize the sapling, to check his leaning. Clever deployment of physical contact, thought Richard, would be evidence of the synergy between him and the young lad. Unfortunately Trudy could not comprehend the virtuous consequences of these sophisticated techniques—how they would catalyze the childish brain into that of an adult's. She did not know the inner workings, mysterious to the layman that she was, of such metamorphoses. But Richard did. He had the social engineering know-how.

Anyway, the boy was denied this guiding hand or foot or whatever, of righteous anger by Trudy. She had, in a way which was quite out of character, told Richard that if she ever saw him touch the boy again, she would let her six-foot-two, ex-husband Quentin know, and that as much as he was a waster, he was not a child beater.

He wouldn't hesitate to beat a man though, and on the occasions when he had been able to pry himself away from his harem of tarts (which the flat he and Trudy once shared had become) to visit his son, he eyed Richard with an eagle-eyed degree of suspicion that was uncannily expectant, as though within that meat-head there was a functioning, anticipating brain.

Well, wonders never cease, Richard thought. But, fair enough, it would be the boy's loss in the long term.

Tsk tsk. She really had no idea, *that woman*—then hmm, as he contemplated being the pupil, rather than the teacher, in the caring, sharing cycle of *interchange of physical energies*, he had cleverly devised.

Three quarters through the tune, Richard was getting bored. It was the same old fare, and Richard liked it a little bit harder, a little bit grittier.

The Corpulent guitarists moshed on either side, as the lead singer continued to grope the model atop the sports car's bonnet.

He gathered the remote and ejected the tape.

Chapter 29

Richard decided to pass away a few more hours contemplating the whereabouts of Trudy as he lay on the fabric settee. It was a little early for her to have gone over to her parents' to collect Jacob.

Four twenty p.m.

In all honesty he didn't much care as to her whereabouts presently. What mattered was that she be present to indulge in the *pleasures of the flesh* he had planned for the night. His desire was carnal and building uncontrollably in anticipation. And after all, a good sex life was at the heart of a strong relationship. He reckoned that that held true even for Juliet and Emlyn (but surmised that their sessions were more about dominance and submission). He briefly giggled to himself.

A couple hours later, Richard was getting a little bored and uncomfortable lying on the couch. His appetite was up again and he had a longing for more of the nourishment that Juliet and Romeo (aka Emlyn) offered out like portions from an oversize apple crumble.

He got up off the settee and ventured back into the garden on the off chance that there would be more action there. Richard hoped that the young night would carry on its reflective breeze a sweet serenade, a moonlight sonata from the vicinity of his *lovebird* neighbours.

There wasn't any activity but the air was cooler and the daylight less glaring. Quite pleasant. With nothing of importance to occupy his mind, his thoughts turned again to the fun and frolics he would indulge in later. He visualized himself standing naked before Trudy, an Adonis before a suppliant, kneeling maid.

For some reason this image forced the blackberry bush into his perception. He considered whether the sexual favours would be enhanced if he did what Trudy wanted and cut it down.

It presented for him at that moment, a strange fascination. As though that night it had a particular significance, which it held to its prickly heart, which he had to unravel. He padded towards it, and for a little while absorbed himself within it. At first glances, it was a bleak, colourless experience, and he found the bush's close proximity slightly disconcerting, due to its sheer size. But it was forbidding and yet tantalizingly familiar.

He ventured even closer, seeking to verify something playing on his mind. A small gust and the blackberry bush writhed like a huge medusa's head, as if expectant of being downsized with shears that Richard had so often "forgotten" to buy for the purpose. But Richard had no such plans to stamp his authority on the virulent shrub. He was snagged by its *nastiness,* and decided to conduct a little study.

He gingerly approached it with the respect for an equal, which he was, so long as he kept arm's distance. It was, from close up, quite a thriving, thrumming, self-contained ecosystem, which he soon became caught up in. With an enthusiasm he never knew could be kindled within him for the pronged Gordian knot, he pushed aside the stems tenderly, as though he were a rubber balloon that would pop with the stab of a single prickle. Carefully avoiding the alert thorns, he peered through the garden hydra's snarled stems into its shaded nucleus.

The tangle in perspective was a miniature Amazon rainforest to Richard's eyes but somewhat less exotic, he thought, willfully tempering his curiosity. He would never have conceived that such an array of insects (albeit small and mundane) could proliferate over and within it, a fact of which he had been so unaware (that is, unaware that in his garden there was a microcosmic facsimile of the winding roads, streets and alleys, the knots of buildings and bridges and tunnels, of the city he lived in).

He was quite finding the botanical scribble of interest and studied the gyrating vegetation, the caterpillars, ants and greenfly, winding their way along branches, like an insectivorous spaghetti junction, around leaves and through the webs—between the shifting tangles of chutes, like gossamer scaffolding . . .

His eyeballs twitched as if accidentally twanging the web strands he viewed. A little flutter of his heart and he was free, watching just their vibration in the breeze. He traced the shimmering power lines that converged towards the centers.

The spiders were supreme—arachnid law enforcers, devouring anything that broke the cruel laws of the insect world, brutal sentinels, quietly watching the crawling cityscape about them, dispatching felons too slow, weak or dumb. He was an arachnaphobe, but he allowed himself to detach from the civilized society of

Homo sapiens to indulge, temporarily, in this alternative world, and to admire the eight-legged carnivore.

He looked into the infinity of the complex molecular model in sour green, and he saw the spiders everywhere, at intervals, harvesting sectors of the labyrinth of its spiritedly itinerant food source. It was an endless repeat pattern, the food chain and accordingly, the balance of power, visually and understandably described. Richard mirthfully equated it to Trudy's return from a shopping expedition, the piles of shopping stacked around her. It was an easy matter to calculate *her* food consumption for the week, as it was to calculate the spider's.

His eyes, reconciled to the brutal beauty of nature that filled his view, settled on one particularly plump spider. Unlike its sisters, suspended elsewhere in their shared habitat, this one was a rather dull green, almost as if it was intent on blending in to the fungus-ridden backdrop of receding stems. Richard thought this peculiar—all the others were power dressed, with vicious stripes emblazoned across their backs, an emphatic declaration of their dominion.

Nevertheless, this was a particularly well-fed spider, riding a virtuous cycle no doubt, the likes of which were so obvious in the world of bugs. Where else was life among the lesser animals better simplified? The more the spider eats, the fatter and stronger it becomes. The fatter and stronger it becomes, the more it eats. The reverse cycle was true for a smaller, weaker spider—the less it eats, the smaller it becomes, the less it eats.

He cocooned the miniature predator with his attentive eyes, watching its twitchy robotic movements, and it lulled his mind. The plump spider bobbled at the center of its skeined platform in endless, silent patience. He analyzed its numerous eyeballs, shining in the shadowy fronds, as it became static, a multi-eyed, steel trap for any ill-fated insects to become gobbled by—Richard closed in on its retracted fangs, appalled, even as a vague, relaxing feeling of recognition soothed his inner mind, something confirming and reassuring.

Then, in the corner of Richard's eye; it was an ant of atypical appearance to those he had until now seen. It rather strangely had over its spindly, segmented anatomy, the yellow and black stripes he had elsewhere noticed on wasps. It was a very distinct marking, on what was usually such a monotone insect. The finely delineated feature made the little creature quite a striking looking, oven-ready meal, if perhaps a little meager, he thought.

The spider, spread-eagled and motionless at the epicenter of the tremulous silk net, a livid green death's-head on crossed bones, bided its time and in no time, the frenetic ant jittered off a nearby leaf and sprung the trap, via the few strands it had triggered, with the deftest of touches. The web, as though a living extension of the spider, was brought to life, strumming and thronging, as if with an independent sentience to intentionally ensnare the doomed ant. It activated the spider, like the flick of a switch turning on a torch. The ant squirmed and twisted as the spider, many times its size, pounced.

It seemed to Richard that the loud colouration on the ant's exoskeleton could only hasten its demise, transmitting its gaudy image along the optic fibres of the web, to reach the fat eight-legged microchip of a spider at the center, at the speed of light. It would then process the information in equally quick time and dispatch the ant.

He marveled at the spider's quartz movement, the way its tapered legs scuttled independently, as though each were animated by their own brain, permitting them to span the silver threads with ease.

Richard expected it to engage in a feeding frenzy there and then. Instead, it perched over the ant, and after precisely measured seconds, twirled it around between its frontal arms. The spider spun the victim like yarn over a spindle, and its wriggling ended as it became mummified in webbing—the cellophane wrap over a turkey sandwich.

The leafy stem of Richard's persona looked to the warm sun of society, but something in the bowels of his being stirred, as he watched on. The dark, gnarled roots of his unconscious sucked deep down, within the dirt, as they seized the moment to bolster his hidden beliefs:

It was all about winners and losers in the insect world, he thought; carnal hungering slaked for the winner and cruel, ripping, tearing death for the loser. Richard bore down on the wretched ant, soon to be drained of all its viscera by the spider, to experience the process while fully conscious. With a raise of his eyebrows, he gave a mini shrug at the diminutive death-row prisoner. The analogy triggered within him a recognition, an awareness, of something this scene had in common with another relationship nearby, also between a fascist and one tyrannized, that Richard had the morbid pleasure of being au fait with.

He half closed his eyes to the exclusion of the dwindling photons of light, to conjure with a mental twitch and a nod and a rub of his cerebral tummy *and* a little bit of gymnastic contortion of the imagination, an alternative scene of a man in the dungeon of a taciturn and murderous queen.

A water droplet appeared at the twisting head of the ant trapped in its blanket, and began fattening, like it might be sweating in its silky bed. Richard wondered what this strange exudation from the ant's head actually was, and traced through in his head the few David Attenborough "Life on Earth" programs he had seen in the past, but nothing came to mind. But he did remember from that second-hand nature watching, that the insect world was like the movie *Alien* scaled down, and settled for that to end further wondering.

The drop continued to swell and Richard noticed that it began to acquire some definition. The ant's head distorted in the liquid lens around it, and began to separate into spectral colours. Simultaneously the features moved under the watery surface and rearranged like colloids in a solution, meeting in altered positions, as though by chemical attraction, and reforming the head of the ant. Between the head and thorax appeared a neck growing gradually, and pushing away what was the head of the creature.

The spectral colours recombined, to give the emerging shape a buff colour, as the mandibles, also chromatically altered, tweaked here and there to form a chin. The eyes reduced and sank in their orbits, and a brow bulged above them. The antennae retracted like a snail's to half their length and multiplied, thinning out into squirming strands, of what seemed to be *human hair*. The living hair suddenly stopped wriggling, like it had been given a blow, the way a hapless tuna might on a fishing boat, and sunk lankly about the sides of what now looked to Richard very much like a human head, atop the disproportionately small body, still wrapped in its silken blanket, within the deathbed of the web.

Richard, totally absorbed in this mentally induced spectacle, momentarily disregarded the spider, as threatening as it was. It now began, with tentative steps, to span the web, making it wobble under its weight, back to the ant.

The fat spider approached, creaking the strands with each cyclical movement of its eight legs and hovered above the ant as though it were about to descend upon it.

The ant's head was now Emlyn's head. It writhed in dread, underneath the bulging torso of the spider, being the only part of his body that was not immobilized. Every muscle in that terrified face moved of its own volition, describing the unsyncopated thoughts of panic within. The spider straddled across his head now, seemed almost to be intentionally tormenting him, lowering and raising its head and midsection, lowering and raising, casting a ghastly, splodgy shadow over his face.

Richard concentrated his attention to try to hear what it was, if it was anything intelligible, that Emlyn was saying. He even turned his ear slightly towards the ant-man to kindly receive what the condemned might ask for. As the forlorn writhing continued below the formidable body of the spider, more droplets emitted from Emlyn's face and met to form streams of sweat, that settled on the web below him, like translucent drops of blood, preempting the real blood that would

261

flow once the spider decided to crunch into Emlyn's cranium. Before Richard was able to satisfactorily turn up the volume in his head, Emlyn's head slumped to the side. He was out cold.

The spider waited for moments, as though expecting a quick revival and after half a minute, at the same time as Richard became resigned to the fact that Emlyn was not going to come around, suddenly lost interest in the morsel. She without further hesitation dislocated from the man-ant and scuttled off to the center of the web.

What a horrid, brutal world, bristling with hairs and antennae and proboscii and compound eyes and ovipositors and thoraxes and mandibles, thought Richard, taking a heavy breath.

Of course, the structure of human society was somewhat different, Richard comforted himself, men being creatures of intellect and emotion and social—to an extent. The fangs were there, but they were kept retracted, there only to threaten or deter.

A weapon of some sort—some means by which to dominate by only the suggestion of using it . . .

Physical size and strength was not a requisite for authority, or the yardstick by which authority could be measured, *supposedly*, but there could be no doubt that a six-foot-five individual could influence a conversation, command an argument, just by intimidating his shorter opposition with his physical stature. It happened all the time. That the physically well-endowed could, without warning, become upset and fly off the handle, was always a possibility. Or at least, this was society's perception.

A for-instance: whenever Quentin, Trudy's ex, was around, he *always* threatened Richard with his physical manner and *he* had the IQ of a lobotomized peanut. They never much engaged in conversation, it was merely brusque hellos and thank yous and nods here and there. He didn't like Richard much and Richard him neither. Quentin was happy enough to keep distance between them, as long as there was space for him to access his son.

He maintained this uninterfered with contact with his boy by virtue of his burlesque build (or so he thought) but Richard would have liked him to know that he had no intention of coming between them anyway, no more than he would have any intention of preventing a dog from returning to its vomit. For some reason Jacob had not caught on to his real father's sordid secret life. He could learn the hard way who to avoid in this world—hard and bitter lessons were the ones most vividly remembered after all.

But Richard hated to think that the muscle-head Quentin believed he had assumed control over the matter through physical intimidation. It was so humiliating to think that he could belittle Richard's intellect to the point of insignificance by preventing any conversation from happening. That would be where Richard could come into his own, where he could shine. Where his silver tongue could dazzle, hypnotize and confuse Quentin and make him become embarrassed by his lack of an education, chisel his statuesque physique down to size and then scuff them both, he and his son, off his plate with the chicken bones.

He'd love to see that look of bamboozlement over Quentin's rugged face, get him to raise his meaty hands to his flowing blond hair in awe, as he tried to unravel Richard's devious argument, stun Quentin to speechlessness, to be able to then pierce him with needles of wit and finish him off.

But for now, Quentin kept the upper hand with his forbidding physical presence like some walking six-foot-two cactus Richard had to steer clear of, much to his chagrin.

But was this, Richard asked himself, *too* extreme an opinion of Quentin? There was no way such an imbalanced structure could not topple over before long. It was obvious that the tall man *with intellect* had the advantage over his shorter counterpart, but of course, he would never *obviously* exploit his physical superiority—he would be exploiting *himself* in a society whose ethos was to promote civility and gentleness. He simply *implied* that he had the weapon and made it clear, whether it was true or not, that there was a point after which he would use it—if he were pushed too far. It was the secret between him and the associated. This always kept the conversations manageable and assured compliancy.

But Quentin's authority was entirely and *brazenly* derived from his brawn and he implied he would use it, without guile or subtlety, and without shame for that matter. Richard was always polite to the man, disarmingly polite, he hoped, but ultimately more polite than Quentin could appreciate. How could he reconcile this behaviour with his general behaviour in society? Didn't he *know* to respect intelligence—Richard's intelligence?

But the man had no intention of bowing. He frustrated Richard. What was it that made him so secure in his behaviour? What was backing him up? Why did he withhold the hand of friendship (into which Richard could prick his poisonous syringe)?

Certainly Jacob, his son, was no chip off the old block. He readily accepted Richard's superior intelligence. Or was he seceding to the "cruel to be kind" use of insult and intimidation?

Anyway, it wasn't right. Quentin would learn someday. He could ride his luck for only so long.

No, despite Quentin's temporary successes, they would not go on forever. This was not the way of polite society. It was one thing to have a tall, commanding physique but quite another to be a bully with it.

Then came to his mind, his, Richard's, relationship with Jacob . . .

Going to the extreme (which seemed to be Quentin's inclination), a human equivalent of a spider would be a *psychopathic killer*, and they were hardly the success stories of modern society, often lonesome, brooding and outcast. They weren't achievers in any sense of the word other than in the impressive number of humans they culled.

There was no correlation with the successes of the spiders through *their* lack of emotional attachments to the surrounding living environment, compared with the psychopath's lack of emotional attachments to those in *his* midst. His indurated predisposition seemed to diminish and reduce him in effectiveness and he would end up too reclusive and fearful to function in society. Not forgetting, of course, that if he were caught, he would find himself wasting in prison, rather than fattening and thriving like the spider.

Richard couldn't understand *their* world, other than as an objective observer. There was no way he could appreciate it from the subjectivity of either the spider or the fly or ant. He himself was a *social* animal. He only hoped that Quentin would go the whole hog (or the whole spider), and try it on with his boss at work. Being penniless would sober him up. After that, it would be payback time upon Quentin the Dullard.

Chapter 30

Richard, perplexed, had taken his focus off Emlyn who now began to return to consciousness. His head dangled from side to side, the thin neck beginning to provide some sort of support for the head and the hair clinging to the sticky threads of white behind, twitching them and sending off the signals to the spider, which for some reason, waited motionlessly.

He seemed to be mumbling something, telling from the wobble of his Adam's apple and the parted lips and now Richard exerted himself to hear what it was that the man was saying, without getting too close to the web, that a shift within the bush could fling the web and its contents onto his face.

"Oooaah, heck, what is this? Where am I?" said the lettuce leaf voice as his head swirled. "Wha', what is this place? Why can't I move? Why am I in the air?"

"You're suspended, Emlyn. You've been suspended, pending enquiry. I'm enquiring as to your condition, hanging as you are on this web—"

"Wha', wait, wait, just a minute, what do you mean I'm on, I'm on this web? Wha', what web? I don't see any web . . ."

Richard had to listen hard to catch his watery thin voice and this combined with his Swansea accent, he found he could only understand if he turned his ear to funnel in the sonic trickle emitting from Emlyn. "The web behind you, Emlyn . . . Don't you see it?"

Emlyn yanked hairs from off the web as he struggled to turn his head enough to see. When he could get enough movement, what he saw baffled him. "Richard . . . what kind of crazy scene is this . . . is this some sort of funfair ride? I'm not thinking straight . . . it seems so unreal . . ."

"Oh, it's very real, Emlyn, and the realism will intensify in a little while, I think you'll find . . ." Richard closed his eyes, as though what he had clued Emlyn up on was something of grave concern to him.

"You're confusing me even more, Richard . . . You're too close to me . . . crowding me. You look huge. Stand back a bit, mate."

"I *am* standing back, Emlyn. It's not that I'm so big, it's more to do with the fact that you're so miniscule."

Emlyn winced and popped his eyes, trying to clear away the vagueness but was still unable to comprehend his circumstance, even as his voice became a little clearer. "No, no, it must be that I'm drunk . . . I'm wearing bottle-bottom glasses or something . . . someone's drugged me up somehow . . ."

Richard spoke slowly and deliberately, "You think so? I can assure you that that isn't the case. You've just assumed the physical characteristics of your personality, you—"

"What're you on about, Richard, you're talking gobbledygook . . . c'mon, don't mess about . . . I'm getting vertigo up here . . . if I am *up* at all, it might just be in my head."

"For someone of your diminutive stature, Emlyn, the height you are off the ground is indeed considerable, but then you are well harnessed, so don't fret your little head, for now—"

Emlyn awkwardly pulled his head from the wispy strands, which to him appeared as multi-ply ropes, to view the drop. "Eeeugh, this is too much, heeeugh, huughh," a stream of vomit poured from his mouth over his web straight jacket. As he looked down, it seemed to disappear into infinity, "This is a nightmare . . . I'm just dreaming I'm up here."

Richard wagged his finger in front of Emlyn in disagreement, "Perhaps *I* am, but *you're* not dreaming, I can guarantee you that."

Above Emlyn, Richard could see the spider, which had seemed to be in a sort of torpor, gently rustle.

"Hugghh, why can't I move my body? Hikk, this stuff around me is cutting off my circulation," he strained and wriggled to no avail. "Get me out of this thing—"

"As I was saying, Emlyn, before you rather rudely interrupted me, you've assumed the physical characteristics of your personality, that being the personality of an ant, and as such, you've become the victim of—"

"Richard, old friend, please, I feel queasy, it's no time for practical jokes, if that's what this is . . . It's magic mushrooms, I tried them once at this party and I grew a metre taller, I—" Emlyn was babbling inanely, phlegm bubbling at his lips.

"Emlyn, no, it's not magic mushrooms that are conjuring the setting you find yourself in, I only wish for your sake that it was. I can understand why you think that might be the case, their being so abundant in your quaint, Welsh, green valleys, but certainly I wouldn't have messied my fingers with those grubby things, passing them onto you. Neither are you in some alcoholic stupor, to answer an earlier question, though I am more inclined myself to a bevy than 'shrooms'."

"Heeeuugh," another trickle guzzled from Emlyn's open mouth.

Richard ignored the convulsing and continued, "Emlyn, I don't know how to break this too you. Perhaps I shouldn't let you know at all—that would probably be more humane, but you're insisting, so I'll tell you." He paused to gather his thoughts and to consider how to put it to him.

"Emlyn, very shortly, you're going to become the evening snack of a rather enormous, green spider which is sharing this web with you."

"Eh? What do you mean spider? A tarantula?" His glib appearance revealed his lack of comprehension.

"A common garden spider, Emlyn."

Emlyn laughed dryly in between wretches.

Richard frowned in seriousness as he went on, "When you experience the fangs enter your brain via your haircut and skull, I think the reality of your predicament will hit home . . ."

Emlyn's goofy expression annoyed Richard, who was going to pains to explain.

"Now, young man," said Richard, "take a look above you."

Emlyn strained and saw above him the huge, spherical bottom of the arachnid, some ten metres (or ten centimeters from Richard's viewpoint) away. "Huh, hah, it's a balloon, a huge green balloon . . . I knew I was in the air, this is some sort of balloon ride . . . Hey,

I hope we're not gonna be up here much longer though, I'm petrified of heights and—"

"And I'm scared of spiders, Emlyn." He muttered in mild exasperation, but went on, "Now if you would, look to the sides of that sphere. See there those black twisted pipe cleaners? They, Emlyn, are the legs of the spider."

Emlyn looked and could see, juxtaposed against the balloon, what appeared to be huge, black rafters, with large splinters—the hairs, coming off their surface. "No Richard buddy, I'm not convinced . . ."

"Okay then, Emlyn, how about this." Richard, without getting any closer to the spider, gently blew on its rump. It excreted some peculiar gunk from its mouth, which tumbled down the crossed strands like small jellified rocks from a precipice, and crashed semi-solidly onto Emlyn's upturned head. It trickled like large balls of liquid mercury over Emlyn's face, some entering his wailing mouth, and he spat and hacked miserably as the odd, digestive fluid seared his eyes, which watered profusely.

"My dear fellow, if you breathed through your nose, that wouldn't have happened, would it?" He didn't wait for the reply, instead just continuing to blow.

The spider, slightly aroused from its state of inactivity, flinched and turned a quarter circle on the center of the web.

Emlyn, tiredly contorting his head, could see the spider move in its entirety, and could see the foreshortened body and black-eyed head of the beast. Emlyn's eyes boggled as his jaw dropped at the woeful sight. His facial muscles were paralyzed. He was unable to speak, as though he had already been injected with the spider's venom.

"We get what we deserve, my friend," said Richard morosely, and with a wistful finality, suggesting there was nothing he could do for the hapless Emlyn.

Emlyn gagged a bunch of indecipherable words and then found the frequency, "Richard, you've got to get me off this, this *web*!" he struggled to tear his hair off the web which reattached whenever he leaned back his head. He was delirious with fright. "Please, Richard, get me off—"

"And what would your suggestion be, as to how I should do that, Emlyn?"

"I dunno, maybe break the web, tear it!"

"And with what?"

Emlyn groaned, "With your hands, mate, your hands—"

"My dear Emlyn, I have, how can I put it, an *aversion* to spiders."

"You mean you won't touch the web?"

"That's right, Emlyn, I can't permit the web to touch my fingers—it just makes me shudder thinking about it. Out of the question." Richard pursed his lips and brusquely shook his head, his eyes looking to his upper lids.

"Please Richard," he shrieked, "you must do something . . . you can't leave me here to die so horribly. You wouldn't leave me like this." The tendons in his neck stood out as he struggled. He had completely snapped.

"Oh yes, I would, Emlyn. I'm not one to interfere with nature. It's heartbreaking to see, yes, but that's how it is." He went on above Emlyn's stunned muttering,

"It's you or the spider. Now, if I were to rescue you, the spider would go hungry, and that wouldn't be right, would it? I'm sure you can understand, Emlyn. No hard feelings, eh?"

"Get a stick, a twig—" he screeched, aghast.

"No-can-do, *old bean*, they've all got thorns on. I don't want to prick my finger any more than you want to be crushed between the fangs of the eight-legged *monster*—"

"Eeeeeeeeeaaaargh!!!"

"Sorry, Emlyn—eight-legged *garden-spider*."

For a half minute all sound subsided as both meditated upon their plight. Richard was getting a cramp in the back of his neck, hunched as he was over the threadbare gladiatorial arena and Emlyn, well he just softly mumbled to himself words which Richard could not hear.

Then he resumed his fight for survival. "Richard, get a stick—look beyond the bush—"

"None come to hand, Emlyn," he said tersely.

"Look around you, man!"

He looked to his left and right briefly, just moving his head, "Nope, none around." He folded his arms.

"For flip-sake you have to get me off this thing!"

"Loooook, Emlyn! Don't whine! I'm sure it will be a quick and painless death. Be over in a matter of seconds. It's about as good a death as an insect can expect."

"Please," he shrieked, "I know something about spiders, they'll inject me with some sort of acid and dissolve my innards and then suck them out! You could never allow that to happen!"

"That may be, my dear Emlyn. But that is just how life is. If you're not a man you can't share in the camaraderie of men. You can't expect the sympathy of men."

"But if I'm an ant like you say, why are you calling me by my name, Emlyn?"

"You are merely an ant named Emlyn, Emlyn."

"But I am a man, Richard," he sobbed, almost resigned now to his fate.

Richard lowered his head, holding his hands, letting them rest on his stomach. "Better to let nature take its course," he said, now with dispassion.

"You're just going to watch me die?"

"Yes I am, Emlyn."

A silence of emotional exhaustion for Emlyn and one in which Richard collected his thoughts, then ending with sadistic proclivity, "We all die, after all—perhaps not as horrifically as you will, by the standards of men, Emlyn—but we all die."

Emlyn had the energy for one more ghastly scream, and then mercifully lost consciousness again, as the spider lurched and turned its sparkling black, expressionless, unfeeling eyes to him.

Chapter 31

It was a size mismatch, morbidly brutal and unnerving to witness in a microscopic kind of way. Richard followed the proceedings anyway. Yes the spider's fangs were plain to see, two hairy scimitars in its callous head and now they were threateningly hung over Emlyn's centre parting.

Okay, there *were* times, rare occasions when fangs were bared, like the spider's, with the condonence of society, just so that authority would be understood. But *only* under certain conditions. For sure, Richard could understand the value in baring teeth in certain situations, when it was called for.

Perhaps survival situations. There were none that he could recall, that he himself had experienced recently, apart from perhaps just one, when there had been a moment, had been a survival situation . . .

What was at stake was the survival of Richard's *sexual* identity, or so he thought.

It was a couple of nights earlier that week. Trudy had been sleeping in the box room at the back of the house over the recent hot nights and Richard was missing her in body, if not soul.

Why was he being punished by her in this way? He didn't know for sure, but things couldn't go on like they were. It probably had something to do with the odd jobs he failed to do, he told himself, and the more he thought about it, the more *obviously* the reason this became—that was how Trudy was wired.

Undeniably, he was a male, still in his prime and with a libido to go with that but it had nothing to do with that. *His* concern was with the bonds within the family and he could not stand to see them weakened any further. There was that *caring*, *sharing* thing that marked him inescapably as being a social animal, a dependent, a family man . . . He just had to accept what he was—bound to the thing most dear in his life, his family, in need of the reassuring touch, the caress of a caring, understanding woman.

Trudy could be understanding.

He would see that she understood tonight.

Trudy was at her parents, collecting Jacob but would be back shortly.

Richard felt he had a responsibility to take this bull by the horns. *So be it*—if to secure their family Richard would have to pander to Trudy's every foolish whim (bless her misguided soul), then that was just how it was. He could do the chores tomorrow but the matter of sexual satiation was pressing *now*—it required resolving *now*.

Richard lay on the living room couch. On the TV screen two tanned bodies ground together and gyrated in unison, gradually increasing in speed and vigor. The sound effects were stock-in-trade oohs and aahs between dubbed English dialogue. There was a thirty-second burst where the male on top seemed as though a cattle prod had been stuck up his anus, such were his convulsions. He gratified himself, releasing a gasp, which rasped like the release of air from a pinched balloon, and wilted away. The copulation lasted ten minutes precisely after which time the camera shuffled, as the camera operators—two toneless, latex-blob-like men, abandoned their equipment, bashing-off furiously all the way to the bank. They thrust and rubbed and oozed for a further ten minutes exactly. Then she paid for the decorating, they smiled cheesily at each other and parted company.

Richard picked the remote and turned down the volume.

It had been three long days and he was feeling eager. With that eagerness perhaps irritable—more so than normal—perhaps excessively so, which was why he had to approach her, apprehend her if necessary . . .

She had returned with Jacob from her parents late that night. It was about 9:15 and she took Jacob up to his room to settle him in. Richard thought that she moonwalked up the stairs, she was so quiet. He wouldn't have even known that she had arrived (even though he was keenly expectant) if Jacob wasn't such a clod-hopping kid. Richard could hear him walking on the wooden block floor along the corridor in his squeaky trainers.

Now in his bedroom, Jacob was tucked away and on his way to slumber land, Richard was sure.

"Trude, darling, we really need to talk." He had somehow crept to the first of the three steps, on the first floor landing, without creaking the timbers, to confront Trudy.

She averted her gaze, switching between looks to his left, to the right, above him and to the floor.

"C'mon, Trude, this is silly! It's not what family is about. Let's talk."

She tensed herself, resentful of the ventriloquist that had fingered her for a hand opening. Beneath her pursed lips, her teeth clenched. She moved forward to pass but Richard obstructed her passage, stretching his arms between the stair banister and the wall.

She stood still momentarily, buffered by his slovenly mass, then moved forward again. Richard blocked her way. He was by no means a physical man but he was more than big enough to obstruct her escape route.

He looked a little bit darker in the warm oily light, like the charred wick of a candle after its flame had been snuffed out. His face took on a bedraggled, ruffled look, that betrayed his anger, crawling beneath the trite veneer. He was working on remote—the etiquette a series of *New Man* clichés, stitched together like a crude patchwork.

Seeming wearied, "C'mon Trude, we need to sort this out. Why don't you speak to me?"

A pause. Then she said, "Out of my way, Richard."

"Trudy darling, don't be like this. Let's act like the adults we are . . ."

There was a sinister haminess about his dialogue, as though it was a cover—an imitation of TV melodrama speak, expected to persuade. The way he persisted in the smooth, false voice, while his eyes shone with subhuman anger unnerved her. Perhaps she should act like a soap opera lover in response?

He stood, blocking her pathway like a Minotaur between two pillars, as the skin of humanity fell around him in drapes. In his eye, she could see the glint of the colour red.

She would have said, "No Richard, you're not rational, you're scaring me," but she couldn't make such a reference while he continued the perversely pretentious spiel, too enraged to realize his mind had become a grizzly, hiding behind the narrowest tree trunk.

He moved forward, his arms still outstretched to the stair banister and wall, forcing her to edge back to keep her distance, her personal space.

"Get out of my way, Richard. Get out now!"

She remained expressionlessly stern but there was a tremor of fear in her voice.

Then the dam burst, his entire face was struggling to resist the grimace creepily morphing over—it gushed red, the corner of his eyelid twitched as the side of his mouth quivered, taut in spite of his effort to appear relaxed, it was like the first stage of transformation to a werewolf. With every gram of his will he resisted the beast intent on claiming him, as though he were fighting for his very soul. Trudy held out some hope even as her body seemed to age a hundred years.

His breathing had become shallower and faster after it seemed he had successfully exorcised himself. Then, a smile, that was more a grin in a dinner suit. He moved forward again, forcing her backward to the door of the bedroom.

With a lower, soft voice to cancel her raised one, "I love you darling, you know I do."

The return of the sickly schmooze unhinged her. "You're acting weird, Richard, get away from me," she said less forcefully, her eyes like large white marbles staring, trying to see a way around him.

"I'm asking you politely to go into the bedroom, Trudy . . ." slowly moving forward.

There was no response as she sidled her way back.

"I'm not going to hit you and I'm not going to shout but I'm not letting you past me. I just want to talk . . ."

Her will to resist was becoming depleted. She felt physically exhausted, her limbs had atrophied. The posture she had so assiduously maintained, meant to safeguard her personal space, flagged. Timidly, "No I won't . . ."

His right arm closed against the wall as his left reached for the door handle. He pushed it open. He walked forward, blocking off her view of the corridor with his chest.

He shut the door behind him slowly and turned on the light at the door side, sparkling the tears running down her rubescent cheeks. She stood tremulously like a schoolgirl before the cane holding headmaster.

"There's no need to cry." He wound over to her and held her upper arms gently.

"I don't want to. You hurt me . . ." She sobbed, seemingly prepared to accept.

Softly, "I'm not going to hurt you, I just want to make it right." He massaged her arms and shoulders, assessing the compliancy of her body.

She knew what would shortly happen but fear and pride compelled her to make another attempt to resist. She wiped her eyes with the back of her hand and vulcanized her body. "I'm telling you no! Let me out of here! I don't want to be with you!"

He narrowed his eyes to gleaming pinpoints trying to lock onto her thought process, squirming like a netted eel, then with lulling softness, he skewered it, "Don't raise your voice, you'll wake Jacob up. I don't want him traumatized by what would appear like quarrel . . ." An affirmation. The opportunity to confirm his commitment to her son—he was violating them both and passing it off as an involved and necessary medical check over.

The tears streamed in the heavy oxygen depleted air, as she floppily tried to push past him, as though over the last ten minutes she had starved to frailty. "Let me out of this room, don't touch me or I'll call Quentin . . ." A last-ditch, desperate attempt.

The grin scored across his face once more. "You just threatened me with Bungle Bear," he said deceitfully. He lowered his head over hers, looking directly into her eyes and said softly, "It's not a matter of what *you* want, not a matter of what the householder can do for *you*—it's what *you* can do for the householder, isn't it?"

She stood dumbfounded, staggering in the final round. She mustered her bantam body and threw a flaccid punch against the cruiser-weight, "I'll call him, I swear, or I'll call the police . . ."

The experience on the stair landing had brought him to the brink but he hadn't gone over the narrow line, which separated the human from the brute. But the human from the reptile . . .

"Okay, now I'll admit that Quentin *could*, how shall we say, cause me a degree of physical discomfort. I don't want to invoke that upon myself, by ruffling your lovely barley hair and the police *could* arrest me for grievous bodily harm, throw me in a cell etcetera if I were to do so, so instead I'll reiterate my point, bearing in mind that sticks and stones break bones but words won't hurt you, which is:

"That you had better get naked and on that bed right now, or you and that bastard boy of yours can get the fuck out of *my* house!"

Richard ended his reminiscing there and felt kind of oily in a sensual way; his skin tingled above the suntan and he felt as though endorphins had been released into his body, giving him a high. He took in some breaths of the musty, damp smell of the blackberry bush which mingled with the aroma of his own contributing and felt pleasure. He was so aroused and invigorated that he had to adjust the stiff, tumescent bulge in his Bermudas.

Aah, yes, Richard too had fangs like the spider, hidden in the soft, social flesh of his human form and he had used them only recently.

They were masters of their domain—the ancient predator was an utterly instinctive, simplified version of a dinosaur, lion or eagle—all masters of theirs. Reflexive, machine-like, obeying the most basic computer program within its brain, it was a nano killing engine. It was *the* essential killer, the *purest* killer, unfeeling, unthinking. There was no thought process involved in its hunting and that's what made it ruler of its microscopic world. Its supremacy in its habitat was due entirely to its simplicity, uncomplicated by emotion; its mind was one track. It didn't analyze, it just acted.

A small, rainbow coloured bird, its wings feverishly blurred, suddenly landed on one of the fatter branches reclined before the web (from behind which Richard observed, keeping a barrier between himself and the macabre events on the silken gridiron). It perched for split seconds, gave a trill, melodic chirp and twitched, plucking the drab green spider from the center of the web, and within the same breath, Richard saw it flicker and alight.

Richard was staggered. The rip in the web resembled a bullet hole in glass. He wondered why nature had fired it and why he and the spider were at the receiving end.

As he swung back in dismay at the ignominious way in which the master predator had been pecked to death, he brushed a branch, which was particularly well endowed with solid, cellulous thorns, and felt it nab him. He had brushed it in the wrong direction and as he pulled away, the section of the branch lashed onto his forearm, the thorns vanishing into his delicate skin. He winced in pain, screaming, "Aaah, fucking hell," and swung around, thrashing at the branches that were exacting a toll now for his brief incursion into their secret, shady world.

The blackberries, caterpillars, ants, ladybirds—and the spiders, fell about him like wriggling confetti. A bull in a hall of diaphanous mirrors, he tore the spider webs in his frenzied arm flailing, smashing the fulsome blackberries against his skin, the silk doilies resting on the thorns attaching wispily, and with the thorns, to his bare, splattered skin and hair, as his eyes bulged with fright, "Eeaaah, get the fuckers off me, eeaaagh!"

Thoroughly tarred and feathered, he collected himself just enough to realize what he needed to do. Shuddering, he began desperately to fiddle with the branch snagged to his arm and managed to release it, perhaps giving up a little more flesh to its fierce prickles than he would have liked. Thrashing and slapping himself wildly, he collapsed to the ground and rolled on the grass as though he were ablaze, for a full two minutes. He got up sweating and heaving, his skin strangely ruffled, part blanched with fear, part reddened by the exertion and his earlier sun tanning.

"Fuck! Shit!" he got back onto the ground and rolled some more, appearing to the winged observers on the roof guttering above the house as though he *had* finally got around to doing the lawn, perhaps in a more unconventional way—a self-propelled lawn mowing gizmo, traversing the disheveled grassy escarpment below.

Richard suddenly lost his only recently acquired interest in etymology and dismissed the arachnids as a glorified trapeze act for his feathered friends.

He had to admit, he had bared his teeth recently with Trudy but then revised the analogy. Not so much the grotesquely hairy, oversize mandibles of a spider, more perhaps the slick, razor fangs of the cobra. With a contrived smug easiness, he padded back to the vacant terraced house.

Chapter 32

Trudy and Jacob did not return that night. Nor the next, nor the next. In fact, it was four days since Trudy had supposedly left the house to collect Jacob.

Four long days and three long nights without sex.

Richard was livid that Trudy should deny him what was his right to have, as a married man. He vowed he would get triple his fill when she returned from her parents'. He'd phoned them countless times over the last few days but the liars flatly denied that Trudy and Jacob were with them. Clearly, they were trying to protect and hide their daughter and grandson. It was probable that she had hinted to them about what had happened between her and Richard a few nights before, when he had insisted on his rights (as he liked to think of it). The kid was Trudy's excuse to be away and Richard swore he would get a good kicking when he returned, whether or not the Sword of Damocles named Quentin hung over his head. Having a baby face was no waiver for Jacob when it came to disloyalty. Richard's guiding hand would be called into play.

Triple the sex, triple the hiding.

But again, that night, Richard seethed alone in the double bed.

Four nights ungratified. *Quadruple the sex and quadruple the hiding*, he promised.

The next morning, Richard awoke feeling quite rough, having spent the night cursing under the duvet his "beloved" and her wretched son. He had exorcised his lust by the improper method but was still as highly strung as a Sampras tennis racket.

He considered paying Trudy's folks a visit, to forcibly collect the renegades, but then abandoned the idea remembering how Trudy's father, despite his advanced years, could still wield a cricket bat as staunchly as he could in his younger days. The whole marriage was turning shitty, or more accurately, shittier and he knew that Trudy's parents would protect her by any method. Even violent ones, if need be.

No, visiting them was out of the question.

Well, at least he still had his tins of *amber nectar* as a consolation, even though it had been a bit of a pain in the arse to have to go to the off-license to replenish them a couple days before. That and the journeys for takeaways. He could hold out, as long as the beers were forthcoming and so long as he had a right hand with which to pleasure himself.

The sun was still beating down furiously and Richard, still feeling his skin prickle from the mild roasting it had received a few days earlier, decided he would mope and fume, fume and mope in the shade and cool of the house, mostly reclined on the sofa watching porn and metal music videos from his extensive collections of both.

It didn't really take his mind off the issue though.

He was halfway through 'Fifi and Helmut, *full-on*', when an impertinent interruption from his vicinity forced him up from his relaxed posture on the settee.

Blaring from a hi-fi nearby, like an eruption of wild celebration in a shantytown after the downfall of a ruthless dictatorship, was the most rude, filthy, uncensored vitriol that Richard had ever had the displeasure of hearing. It was heavy-rock music.

He ventured over, through the kitchen and stood at the door, trying not to be conspicuous, as he pried.

It was all well and good when *he* played it. He was one of the *elite*, chosen to play it. But it didn't sound half as good coming from a decrepit neighbour's sound system. Who, what could it be, that this noise was being pumped out so unashamedly? Fair play, Richard listened to the stuff often, when he was out in his "garden", but only at half the volume (considerate soul that he was). What would the neighbours think? What the heck, it was a neighbour pushing out this sonic battering ram right now! Who was this audacious individual, this rebel, who would risk incurring the wrath of a largely aged community, to satisfy his or her depraved, mutant musical taste?

At first, Richard assumed it was from one of the gardens in the terrace beyond Emlyn and Juliet's, but, in fact, it seemed, as he listened, to be actually coming from *theirs*. Richard peered intently, standing at his garden/kitchen door, over their wall, trying to fathom the meaning of what was occurring.

It was Emlyn no less! He walked over to the silver and black sound machine on his patio and twiddled a knob. His portable CD bellowed out sonic waves from a plethora of the heaviest metal music bands. The sonic assault was not really music to Richard's ears, as a passive observer might have expected. Far from being impressed, Richard felt resentful. Who was Emlyn, wimpy, prudish Emlyn, to be gracing his CD player with the music of the specially selected, those with that special mentality who could fly the flag of rock music, the fearless, chosen ones?

The ear splitting sound, ripping through the air, shattered the summer stillness like a fat drunkard belching vomit over the bust of a pristine nun, *in a nunnery*!

On seeing Richard, Emlyn strutted (strutted?) over to the super woofer and cranked up the volume—it seemed to the maximum. Kieran couldn't fathom the meaning of this gesture. For one thing it precluded any possibility of their having a conversation, but also Emlyn seemed to be conducting himself in an altogether different manner to that displayed on previous occasions, when they had the pleasure (at least it was that for Richard) of meeting, as it happened, always, just after Emlyn had had some form of beating off his fiancée. This time round Emlyn completely blanked out, ignored Richard.

And what of his fiancée? How was it that Emlyn was being allowed to do what he was doing without reprimand?

Richard felt quite indignant. He was unsettled and shocked by this behaviour—this just wasn't the behaviour of an Emlyn, it wasn't in his character profile. Richard was startled and upset, especially in the light of what recently had happened with his fair Trudy. He knew people so well; there were personality types that were unbreakable, there were guaranteed traits in a person's character and he never assumed Trudy was one that would have the balls, so to speak, to get up and go, to leave him for as long as she had, rather than give

288

him his nighttime pleasure. Now it seemed that Emlyn too was contradicting the character breakdown Richard had knocked up for him. This was just too much. This was incomprehensible. It was unacceptable.

The music blared for at least a solid half hour as a disturbed Richard peered from behind the kitchen/garden doorway, hoping for the arrival of a club-wielding Yeti, called Juliet. He thought about complaining but then acceded, reminding himself that even as he kept in line those in his domestic setting, he rarely asserted himself with those outside. Being assertive could be misconstrued as being arrogant and he feared reprimand even from someone he had diminished to insignificance, namely Emlyn.

Juliet must be out, she must be at her aerobics class or down at the pub—goodness knows she liked her beer as much as Richard liked his—which is why she did aerobics. Or perhaps she was window shopping, deciding which presies Emlyn Claus would be getting her for the next of the many personal Christmases she had instigated for herself throughout the year. No, that's ridiculous, you're unsettled, disoriented. That's just too fantastical. She's around. She was always around to chastise Emlyn. She'll have you, boy. He suddenly whip-lashed his despondency into vicious hope, a toothy grin shining out like a malicious beacon within the garden doorway. He watched and waited.

Then he noticed a difference in Emlyn's demeanor, from appearing almost arrogant, to one of deference, of almost coming down to kneel in reverence to a hidden goddess alighting from the heavens or a harpy ascending from Hell!

"You wait, she'll have you soon enough. You're dead meat, boy. She's going to batter you now," Richard thought gleefully.

He carefully edged his way into the shed and stood where the lawnmower had been positioned for days on end, like a beckoning lady of the night at a street corner. Kieran delicately walked into the junk disposal room and stood framed within the doorway, with a clear view of what was happening next door but ready if necessary to vanish inside the shed out of view from the outside world, if noticed by the new arrival.

Then, wafting into view, seeming to shimmer in the summer heat, appeared TRUDY!!!

Emlyn was seated on a deckchair by the radio/CD player. He stood and moved toward Trudy as she walked toward him. They were smiling warmly at each other with a familiarity which beguiled Richard, sneakily observing from the shed doorway in his garden.

The two made physical contact on the patio and EMBRACED!!!

Richard's mind raced and feverishly conjectured over this, as he saw it, abominable vision. For brief moments he was silently furious, outraged.

Then it all made sense.

He knew that sometimes opposites attract but really, were Emlyn and Trudy all that different from each other? Perhaps when Emlyn had recently moved in, it had been love at first sight. Who could say?

The tapestry was coming together now. Not a simple jigsaw but a tapestry. Something artful and elaborate coming to fruition. He bitterly reminded himself that even though Juliet cohabited, it was Emlyn who was the owner of the property. It brought to mind the fateful night, days before, when Richard had confronted Trudy in the bedroom and had given her the ultimatum.

He drew the can of lager to his lips, standing forlornly in the doorway of the shed. The can was empty.

Looking despairingly into the adjacent garden from his secret vantage point, he now saw Jacob run out and embrace the two, still hugging, around their legs, an expression of joy on his face which Richard was unfamiliar with. Then Jacob's face turned toward Richard, slouched in the scruffy shed doorway. Both stared knowingly at each other.

Richard pulled away from the psychological duel first. "The little bastard winked at me," he mused.

He'd seen it all.

What he had witnessed, combined with the sneering, jeering metal music, still obliterating the oppressive summer air, was causing Richard's knees to weaken and his posture to hunch miserably.

He'd seen enough.

Resigned to the fact that he would have to find another concubine on which to satisfy his masculine penchant—not an easy task when you looked like Richard and was as randy as he was—he raggedly wandered into the shed, away from the persecutory gaze of Jacob, lest he might alert the lovebirds on the patio of his presence in the shed.

Richard crouched down amongst the debris and sat, condemned to the unwanted scrap heap of life, despairingly pondering his future life without the creature comforts Trudy had provided. For that matter, who would now do the cleaning and shopping and ironing?

Amongst the junk, propped lopsidedly against the wall was a dusty old mirror. Richard rested his worried stare on its reflection—the plump, slouching, potato-faced specimen that was himself. Still that blasted cacophony prevailed. He didn't find solace in what he saw. The image humbled him somewhat and with this he felt a forced affinity with his spiritual nature, a side of himself which he had almost forgotten about, as self-assured as he had always been. He didn't like this occurrence in the slightest.

The more he stared the more he felt uncomfortable and yet mesmerized. At some point during this visually hypnotic experience, almost imperceptibly to his eyes, the mirror enlarged in his peripheral vision, so that it almost seemed to resemble a doorway.

In place of the disheveled looking Richard, who had been positioned in the centre of the reflective pane, stood a pinstripe suited man, wearing a bowler hat. This transition from the slob to the executive puzzled Richard. The besuited individual standing upright in the mirror seemed very much out of place amongst all the rubbish of the shed, swimming in the flood of thrash metal, still bellowing from Emlyn's woofer next door.

Richard wondered if this fellow in the mirror was his alter-ego. He was slim, tall and quite handsome. Richard liked to think that it was himself. The mirror seemed to edge its way towards him and soon he was practically on the "doorstep".

The man in the doorway reached out to Richard and took his hand, at the same time gesturing to him to come within with his other hand. Richard felt no fear or surprise but he felt compelled to follow this dashing individual inside. He got up and left behind the shambles of his life, hopefully to follow in the footsteps of this bourgeois stranger, leading him through the portal, apparently to a better place.

Chapter 33

Kieran resurfaced once again but his focus wasn't clear as to who, this time, if indeed there was someone else, was sitting next to him. It may well have been Terry Lee still bashing on about his kung fu.

Kieran wasn't sure. He didn't know and didn't care at this point, as he wrestled with the drug inebriating his hallucinating brain. Though seated (more like teetering on his chair, swaying and yawing), he tried to find balance, gripping the edge of the table above his knees with all his strength, trying to resist the whirlpool effect of that enigmatic and attention commanding timepiece, vying for his soul yet again. With all his diminished strength he fought against the soul devouring device, wanting to educate him with the knowledge of yet another unscrupulous individual's "Godforsaken" life. Kieran couldn't fathom why this information was being imparted by the chronograph, stationed on the wall before him and to where the subjects of these documentaries were destined to end up.

Kieran turned his head from the mysterious, enchanting device, so that his face was facing in the opposite direction. He didn't care as to how his exaggerated and antisocial manner might appear to those, whoever they might be, around him, just so long as he wasn't sucked again into that confounded creation, which he was sure wasn't the making of earthly hands.

Nevertheless, though he tried desperately to discern, to decipher, the meaning of the mumbling coming from someone next to him, in order to regain his faculties, he found that his neck muscles numbed, as the strength to control his head dissipated, so that his unwilling face, desperate eyes, once again turned to the demon or angel spawned (he wasn't sure which) contraption on the wall nearby, to again witness the story of a doomed stranger's life, on the earthly, or otherwise, plane of existence . . .

Chapter 34

The dinosaur, a particularly fearsome one, with deep, red-centered, glistening eyes, burned with rage.

He hustled awkwardly under the heavy metallic cage restraints, the bars equally spaced, pressing down but leaving no impression on its hard, green-blue scaled back. The bony spikes along it, poking above the steely latticework, stretched in a line from its head (which was very little other than a massive dagger toothed pair of jaws), to its tail, only the tip of which was free to swoop back and forth, slapping the polished steel floor wildly, lashing the air like a whip.

The floor beneath the dinosaur was molded so that it more effectively contained the prehistoric predator, making it seem as though its belly was part submerged in liquid metal. It was in fact the hardest crystalline substance that the technologists in this sector of Satan's Hell could come up with, being that it was probably the hardest known substance in the universe—Satan prided himself in his advanced scientific discoveries (for torturing purposes), and his technologists were damn good.

The dinosaur's muscles contracted suddenly, as it released another gust of aggression, jarring the steel cage over its back so violently that it quivered and thrummed. Its tail end went blurry-fast and its strikingly small upper arms (in comparison to its oversize haunches), with its hook-nails clawed, sliding over the semi-reflective flooring.

Further bursts of brute force only caused the cage above it to ping and creak. The dinosaur's eyeballs all the while writhed in their sockets like gyroscopes of a plane in freefall, trying to compensate for the lack of permitted movement in the rest of its mountainous body.

An android—a human-shaped robot—stood over the virtually immobile head of the trapped beast, and looked down disdainfully. It kicked the saur in the mouth, its glassy foot clinking as it bounced off one of the whiter than white, foot-high teeth in the creature's lower jaw. It looked into the aperture at the top of the monster's skull. It went deep and ended where its walnut brain was positioned, in the epicenter of the cranium that contained the most basic, wild and vicious thoughts of the angriest creature that ever existed.

The aperture looked like a spaceship-docking bay, miniaturized, a peculiar feature on such an ancient creature to one not appreciating the whole scene, which juxtaposed life forms and technologies millions of years apart.

The only tools possessed by the dinosaur, the most basic conceivable, were its exaggerated teeth and claws, as though the fact that they were so very simple was compensated for by their magnified size.

The robot, on the other hand, had a number of complex devices. Its "tools", more a veritable menagerie of whirring and clicking, mechanical, insect-like creations, were being brought toward it on a trolley, pushed by a humming drone over the immaculate polished floor.

Each of the components, about half a meter in length, were neatly arranged over the trolley's surface, in readiness of the robot's unblinking attention (its eye sockets were lidless, filled with a bluish white glow), that he gave them, turning from his gargantuan captive. He fumbled with his lower lip (pointlessly perhaps because his mouth was a totally inflexible inmoulded orifice). Simultaneously with the other hand he did an eeny-meenie over the technology on offer, with the wag of a finger.

The android was one of the types vigorously multiplying elsewhere in the galaxy of, and those surrounding, Earth. This particular version was a task-specific android, even though it resembled many of its race outside of Hell. It had been custom "birthed" in an industrial factory in some sector of TechnoHell as Satan described it, the Silicon Valley of the Underworld.

The homiform robots (remember Satan's attraction to the human species), that were turned off its production lines were suitably complex a mechanism for the soul (which very possibly inhabited a complex biological body as a previous incarnation) to utilize for its further journeys in material existence.

The robots were stockpiled in their millions, in Satan's factories awaiting the wispy, evil souls, like acrid farts, also in the millions, to circulate, choose, and harness one for its further material experiences. Whereupon, the robot within the stockpile would suddenly animate, whereupon, it would be immediately seized by Satan's factory police to be taken away for baptismal torturing.

The robots were a relatively new development everywhere, including Hell, but they were keenly seized by the souls of Hell's recently departed. Because the new robots were sophisticated mechanisms. Very sophisticated. They would be a great vehicle for the greedy soul to experience material delights, new sensory pleasures.

Or so they thought.

The materialistic souls, having forgotten their suffering in their previous corporeal existence in Hell, transmigrated into the new, lifeless mechanism. But they should really have left Hell, should've left the material sphere which was a fool's gold for the free soul, and the cause of its suffering.

Some souls never learn. Unfortunately for these souls, now bound for a lifetime to the android frame (and that was a very long one for the robot shell of super-strong alloy), they would experience not one ounce of pleasure. Their exquisitely developed nervous systems had been designed by Hell's techno wizards, under Satan's precise orders, to experience only ultimate pains.

The robot would throughout the course of its life experience the pains of the likes of sciatica, trapped nerves and sensitive teeth, but multiplied a hundredfold, numbing its brain to any possibilities of pleasurable experiences—and there weren't any to be had in Hell anyway.

So the robots were chastised from within and without.

Born into Hell, these robots and androids struggled just like any other life form, but despite all their suffering, many had been assigned functions and tasks.

The one attending the restrained dinosaur was experiencing torment—he had, as part of the architecture of his own brain, an integral module purposely designed to allow the robust, long-lived android to be perpetually awash with agony. But it did not impede his performance as one of the Devil's Brain Enhancement Technicians.

With a crystalline click, his fingers landed on the Brain Enhancement Unit of Noctonomicus the Cyborg's design (which too had pain inflictor capability), resting on the steel trolley before it.

He turned his head back to the dinosaur with a whir and a soft clack.

The monster was still straining against his harness, eyes spinning madly, clenched teeth bared and its tale lashing furiously.

"Well, here goes, my friend, you're about to undergo a million years' evolution in an instant—and experience a million times more pain than you ever have," the android said sardonically.

The dinosaur's eyes stopped rolling for a moment, unaware of what the artificial life form had said, but brought to attention by the unexpected monotone whine of its voice.

The robot tapped along the floor with dainty steps and again pivoted over the bulk of the dinosaur's skull, slabbed in layers of jaw muscle, gleaming fangs juggling from its giant crocodilian cake-hole.

The crystal android carefully lowered the substantial, light spotted unit, which looked like a cross between a huge TV remote and a metallic-black cockroach, into the slot, without touching the mouth of the aperture. It slid in smoothly and clipped into place when the black, anodized tip of the unit came flush with the stretched hide of scales over the dinosaur's head.

It snarled in rage, "YOU FUCKING BASTARD! I'LL TEAR YOU TO PIECES, YOU SON OF A BITCH!" The dinosaur's newly acquired powers of speech were in evidence, as his brain was instantly enhanced from that with an IQ of seven, to one of a hundred seventy. So too was his sensitivity to pain—now focused as a scorching finger poke at the base of its brain, causing a splintering headache, right off the scale.

A further volley of insults was followed by an eardrum-searing yowl.

The sound effects didn't overly trouble the humanoid droid whose ears he had hitherto calibrated for such an occurrence. The android knew what to expect—he had applied many such brain/pain enhancement units to dinosaurs in recent times. The android stood back and processed the sound and visual information from the nerve-racked prehistoric creature, even so, still extremely dangerous.

"There, there, my scaly friend," said the android, gleaming in the laboratory's clinical white strip lighting. "How must it feel?" he asked rhetorically, almost to himself.

"OwwwwOwwwwOwwwwOwwww, my head hurts, jumping Jehoshaphat it hurts!" It was clear that along with the advanced intellect, the dinosaur's brain had also been augmented with knowledge of the Christian religion for the purpose of denigrating it, via such profanities.

"Take it easy!" said the sparkling android, its electromechanical entrails and pneumatic limbs seeming to be suspended in the purest, coldest ice. "You're going up in the world! Now you can do sums, have a dress sense, appreciate music and lie. Lucky you!"

The dinosaur, struggling in its cage, roared, the blast of air skimming off the glassy streamlined form of the android as though it were a man-shaped car, undergoing testing in a wind tunnel. The robot processed the contents of a sample of this air it had taken while within the brief gale. A human would liken the smell to that of a well-stocked butcher's shop, but the sophisticated android could more precisely examine the air's chemical contents with a minute chemical identification apparatus in its nifty artificial brain.

But finally it said, "We'll have to do something about that halitosis," with an electronic dryness.

The dinosaur's eyes narrowed to red slits, red gums showing above its bayonet dentition.

From the belt around its waist, the robot unclipped a complex looking remote control, the size of a videocassette. It pressed a combination of the buttons, and a droid like an enlarged child's toy tank, with an upper section that was a mechanical version of a human torso (or at least, a *humanoid* one), head and arms, appeared. It trundled around the restrained dinosaur and sprayed eucalyptus scent from an aerosol, while the dinosaur yowled some more.

If only Satan knew of the crystal android's attempts at making the habitat a more accommodating one with this perfume! He'd come down on the mandroid like a ton of fiery, soul-imprisoning bricks.

Another robot was called upon via the remote control—it approached looking like a pageboy, seemingly made of aluminium spanners of mixed size. Precise clicks about his body were audible within the precise steps of his walk. Before him he held a gold-tassled, red, velvet pillow, on which rested a silver tray. In it was a collection of fluffy balls, each about the size of a peanut. The pagedroid, with biddy steps traversed the area about the decked dinosaur. The robots the page approached looked upon this silver dish reverently, at the intriguing objects thereupon. For moments they analyzed the plate the small robotic fellow held before them. Then each respectfully picked up one of the fibrous, perfectly spherical balls, and looked it over with their analytical, photoelectric eyes—they raised them to their heads (if they had heads). What were these remarkable and mysterious objects?

Earplugs.

They placed the earplugs in their ear holes.

Their auditory sensors (ear holes), suitably protected from the sound battery (which was the restrained dinosaur), they went about their duties, uninterrupted within the vicinity.

The droids who hadn't calibrated their hearing, who didn't have a head (and therefore had no ears in which to apply earplugs) in the way that the Brain Enhancement Technician had, loaded into their onboard computer banks the advanced software which had the same effect as the cotton wool plugs, rendering their auditory apparatus impervious to the dinosaur's sonic assault.

They tended the various hi-tech artifacts in their midst, as the dinosaur roared out mini cyclones of sound. Within the percolated atmosphere of the laboratory dedicated to brain enhancement, there was a split screen, about the size of a squash court, onto which stared a huddle of droids, carrying laptops. They would every now and again turn from the screen and input data relating to its images into their computers. They seemed completely engrossed in their activity.

On that screen were camera views of two new arrivals at this technology steeped sector of Hell.

The glassy android, which had bestowed with the same hand upon the wretched dinosaur intellect and appalling pain, looked to the split screen with extreme enthusiasm. It seemed he had two new arrivals, two new candidates for his brain enhancement expertise to be unleashed upon.

He announced with a temporary glee (though there was no audible intonation in his voice) to the agonized and uncaring dinosaur, "It seems we have two newcomers in our midst!" He read the subtitles on the screen, "One Divinity Callisto and one Richard Pritchard. Well, Well."

The crystalline robot analyzed the two, naked and looking petrified, shoved and prodded forward by their mechanical captors, swarming threateningly around them. The twosome were unaware of their being under surveillance. The observing android wondered whether, going by their superficial appearances, they needed brain-power enhancement. After all, Satan often liked to see those in Hell do each other over in artful, sophisticated ways, rather than as cartoon-like slapstick. Evil expressed through intellect.

But apparently neither needed such enhancement. Both were human life forms which the android knew were already well endowed with reason. The one named Divinity, who in a previous existence had been a man-killing Aphrodite, had transmigrated into a more humble, dowdy, bodily vehicle. She was short and fat and haggard. She only needed a cauldron or broomstick for the witchly transformation to be complete.

However, as ugly as she was, she seemed the ideal partner for Richard, the hitherto indolent sex-maniac and psychological manipulator, who had ventured into Hell of his own accord, tempted through the cross-dimensional door by a deceitfully dapper looking recruitment-stooge of Satan.

Richard's appearance was unchanged, like an elongated sack of spuds just as he had been back in Surrey, England, Earth.

The transparent android, had he had flexible lips, would have smiled at the *Antony* and *Cleopatra* of Hell with the sadistic proclivities, whose brains he would shortly scrutinize.

They were certainly intellectually bright enough already, but he savoured the prospect of sensitizing their pain receptors a thousandfold. He already had in mind the pain enhancement equipment he would trouble them both with. For but brief moments he was distracted by the prospect of immersing the two into a world of pain, no sooner than he himself felt the grasp of suffering from the inbuilt agony module in his diamond-like skull.

Chapter 35

Kieran had become a chain coffee drinker despite being quite aware of its mind-altering attribute. Something had compelled him to drink, drink, drink! He wasn't sure whether it was something from within his deeper being or the clock. Maybe both. But no more replenishments were forthcoming for as long ago as six hours (not that he was aware of the duration of events he had been experiencing).

His jaw dropped as his eyes boggled under furrowed brows. He stared at the couple of empty Styrofoam cups on the table. A shiver rippled out from his spinal column, becoming a sharp coldness evenly coating his back, spreading through his whole body.

He continued to bear down over the innocuous looking cups. A couple of droplets of sweat impacted on the wood effect vinyl, a Boolean addition taking place before his eyes as they got sucked up into the spilled pool of "coffee", and blended into it.

He hadn't noticed anything in the taste—nothing untoward, apart perhaps from a slight bitterness. They were after all from an office vending machine. But he knew despite being virtually catatonic, that they had been spiked.

He put both hands on the edge of the table, holding firm, trying to steady his reeling thoughts, and raised his eyes to *them*.

They were all there now, all eleven members of staff, washed colourless in the harsh strip lighting. Kieran stared at the plastic mannequins, seesawing in the unearthly light.

He had a sense of foreboding danger. Maybe, despite his shaking, this free fall was the time of merciful ignorance. Maybe the swirling room was a blindfold. To regain his mind would be its removal, whereupon he would be transported again, sober within his altered perception, in the midst of yet another story from a ruined life. He could not tell whether they were someone else's, his former existences, or lives to come.

Now he didn't want everything to make grim sense, didn't want a new, seemingly Godforsaken world to be revealed to him in glorious Technicolor.

But deep within he knew why Alice had left him, and had to see her again. But he never would if he didn't get his butt into gear. He might just be a lamb for the slaughter—he didn't know exactly what was coming next on this perilous path.

Kieran took the devil by the horns. Gripping the table harder, he tried with all his will to stop the room yawing. Rivulets poured from all over his skin, the sweat matting his hair and clothing to his bloodless body. He wobbled uncertainly. His glazed eyes flickered like a drunkards, as he struggled to get control.

They weren't slouching anymore. They were sitting forward looking at him anxiously, hoping for his emergence from the eclipse.

Gradually he did so, piecing himself together like a cadaver refitting its dissected organs. He brought his hyperventilation under control. His vision clarified. The room stopped lurching.

He looked at each in turn—all of them were solemnly clay faced, as though the vivacity they had on loan had been taken back, having extolled their yarns. Forlorn and lost now, they seemed reclaimed by a harsh master.

All of them except for Gabriella, standing close to him, bearing that enigmatic, enduring smile that comforted them all throughout what had become a *very long day*.

But what sort of landscape lay around, away from her shelter, in the nuclear winter?

Gabriella's soft voice ended the dead silence. "Do you have any questions, Kieran?"

Kieran gaped at her but didn't reply, still somewhat groggy.

She said, "Soon you'll meet the director, Maureen. That's Ms. Lock's *Christian* name . . ."

The other ten exchanged glances with penitent eyes, resigned to the contrary fact.

Gabriella corrected herself. "Uh, well, her *first* name. But we're not allowed to address her by that."

Kieran's sudden realization:

"Mau, Mau, Mo . . . Maureeeen . . . Mm, Maureeeen . . . Loch . . . Mm, Mo . . . L, Lock . . ." His lips were numb as though he had spent all the day in a freezer chest. The hairs prickled like icy filaments on the back of his neck, his body flash-froze. His heart thumped like a galloping nightmare.

He looked to the monitor on the table before him, at the puzzle that earlier buzzed in his head, like an unswattable fly. The secret image spewed slowly from the back of his mind, where it had always lurked, from the moment he had set eyes on that damned pixilated enigma. It materialized surreptitiously, a black plague in a medieval citadel, stunning him so that he emitted a measure of urine into his pants as he released a long gasp of horror. Now it filled the screen, as though the monitor's electric innards had vomited.

It filled his wide, terrified eyes too.

Gabriella interjected solemnly. "You've sussed the screen saver secret. It's actually a portrait of Ms. Lock, revealing her in her preferred exterior manifestation—as the Devil."

She continued her grave revelation. "The regulars here have known it for a long time, but it was completely indecipherable to newcomers. That is until I recently received e-mail carrying the CHERUB virus. It's affected the network in all sorts of odd ways (and the screensaver, to some who are more spiritually attuned, is now understandable). Ms. Lock can't get rid of the malware."

Kieran was more than satisfied that he was beholding a snapshot of the incarnation of evil. The hideous, horned, red grinning head on the screen was so vivid, it seemed to rise off its surface like a diabolic hologram.

He knew it to be the personification of pure wickedness, known by many names: Satan, Lucifer, Mammon, Beelzebub.

Kieran, from the outset, had had intuitive suspicions about the director of Candlelight Ltd. and now revealed to him was the unholy fact of Maureen Lock's, Mo Lock's, *Moloch's* true identity.

He cast his mind back to John Milton's *Paradise Lost*, remembering that Moloch was one of Satan's angels. A pun if ever there was one but somewhat downsizing the King of Evil that Ms. Lock certainly was. A witty moniker nevertheless, thought Kieran wryly.

So the Devil was a cross-dresser.

Gabriella looked serious. "Though I shouldn't say it (but is it so surprising), Ms. Lock's *so* vain. She insists that all her staff have the screensaver installed on their monitors to remind them who owns them." She added sarcastically, "In an employment sense, that is."

The faces of the seated, many tearful, now that their wretched existence had been revealed, were lit up with the unnatural glow from the monitors, though they chose not to look upon the twisted, saber-fanged face of the one that had imprisoned them in limbo.

Kieran groaned, then mustered his brain for speech. "Uh, why didn't you just explain my situation straightforwardly . . . uh, when I first arrived?"

Gabriella said, "You wouldn't have believed it. Would've been suspicious. Might've contacted Ms. Lock directly, by post or e-mail afterwards. She'd dispose of me, and have someone else introduce you 'properly', have you signed up at Candlelight Ltd., for *The Company*.

"I've been assigned the task by Ms. Lock of recruiting you for Candlelight Ltd. but it was always my intention to clue you up as to what you were really getting into—a one way trip to Hell. I'm on your side, Kieran; I would never let that happen to you!

"It was better to let the ugly truth speak for itself, enhancing your perception with the hallucinogenic *coffee*.

"No offence." No blink or frown indicated guilt.

Kieran was still wrestling to regain his faculties but managed to question, "And, uh, what about that unearthly clock, who or what in hell's name created it? How, uh, why, was I swallowed into its alternative worlds?"

Gabriella answered. "You said it, Kieran. It was manufactured in Ms. Lock's, Beelzebub's, domain—*The Company*, or Hell, by a team of her (or should I say his), most eminent inventors. Having been spawned in Hell it is imbued with supernatural power.

"Ms. Lock and her team of diabolical scientists had envisaged that the clock would actually tempt interviewees, including you, to irrevocably join Candlelight Ltd. and *The Company*, by deceiving your mind with glorious scenarios depicting you at Candlelight Ltd. and then *The Company*, described as a graphic designer's paradise.

"The drug I introduced into your coffee countered the despicable bias of the clock, which would have revealed to you only lies about your prospects and about Candlelight Ltd."

The mobile phone in its holster at Gabriella's side pealed, fracturing the air like glass.

She gathered it from the holder and after a moment's deliberation, lifted it to her ear. "Gabriella Seymour, Candlelight Ltd . . . Hello, Ms. Lock, yes, he's still here. Of course, I did it in exactly the way you wanted . . . Oh yes, he is an eager beaver . . . You thought about putting him on The Float? I see . . . No, it's more a falsetto . . . You've changed your mind . . . I see . . . as your PA to perform favours, yes . . . I don't doubt your prowess, Ms. Lock, but he might not meet your standard . . . Sorry, Ms. Lock . . . but there's no need for haste, Ms. Lock—I thought a little more butter for good measure . . . Sorry, Ms. Lock . . . Good-bye, Ms Lock."

Gabriella returned the phone and looked at Kieran gravely. "That was Ms. Lock. She's on her way up to meet you, Kieran. Wants to make your employment official at Candlelight Ltd. and then set you up at your new office. That's not here at Candlelight Ltd. by the way, but over at *The Company*, our proprietor, *Hell*!"

"Now you know all about Candlelight Ltd., Kieran. Will you stay or leave?"

He had gazed upon the face of evil incarnate in two dimensions—now he would have the opportunity to shake hands with the *real deal*, in three.

The question consolidated his body and mind. Kieran's response, unsurprisingly, was emphatic— "I'M GETTING THE FUCK OUT OF HERE!"

Kieran looked at the clock. He didn't need to, to realize the imminent danger he was in. It still told 11:45.

Folklore has it after midnight is the witching hour.

It figured that Ms. Lock would arrive at the office roundabouts twelve.

Kieran checked, Gabriella confirmed, and then suddenly the clock's second hand was sweeping with deadly new life.

But there was time enough to vacate the building.

312

Sweat dribbled from his forehead, down his cheeks. Some into his mouth. It tasted salty. "I suppose *Mo Lock* will arrive looking less than the paragon female, but I don't suppose quite as bad as that screensaver," he said bitterly, struggling to rise to his feet.

"No, not as rough as that. She'll make up her face a little. But a paragon? That depends on what your idea of one is."

"Anyway, I don't want to be here to find out."

"I knew you'd come around, Kieran," Gabriella said, with that smile again.

"And you? Surely you're coming too?" Kieran asked.

She walked briskly to the door of the meeting room. "Obviously. You didn't think I wanted to spend the night with Ms. Lock, did you? But I wouldn't have left you if you decided to stay. Just would've used more forcible methods to eject you from the premises, *even though you'd only end up coming back*." She grinned and held open the door.

"Me, come back here? Fat chance! Let's get out!" he blurted to her.

He staggered to the door and was almost the first through. Then he realized that the bards behind him, as quiet as mute mice, hadn't made the slightest movement from their chairs.

"What the fuck are you waiting for! The Devil's coming and he, uh, she's going to eat you up for a midnight snack! Come on, get out!"

They didn't move a muscle.

Fred Philadante said somberly, "No-can-do, bro. We're all of us here doin' time for our sins. She can . . . hurt us bad."

Kieran shouted "Sure he, dammit, *she*, will—if you stay! Well, I'm not leaving this place until you do! Come on!"

Saying nothing, Fred turned his head and brought a hand up to his bleached mopatop. He began tousling and pushed his fingers in towards the surface of his scalp. The hair crickled as he did this, the rigid layers of hairspray resisting his effort.

Kieran wondered what he was up to.

Precious time was passing.

Fred had forced up a tuft of the yellow-white growth, looking like weird tumbleweed rolling off the side of his head. He kneaded his temple to remove the remaining flax-like strands.

Kieran had had a full day of crazy occurrences, but this was up there with them.

Fred was holding the wadge of hair away from a silvery rectangular patch, poking slightly above the skin of his head. It had what appeared to be two garish Christmas tree lights within its surface, glowing spookily.

Kieran asked in terror, "Fred, what's that thing embedded in your skullcap!"

Fred, his head still turned sideways towards Kieran, revealing the sunk-in object, said morosely, "It's a brain implant, Kieran."

He turned, looking haggard, and stared at Kieran through his inappropriately funky, scarlet-rimmed spectacles. "We've all got them, 'cept Gabby—she's here on trust, the purdy infiltrator she is.

"Ms. Lock's—*Moloch's* techno wizards put them there to control us. We each had them installed soon after we started with Candlelight Ltd. She took us

314

down into the bowels of Hell, and became a *he*. You could say we went for a walk on the *wild side*. Life ain't ever been the same since.

"Heck, the jobs well paid—ain't no denying that. But money ain't everythin'." For some reason he said this as though he were a wiser man for the experience.

Kieran was gobsmacked.

Terry Lee added to the macabre revelation. "We repackage Hell as though it's a holiday resort. We're the Devil's spin doctors, Kieran. We can't help but be. These implants permit a telepathic link with the Underworld—with Satan's administration. They control us that way. The device destroys our will to resist like a poisonous mushroom. They torture us through it." He passed the parcel to Geeta Patel.

With tears in her eyes, she continued where Terry had left off. "The Devil works us like dogs"—sob—"often into the early hours of the morning. We hardly ever get to see our loved ones"—sob—"but none of us here can leave because if we do, the Devil's detectives will find us and destroy our brains," sob.

She said with finality, "You two go alone. We'll stay here to face the wrath of Ms. Lock."

Kieran was pulling at his hair with both hands. He looked at his newfound cybernetic chums, to the clock, back to them, to the clock.

It told 11:53.

He whimpered something incongruous.

Gabriella, like the arrival of the UN force. "Come on, guys. It's okay. You save Kieran's soul, and you go scot-free. You'll have paid for your sins. The brain link from the Underworld will be broken. Your perdition is over."

"How do you know that"—sob, asked Geeta.

"You followed my instructions today, against Ms. Lock's brief. Haven't you noticed that the implant reception has already become weaker?"

They had to agree that it had.

"Right. We all leave here now, together, and you'll have earned your freedom. You'll be beyond Ms. Lock's jurisdiction. Let's go!"

They looked to one another. Nobody could argue otherwise. Won over, they hastily got to their feet.

"Man," said Fred, "I'd just love to see Ms. Lock's goofy face when she realizes we've done a runner."

"If you don't hurry up, you will, and it'll be her Hell version," said Gabriella.

"C'mon, c'mon, go, go, go!" Kieran jabbered, standing sprightlier on his feet.

It was 11:55.

They scurried through the meeting room door in single file.

Gabriella still held it ajar, waiting for Kieran to walk through.

"Ladies first," he said, taking the door from behind her back.

"Very gallant," she said, and followed the line into the main office.

Kieran stood at the doorway of the meeting room and fleetingly looked through the workspace of Candlelight Ltd., to the expansive sheets of window, spread from corner to corner.

Outside, not even the fog was visible now in the night's blackness. But Kieran resolved the view himself, recreated it in his mind, that breathtaking panorama from his dream that morning, which only now, as perilously close as he was to losing its memory forever, he could appreciate with a degree of objectivity for what it was.

Staying where he was would be its forfeiture, for the dark, thick woods teeming with malevolent creatures, on whose edge he was standing.

He clambered on the heels of the line, going for the main office door.

They walked straight out of Purgatory.

Chapter 36

It was 11:57.

The corridor was dimly lit. To Kieran it appeared even longer than when he had first crossed it. They jostled silently through to the floor landing.

The group gathered by the elevator door. The lit square on its control panel had been frantically pressed many times.

Gabriella arrived just in front of Kieran. She said to those waiting expectantly, "No, stand away from there! We're not taking the lift. Dear Mo Lock will be ascending to this floor, that way."

No one questioned. She had everyone's complete trust.

"We'll take the stairs," she said. "Stay together, we need to move fast. If one of you falls, twists their ankle, I want the others of you to help that person back up, and down the stairs. Fred, Terry, I want you to take hold of Geeta's arms and help her down the steps—take the weight off her feet," she added brusquely.

Three out of the group were elderly—aged sixty plus, and less sure on their pegs. Geeta suffered from arthritis, and traversing a couple flights of stairs was beyond her ability. Nineteen was beyond her ability to *imagine* tackling, even though they were descending.

The men stood beside her, and took a hold of her arms.

It was11:58 and thirty seconds.

"Right," said Gabriella firmly. "Let's make our bid! Down we go!"

Kieran hesitated, waiting for Gabriella to proceed.

She stood firm. Her stern face made her look immoveable this time. "You first, Kieran," she said in a tone he hadn't heard her speak in since they'd met.

Her young appearance was deceptive. Kieran at that moment realized there were layers beneath layers to her personality.

He said nothing more and turned, following closely behind Fred, Geeta and Terry.

The group of fugitives took a left, and rushed through a set of fire doors, scrambling towards the first steps from the landing, the eerie echo of their footsteps in the stairwell the only sound.

It was 11:59.

They clambered in frenzied panic down one, two, three and four flights, sweating and trembling and muttering desperate expletives.

Twelve o'clock midnight.

Tikatakatikatakatikataka was the sound they made swarming down the low-lighted stairwell, petrified, huddled, like lab mice sprung from a cage. Some were moaning tearfully, others were silently gritting their teeth, others were cursing the Devil and all his works with deep-blue slang. All of them were pumping their arms and legs like their lives depended on it, because they did.

A life in Hell was no life.

Gabriella kept the rear guard, looking behind her regularly to see what, if anything, was coming.

It seemed nothing, but they didn't slow up to tie shoelaces.

The building sounded empty apart from them.

Then between floors eleven and twelve, the sort of sound they *were* expecting clamoured through the chasm. Above them they heard a bone-chilling shriek, like a banshee's. It dragged on and on, as though its tone deaf creator had lungs as voluminous as a Zeppelin. It shimmied around them like a cold ghost as they skidaddled down steps, three at a time. Simultaneously they could hear a furious snap, crackle and popping coming from the same direction, as though cockroaches were being crushed, and the sound greatly amplified. They knew Ms. Lock, Satan, was close on their tails.

Their swearing included no blasphemy but was strong stuff just the same. It increased in volume with that of the pursuing creature's, gradually catching on them. Kieran peed his pants some more. A couple of the other crazy, stutter-steppers christened their underwear for the first time.

The screeching above deepened in timbre but didn't cease, becoming one continuous histrionic wail. The crackling sounds were changing though, displaced by a CHACK, CHACK, CHACK which rang off the walls of the stairwell, as though heavy clawed feet were impacting on the concrete steps a floor above them.

As close to death, doom, dismemberment and destruction as they were, descending down that terrible stairway, in their minds they prayed to their God whether he be Christian, Hindu, Muslim or just benevolent Mother Nature.

They alighted onto the ground floor.

Apart from those in their own desperate group, they had not seen a single other soul on their way downward, who could obstruct their escape, or end up confronting the unseen monster hot on their heels. Thankfully.

Under other less chaotic circumstances, on a more regular working day, they may have realized that the time according to their watches was six o'clock.

Their behavior was instead governed by the Hellish, time-measuring instrument in Candlelight Ltd.'s meeting room, the hands of which, threatened doom. They were aligned to the time zone of the Underworld.

The motley bunch had in five minutes flat, scarpered down to the bottom of the staircase, twenty storeys high. They were exhausted but frantic with fear of the pursuing demon at their heels.

The wretched gathering clamoured at the sliding doors, the building's exit, which delayed in opening.

The Arch Fiend was upon them; they didn't turn around to face him, instead barging and clawing at the static doorway in a frenzy. After a delay of about five seconds, by the grace of God, it slid open, relieving the crush against it.

The merciful twelve sprinted, stumbled and fell out into the cold, fog-laden air, out into freedom, running in every direction like headless chickens.

Chapter 37

Kieran didn't stop running until he realized that the Arch Demon, who would've had him captive in Hell, was no longer chasing him. He was head-high in self-preservation instinct and adrenalin but still had thoughts and cares for his fellow escapees. Even so, though he was fairly certain he was not being pursued, he put a couple hundred more meters between himself and the tower block he had just vacated in some style.

Then, some five minutes later, acknowledging his conversion to the spiritual path, he thanked God for this deliverance, and gradually calmed himself down. Of all the things to think about in that condition of surrender, the Bible momentarily came to the fore. He resolved in those moments to make a concerted effort to read, digest and apply practically to his life the Bible and all its lessons, to embrace God, so that his walk would be, from now onward, a Godly one.

That he considered the Bible's only value as a doorstop previously made him convulse inside.

The fog, like cold, stagnant steam washed around him as he moved forward. It was even thicker at ground level and swirled in eddies as he moved his feet. It glowed with a ghostly light from the energy of moonbeams, as his body resumed its corporeal existence.

Kieran was aware of his gut once more; feeling tugs on the bleeding coils of his intestine, as if it were being pulled by invisible strings down into the fog below. He briefly considered taking a pill but then realized he had ingested enough artificial chemicals for one day. Gabriella had doctored his drink—it allowed him a glance, in his trance state, of where he was heading.

Instead, Kieran opted for the low-tech fetal position. The pain was a stinging one and took all his energy to be able to bear it. He collapsed to the floor, doubling over. Thinking of the trickles of blood oozing down the walls of his duodenum brought acuity to his senses. He mustered the strength to stand.

Not even supreme effort could straighten him upright from his hunch, but at least he could attempt to drag himself onwards, to seek out his new spiritual friends, who had scattered in every direction, fleeing from the Devil.

Before moving forward, Kieran twisted his neck to see behind. As he might have expected, the tower block was not visible. The doorway he had passed through, perhaps three hundred meters away, was gone, of course obscured by the fog, of course . . .

He didn't turn back to check.

Driven on by fear and pain—in that order—he staggered on, tangibly displacing the misty miasma, putting distance between himself and the phantom sky rise, looking to find Gabriella and her erstwhile skeleton crew.

A little further on that lonely, eerily untrafficked highway, Kieran came close to what appeared like a crop circle in the fog in the middle of the road. In the centre of the vortex where the fog was strangely absent stood a female figure which Kieran recognized as Gabriella!

Kieran was some two hundred meters away from her when a scintillating white light appeared, about the same in size as the demisted zone in which Gabriella stood, seemingly at the ceiling of the black starry sky and visible from within the rarefied circle. The light flashed for a split second, turning the fog-swamped, surrounding cityscape into a negative image and then, once gone, Kieran observed in startlement the winged creature spiraling downwards from the heavens towards Gabriella. Her head was facing the descending being and her arms were raised to the sky.

The feathered man, unmistakably an angel according to Kieran's Biblical recollection, lent the brilliant white of his wings to Gabriella, highlighted, directly below him. He swooped down gently and alighted next to her.

Kieran, dazzled by what he was witnessing, wondered if he was still stupefied by the adulterated coffee.

The two celestial beings embraced and kissed briefly and then took to the air under the power of the male angel's wings, wafting gently in the frigid air.

Kieran stared in disbelief as the two ascended majestically into the night sky and then disappeared from his view.

How appropriate that Gabriella, whom he had thought of as an angel in a metaphoric sense, be escorted to the Heavens by an archangel—could it be *Gabriel*, he wondered? Perhaps she too was a messenger of

God. Maybe *herself* truly an angel. Perhaps she had been divinely appointed to rescue damsels-in-distress like he had been. Maybe that was her true career.

She had ascended to Heaven with her lover. Now Kieran resolved he must ask forgiveness from his ex-lover, Alice.

Chapter 38

Alice was listening to CDs, lying on the carpet, fumbling through the covers, looking at lyrics.

"*. . . Ride the tiger as it prowls about*
Shout, 'I am an angel, outta my way!' Shout!"

She pictured Roland Megaton for a moment, the musical sensation of the season. Then she thought of David Bowie. Then Mark Bolan.

But finally she imagined Kieran Nichol amongst the stalking, dancing tigers of the song.

She didn't know why. He never danced, never sang. He hated animals with a passion, unless they were on his plate with gravy and mash.

She didn't know why *she* couldn't eat well, sleep well or enjoy her music properly. Didn't know why she was crying all the time.

But her heart knew something her head didn't.

Even so, there was no way she was going to call him.

He'd put her in her place too often. A place where she didn't want to be.

"*. . . The feral beast bares its teeth again . . .*"

He'd dressed her like a doll to his taste. At the same time he had erased her personality. She felt like a sidekick. Or a fashion accessory. Under his arm. The way to be seen (not that they went out anywhere together).

He kept her just so he could satisfy society's expectations of what a thirty-something man should be—married, with a career and children. They would be the first robot couple to produce offspring. That's why they wouldn't be.

Recently when Alice looked at Kieran, back from his workplace, he didn't look like a man. He looked like a diagram of a man. He was dehumanized. She couldn't stand to see it.

The way he worked himself like a dog made her feel ill in *her* mind too.

His chronic psychological sickness he just lived with, accepted.

But he was breaking up physically before her eyes as well, and he couldn't go on for long like that; the headaches, the colds and flu. And the stomach.

For money.

He was becoming the Devil's moneybox. Coins dropped through the slot in his head, and he heard them clink, smug he had something for a rainy day. But he'd be cracked open by Satan before a drop landed in Hell.

He'd celebrate his fortieth with a coronary.

Alice sat up, crossed her legs and wiped tears from her eyes. She blew her nose with a red and blue, mottled, silk handkerchief she had dyed. It was saturated. She kept it to her face anyway.

She wouldn't call him. She couldn't. She had let go—sort of.

She had *tried* but couldn't keep him out of her mind. Especially because he was in danger.

A coronary by his fortieth.

Now he'd have to reevaluate. It was either his pathway to suicide, or her.

Alice didn't know which he'd choose.

She wanted all that schmoose he'd enraptured her with in the first place to be real. She wanted to feel like they felt when they first started going out.

Not like a sucker.

He'd have to phone her up and unsucker her. He made her feel as though she had been suckered in a big way, by a mean big brother.

"Wait 'till your father gets home," she muttered.

Really that was overly flattering. Nowadays he was more like an articulate zombie telling her how to live.

So she took the initiative and said *bye-bye*, shedding no tears and no sweat in front of him.

Maybe she still had it.

Her face creased, and she smothered it again with the hanky.

Maybe she didn't and was the *ultimate* sucker. Every passing day made it less likely he'd call.

All he had to do was call her! It was a simple choice between dying on his feet and her. Surely!

Perhaps not for Kieran. It was three months already.

Evidently not.

She sobbed. Her tears splashed upon the unfolded CD cover between her crossed legs. She wiped it on a denim-clad thigh. The cover's surface was bumpy where the drops had landed.

Alice reached in front of her to the CD player and pressed "eject". She took out the CD and placed it on the carpet under the small glass top table with the hi-fi above. She put in the new CD.

". . . I dreamt of you on a summer's day
As amid the orchids you lay, dreaming of me . . ."

Kieran wanted a woman he could *train*. The way he *insisted*.

He reinforced his arguments with the spiel of a salesman. Only she thought he was selling her shit.

He might tell her that the source of life-giving water was—a tap.

She would correct him, saying that water's origin was in the oceans, glaciers and sky.

Whereupon he would pooh-pooh her, and tell her *get some*. She couldn't.

Kieran would turn the tap and fill a glass, give it to her and say, "I rest my case."

Tap water was his science, always at hand, in plentiful supply. He explained away miracles, the triumph of the human spirit, Heaven, with tap water science. Resisting him was futile. He'd just give her a glass of damn tap water.

With it he reduced life to mundanity.

And he's wrong!

His outlook was so bleak. He winged and whined about the gray skies, but insisted on them, telling her the sun, moon and stars were confabulation. It was a self-fulfilling prophecy. He seemed to become attuned to the clouds. Whenever he looked up they were there, and he only ever looked up when they were.

That was Kieran in a nutshell.

Now he had to make a crunch decision, because Alice had sent a letter to his flat giving her forwarding address for mail. He knew she was living with Mervyn "Merlin" Bates because Kieran had redirected a handful of letters to her there.

And she knew *he* knew Mervyn had the hots for her, because she'd invited him to the flat she was sharing with Kieran when they were still living together and his slavering over her was obvious.

So, she would just have to await Kieran's call, hoping his mind would undergo an epiphany, and in the meantime feel like a career widow.

The CD died and she sat silently, contemplating a future life without the one she truly loved, with only her hanky to comfort her. Not even Mervyn was there at this time. He was out for the night, though her upset wouldn't really have been mollified by Mervyn's contrived, ham-fisted attempts to console her. He wasn't a soul mate. Kieran, she knew, had the potential to be.

The doorbell rang. Breaking away from her reverie, she rose and went to answer.

On the doorstep stood Kieran, bedraggled, stooping and clutching his stomach. He looked to Alice with pleading, sorrowful eyes.

He said, "Please let me in, Alice—I'd like to talk with you . . . I've changed, I've changed . . . I've changed."

She let him enter.

Epilogue

It was a Wednesday Morning.

Dr. Goddelijk, or as he preferred to be known, Mr. Goddelijk, straining hard, was distressed at not hearing the familiar sound of *number twos* plopping into the toilet bowl.

It had been three days since his last fruitful visit to the lavatory, since he had unloaded.

He felt physically weak and mentally groggy, unaware of the mischief the late Divinity Callisto had performed upon him with her Tykhon Y2K a few days earlier.

Mr. Goddelijk, who was a psychiatrist by profession, had taken the day off work at Tewsbury Hospital, because he was feeling so out of sorts, despite having taken an overdose of laxatives the previous day.

Underachieving, he stood from his squat on the toilet seat with the aid of his walking stick and pulled up his baggy pants. After washing his hands, he went to rest in the lounge of his humble dwelling.

The morning's malaise was interrupted by a knock on Mr. Goddelijk's front door.

The postman handed to him a parcel in brown paper. Mr. Goddelijk signed for it with a marked disenthusiasm.

He paid the water closet another visit without getting any results, before returning to the drab parcel.

It was about the size of a Rubik's Cube, a puzzle Mr. Goddelijk would have no problem solving, as high as his IQ was.

That was before he met Ms. Callisto.

Now his faculties were so dulled, as his immune system fought against the toxins buzzing through his body, the result of extreme constipation. He had to edify his brain as best he could, in order to pry open the wrapped box.

He did so and within was a folded note and a small, labeled, glass bottle, with a metal cap.

Mr. Goddelijk unfolded the note. The simple covering letter read as follows:

Dear Mr. Goddelijk,

Please find enclosed the remedy for your ailment.

From a long time admirer.

Gabriella XXX

Mr. Goddelijk, whose brain was swimming in sewage, even so was dismayed at receiving this package. But he had enough of his wits about him to know that he should have the bottle's contents, a bright blue syrup, chemically analyzed at Tewsbury Hospital's labs before even contemplating medicating himself with it. For that matter, he would sooner have a stomach checkover with a specialist at the hospital and would certainly arrange one now.

Not that he would receive any joy from a practitioner of Western Medicine. The solution to Mr. Goddelijk's problem was not in their repertory.

He held the small bottle labeled REMEDY up to his bespectacled eyes and ogled with a degree of suspicion, then tempered his cynical reluctance, considering the proverb which advises that *one shouldn't look a gift horse in the mouth.*

He prized off the top of the bottle and drank from it.

Get in touch with the author

I hope you enjoyed reading this novel; I spent a long time writing it, on and off, over the course of just under a decade.

I was influenced in my writing by different religions—Hinduism, Vaishnavism and Christian teaching.

I also created the book cover. I'll give a brief explanation.

It features an individual (i.e. Kieran Nichol) in a spot of bother (or maybe not)!

On the one hand, the proverbial candle is burning at both ends (Kieran being the candle). His cynical attitude to life is burning him up spiritually and physically. His negative thinking being akin to a forest fire in his head, consuming even the potential for positive attitudes in him—and are those the fires of Hell licking up from beneath him?

On the other hand, in theological circles it is said (truthfully) that "we are all embers from the same fire". God is the fire and we are the sparks thereof. Kieran's conscience—expressing itself as the flame in his head (causing a positive change in his thinking), is bringing him to God—the substantial flames beneath him. They'll soon meet.

So Kieran in my breakdown of the image is either plunging into disaster or is undergoing an epiphany. So it's Hell or Heaven for him. A critical crossroads!

I'd like to get to know my audience better. I would welcome your feedback and other comments, so feel free to contact me at the following e-mail address:

deanvyas@hotmail.co.uk